APR 2 8 2005

LAST CALL
FOR
BLACKFORD OAKES

the hastiness of the cover arrangements the agency would need to undertake.

On the October mission, Blackford had taken with him a young CIA colleague, a Ukrainian-born Iowan called Gus Windels. They had traveled as father and son, "Harry Singleton" and his son, "Jerry," ostensibly engaged on an innocent mission, tracking down Jerry's long-lost aunt. It hadn't been difficult for twenty-eight-year-old Gus to pose as the son of the man he was accompanying. Blackford, at six feet two, was a shade taller than Gus. His hair still showed some of its original dark blond, though it was now mostly gray. Blackford was no longer eye-catchingly handsome, but he was ruggedly attractive, with blue eyes and an inquisitive chin that reinforced the words he spoke, and sometimes energized thoughts that ran through his agile mind. Blackford was spare in frame and moved with habitual ease, though he was not the limber youth he had been, so memorably, for so long. He was plausibly the father of the blond young American at his side on the Pan Am flight to Zurich.

Now, Windels was stationed in Moscow, working under his own name at the United States Embassy. It was he who had alerted Oakes to the suspicion of a fresh plot. He could speak with Blackford in a private shorthand. They had developed a special relationship during the dangerous October days of the exploitation of the covert defector, the preparations to betray the young Russians, and the consummation of a presidential directive. This time, Gus put it all in a discreet few words

"Well, sir, we've got a defense budget of nearly three hundred billion. That's prodding, right?"

"Yes. That's one way to make our point about road signs. Cap Weinberger would like to hear it put that way. Well, he's secretary of defense, and secretaries of defense have a right to think that hundreds of billions on defense are a means of prodding people to do the right thing." He got up from his chair. "If you need to see me again"—he extended his hand— "call Kathy."

Blackford walked to the side door. "Oh, Mr. President, I forgot. Good luck on the Nicaraguan business."

"Black, you want to handle. *that* for me while you're at it?"

Blackford opened the door and left the office.

The meeting he then scheduled with the director had a delicate edge. William Webster, the wise and polished director of the CIA, had never been told about the critical intervention of October 1986. It would have been impossible for Oakes to brief him now in detail on his forthcoming trip without giving him the background on the previous mission. So Blackford, on meeting with Director Webster, said only that he would be away on a confidential mission for the president. He spent an hour with Webster devoted to examining the general political situation in Moscow and Eastern Europe.

"You got any other presidential commissions you're undertaking?" Unlike some of his predecessors, Webster was not looking for ways to reassure himself of his authority as head of the CIA. He quickly accepted that this new mission was somehow linked to an earlier mission. He raised no questions about Blackford's going, though he was ill at ease with

"You don't have to write anything, sir. Just tell me it's okay—"

"Viva voce?" Reagan was visibly pleased to use an old term of the trade.

"Yes." Blackford nodded. "Viva voce."

"Why do they have that rule?"

"Because if an operations chief were captured, he'd have a lot of vital information."

"Which the enemy could get hold of through torture?"

"That's the idea."

"How would you keep that from happening in your case?"

"I'd take precautions. Sir."

Reagan paused. And then nodded.

"I'll pass your word on—if I have to," Blackford continued. "I'll book a flight through Zurich and enter the Soviet Union under cover. That will also make it harder for the bureaucrats in the CIA to remind me where I can't go."

"Okay, okay. You have my word on it. But don't get me crossed up with your director. He's a good man." The afternoon sun broke in through the south window. Reagan's arm reached back and he felt for the cord, bringing the shades down enough to neuter the sun's glare.

"I don't know how it's all going to end up with Gorbachev. You saw what he said on the seventieth anniversary of their revolution?" Reagan reached into his desk for the clipping. "What he said was"—Reagan's voice was detached now, at public-speaking level—"that—I'm quoting him—'In October 1917, we parted the old world, rejecting it once and for all. We are moving toward a new world, the world of Communism. We shall never turn off that road.' Maybe he needs a little prodding."

not *sure,* not like last time. This time it's a real complicated business—"

"I don't want to hear about it." Reagan looked down at his desk, arched his eyebrows, and slowed down the tempo of the conversation. "Just do this: Do whatever you can to protect Gorbachev, do it one more time, abort, abort—"

The president winked and leaned back on his chair. "I had a reputation back in California: I was a *moderate* on the subject of abortion." His creases broke into a smile. "You know the one about the British serial killer who said he was actually astonished by his moderation? My reaction exactly!" He paused and his eyes went to the painting of George Washington. He said deliberately, "There's to be no moderation in anything you have to do to protect Gorbachev. And no reporting to me except as absolutely required."

"I won't report back anything in detail. It could all be just a bag of wind. But I think I ought to go over there and find out."

"What do you need from me? Airplane tickets? Come to think of it, Black, the White House has a pretty good travel agent. I guess it does. My plane is always there when I need it. So, what do you need from me?"

"I do need one thing, Mr. President. Back then, last October, I was still director of covert operations for the agency. Since then, I've had to . . . slow down, so I'm just an agent. But as former operations chief, the rules say I'm not allowed inside enemy territory. You'd have to waive that rule."

The president pulled open his top desk drawer but then slammed it shut again. "I've been sitting here for nearly seven years. The things they want me to write an executive order about! Now this."

Gorbachev held his gaze on Reagan, waited a moment, and then nodded, moving on to another subject. He had heard from the president's own lips what he wanted, and needed, to hear.

But now, in December 1987, would the subject of assassination come up again? Oakes had invoked the oral code over the phone with the critically situated Kathy. *"This is about Freckles."* That meant there was extra-institutional urgency in the requested meeting. The president would see again the man in the Central Intelligence Agency whom he had dealt with before, and had trusted for some years.

The code was used sparingly, only three times during the Reagan years so far. It meant that Blackford needed to move outside the ambit of the director of the CIA, even when that had been Bill Casey, Reagan's closest security adviser until his death in May.

Kathy slotted him in for four forty-five that afternoon.

Neither party wanted routine clerical notice paid to their meeting. The usual approach to the Oval Office was therefore avoided. Kathy led Oakes into the Cabinet Room, and from there knocked on the side door of the Oval Office, bringing Oakes in. The president stayed at his desk and nodded with a friendly smile, pointing to the chair alongside.

"Sir, the business of last October, the plot against Premier Gorbachev—"

"Yes, yes. Why do we need to bring *that* up?"

"Because there's a fresh design on his life—we *think*. Solid enough to bring to your attention. It comes to us from a survivor of the business of last October. But this time we're

He told Oakes—his mouth slightly contracted, as was habitual when Reagan was spitting out instructions—that the plot was to be suppressed. Having made the critical decision, Reagan wanted *the whole thing* to go away. The very last thing he wished ever to be reminded of was that he had once given orders to betray a band of young Russian patriots. After all, weren't these people to be likened to the July 20th plotters against Adolf Hitler? Likened to, well, the Romans who finally did away with Caligula? He stopped himself from deliberating further along such lines. Sic semper tyrannis! was good stuff, but just *not right* in dealing with someone who, with the flick of a finger, could dispatch nuclear bombs that would destroy lives by the tens of millions.

Seven weeks after his fateful meeting with Oakes, Reagan received word. "The affair" had been "taken care of." That could only mean that the young Russian plotters had been frustrated, presumably imprisoned, or executed. Gorbachev was safe on his throne. There had been a moment of high anxiety for Reagan, some while later, when he met with Gorbachev. The premier was in Washington on a state visit, and sat now with his host in the Oval Office, alone except for the two interpreters.

Gorbachev suddenly turned in his chair. He looked Reagan straight in the face. *Had the president known anything about the plot of last October to kill him?* he asked.

Reagan was eternally grateful for his histrionic training. "Mikhail," he said, his face redolent of sincerity, "let me give you my personal and most solemn word that no American official was in any way involved in any attempt on your life." Reagan's answer was formally correct. Reagan had *not* connived, and on deliberation would not have connived, even passively, in any attempted assassination.

Reagan had inclined, at first, to do nothing—let the Russians look after their own affairs. Gorbachev was certainly an improvement on his predecessors, true. Yet he was a blooded successor to a line of tyrants that had begun in 1917 with Lenin, followed by Stalin, a thirty-year curse. And then there had been Bulganin and Khrushchev and Brezhnev, another thirty years among them, followed by Andropov and Chernenko ("elderly guys," Reagan mused, "—about my own age"). They didn't serve for very long, but they did carry on the bloody Afghan war launched by Brezhnev. A war that Gorbachev, soon after his selection as general secretary, vowed to fight to the end.

Should President Reagan do nothing? Say nothing—when he got word through Oakes that an assassination had been plotted?

Reagan sat on the intelligence. While weighing the question of intervention, he reminded himself that the young conspirators were perfecting their plot. What finally influenced him had been the summit at Reykjavik. This was his second meeting with Gorbachev, and this time he sensed that Gorbachev was different enough from other Soviet leaders to be worth going to undiplomatic lengths to protect. So he called Oakes in and told him to intervene. To abort the assassination. If necessary, even if it meant exposing the ring of youthful plotters. Yes—if necessary—even if it meant exposing the deeply hidden Soviet asset, the clandestine defector who had tipped off Blackford Oakes.

That was fourteen months ago, but Blackford vividly recalled the day the president gave him the order. Reagan had come right to the point.

CHAPTER 1

Ronald Reagan, at ease with himself as ever, satisfied himself yet again on summoning the memory of his dealings with Blackford Oakes in October 1986. He had done the right thing. But now, December 1987, Oakes had put in for another meeting with the president.

Their 1986 meeting had had to do with a plot to assassinate Gorbachev. A group of young Russians, weary and demoralized by the brutal Soviet war against Afghanistan, had planned to kill the Communist leader. Oakes, veteran CIA agent, was in secret and unshared touch with a Soviet defector he had long experienced as antagonist, but who was now a hidden ally.

And so Reagan had had to ponder the agonizing question: Is it the business of the United States to get in the way of a plot by native Russians trying to get rid of Mikhail Gorbachev, general secretary of the Soviet Communist Party, and dictator?

BOOK ONE

LAST CALL
FOR
BLACKFORD OAKES

For Joseph W. Donner,
gratefully and affectionately

*This is a work of fiction. All names, characters, places, organizations,
and events are either the products of the author's imagination or
are used fictitiously for verisimilitude.*

Photo on page 130 used by permission of the Ethics
and Public Policy Center.

Library of Congress Cataloging-in-Publication Data
Buckley, William F. (William Frank), 1925–
Last call for Blackford Oakes/William F. Buckley Jr.—1st ed.
p. cm.
ISBN 0-15-101085-4
1. Oakes, Blackford (Fictitious character)—Fiction. 2. Americans—Soviet
Union—Fiction. 3. Philby, Kim (1912–1988)—Fiction. 4. Intelligence officers—
Fiction. 5. Soviet Union—Fiction. 6. Cold War—Fiction.   I. Title.
PS3552.U344L37   2005
813'.54—dc22   2004025580

Text set in Sabon
Designed by Cathy Riggs

Printed in the United States of America
First edition
A C E G I K J H F D B

LAST CALL
FOR
BLACKFORD OAKES

William F. Buckley Jr.

HARCOURT, INC.
Orlando   Austin   New York   San Diego   Toronto   London

cabled to Blackford's private number. What he said was: "It's come up again, possible threat to #1. No way to upload this through official channels. You must come."

Blackford trusted Gus Windels's judgment, trusted it enough to take the case to the president.

CHAPTER 2

Ursina Chadinov was six years old before it occurred to her to wonder about the rule of the house.

The house in question comprised one and a half rooms in the crowded Gostiny Dvor district of Leningrad. During the great siege, just over ten years earlier, the apartment had belonged to a Jewish violinist. He performed with the symphony, until such concerts were simply excluded by the fighting and the starvation. Even after the long postwar years that had gone into the reconstruction of the lustrous city founded by Peter the Great at the turn of the eighteenth century, Gostiny Dvor, like many other living areas, had to put up with inconsistent supplies of water and electricity.

Still, it was home, and welcome to the Chadinovs. The rule of the house, which Ursina now questioned, was that only the English language would be spoken at mealtimes. What had brought her question to the table was the dispensation of the rule the day Josef Stalin died. Dmitri Chadinov thought that some gesture was appropriate, on the death of the general secretary. Chadinov had spent many hours, over two decades, defending Stalin at postings abroad, in England, in Turkey, and in France. He had harnessed his skills as a diplomat to celebrate the accomplishments of the Soviet leader. He was not himself persuaded that the death of Stalin was a terrible event for the Soviet Union, but such thoughts were never shared, not with his wife, Simona, and certainly not with Ursina, his precocious daughter.

"The reason we speak in English during meals is to teach you the language, Ursina. The English language—after Russian—will be the most important language in the world, and not only in diplomacy, but as—" He turned to his wife. "Simona, how do you translate lingua franca?"

The fifty-year-old Lithuanian ran a big spoon around the pot of simmering potato soup and furrowed her wide brow. "You treat me like a Latin–Russian dictionary. It is more than thirty years since I studied at the nunnery. You would translate that, roughly, as 'universal language.'"

"If it is universal, why don't my friends also speak English when they eat?"

"Because," Dmitri Chadinov answered, "you're more special than other little girls."

"If I'm so special, why do you take me to dancing classes only one day every week? Tamara goes Mondays, Wednesdays, and Fridays."

"Because," Simona interrupted, "Tamara's mother is with the Maly Opera and has special privileges."

"Our teacher, Comrade Uziev, says nobody has special

privileges in a classless society. How do you say that in Latin, Mama?"

Dmitri laughed. "Even in a classless society everyone has a responsibility to develop what skills they can. Like mine. I can speak English, you know that, and I can also speak Turkish and Norwegian and French. And your mother can—"

"Teach religion." Simona served up the potato soup. She smiled at her husband, but it was a tired smile, after three decades of renouncing the religious faith in which she had been trained, but which she could no longer practice. The revolution had ended all that. All that bourgeois superstition.

"Anyway, tomorrow we will resume our rule," Dmitri concluded the discussion. "Only English at mealtimes."

Ursina cocked her head and brushed the light blond bangs to one side. "I don't think I will speak English with you tomorrow."

The senior Chadinovs stared at her, speechless.

"Well," said Dmitri, "maybe tomorrow you won't be eating anything."

"I don't care."

"Leave her alone," Simona addressed her husband in French. "She'll have forgotten the whole thing by tomorrow."

"D'accord," Dmitri said. And to Ursina, in Russian, "Tomorrow we will attend the memorial ceremony for Comrade Stalin in Palace Square."

"All right," Ursina said. "Do you think they will ask me to dance at the celebration?"

Dmitri smiled. "It isn't a 'celebration,' Ursina. It's a—" he motioned to Simona for help.

"A requiem."

"No, no, Simona. That is a *religious* term. It is a . . .

meeting to register our . . . grief . . . at the loss of our leader. Do you understand, Ursina?"

"All right. I'll recite the poem, 'Humpty Dumpty had a great fall; / All the king's horses / And all the king's men—'"

"Ursina!" Simona looked at her daughter and thought: What will she be when she's sixteen, not six? Whatever else, Simona thought, Ursina would be very beautiful, and her inquisitive eyes would shine very bright.

CHAPTER 3

Ursina was twelve when her father gave himself the lethal dose. She was disconsolate, but also curious as to why he would do such a thing, and she managed, one day when her mother was out shopping, to unearth the folder containing the medical records. She learned that her father had been diagnosed with syphilis.

Simona was surprised and cross on being told by her daughter that she had learned the reason for her father's suicide.

"I'm going to read up about syphilis," Ursina said. "I know a library that has *all kinds* of medical books. How did Papa get syphilis?"

Her mother said that it was a disease her father had contracted while in diplomatic service in Turkey.

"Is Turkey very full of syphilis, Mama?"

Simona knew by now that evasions didn't work with

Ursina. She replied simply, "Yes. It is a deadly and very painful disease. Winston Churchill's father died from it."

"Was he in Turkey?"

"Yes," Simona said. *Why not just "yes"?* She succeeded. Ursina didn't come back for more, didn't ask when the elder Churchill had visited Turkey.

At school, Ursina focused her enormous energies on science, and one day she announced to her mother that she would become a doctor. But she didn't spend all her afternoons in libraries and laboratories. She was intensely curious about the splendid city she lived in, and bicycled studiously about the city and its outskirts with Tamara, her schoolmate, who had qualified for special training in ballet.

"I must be very careful when bicycling not to do any damage to my legs," Tamara said.

Ursina teased her. "If you do, I will operate on them."

Tamara laughed, half-heartedly. The very idea of turning over the care of her legs, destined to be seen in the Kirov Ballet, to Ursina! But after feigning concern, she bicycled along vigorously with her friend on this bright afternoon in early October. It took them nearly an hour to reach the deserted palace at Tsarskoe Selo.

Tamara was reluctant to walk through the tall grass surrounded with NO TRESPASSING signs, toward the old palace, but Ursina persisted.

"This"—Ursina, standing by a tree halfway to the building, looked excitedly about her—"was where the czar and czarina and their four daughters and the little czarevich strolled." She closed her eyes, conjuring the scene forty-five years ago. Motioning to Tamara to follow her, she walked resolutely toward the deserted mansion.

There was a guard sitting, legs outstretched, in a guard-house outside. He hailed them to stop. But after a brief conversation with Ursina, he motioned the girls to go ahead and explore, but told them to be back in twenty minutes. "Or I will apprehend you and have you flogged!" Ursina laughed, and the guard laughed with her, wondering if he had ever seen a more beautiful fifteen-year-old than this one, with the oval face, large brown eyes, and mischievous mouth.

The ghostly palace had been mostly living quarters, Ursina remarked as they walked about the ground floor. "But there were public rooms—this was obviously one of those, look how long it is—for the ministers who waited on the imperial presence. They were made ministers because the czar tolerated a lot of parliamentary agencies around him."

"What did they do?" Tamara asked.

"Not much." Ursina showed off the knowledge she had picked up from the library book on Leningrad's palaces. "Remember, the czar was crowned as *Autocrat of All the Russias*. He did what he wanted—until our people came to the rescue."

They looked about and then, on the way back across the park to their bicycles, stopped again at the guardhouse, where Ursina gave the old guard a piece of the rock candy she carried. "That was very interesting. Thank you, comrade." He smiled and took the candy.

Ursina didn't linger over imperial history and didn't pause, after her early bicycle tours, to study palaces. Year by year she immersed herself more deeply in her study of science. She took to spending her free hours, after school, at army hospitals, the closest being the hospital at Moskovsky Avenue 1072. It was one of six charged with tending to the broken bodies of four thousand survivors of the long and bloody war with the Nazis, a war that ended the year before Ursina was born. She contrived to look older than seventeen by pulling back her hair, wearing a babushka, and applying a thin layer of lipstick.

She paid special attention to Ward 14. That ward was maintained as a hospice. Its patients were all dying, some more quickly than others. Ursina lingered regularly with Lutz, nearly every part of whom—excepting only his smile, which Ursina thought indestructible—had been shattered by a land mine. He managed to smile even when being fed potions that made other patients gag.

But Lutz was not a smiling scarecrow. He spoke with great absorption of his own story, and his expression was sometimes overtly melancholy.

"You know, Miss Ursina, I stepped on that mine eighteen years and four months ago and have been in hospitals all that time. Yes, I remember the day and the hour and the minute, January 11, 1945, at 1406. But you know what, Miss Ursina, what I remember most was the pain of the weeks *before* we set out on that road."

"From another wound?"

"No," Lutz smiled. "Unless you call hunger a wound. We were eating bark from trees. One day, Miss Ursina, you will permit me to make you a birch stew. . . . Don't stick out your tongue on your pretty face! Birch stew can be delicious, if you're hungry enough, and if you are allowed to sleep after eating it. Sleep was difficult for the Fifth Motorized Rifle Division because the artillery batteries were only a few kilometers behind us."

What work had he done before he was conscripted?

His face brightened sharply. "I served at the Bistro By-talso. Through the kindness of the great gentleman who played the accordion for the guests, I was myself learning to play. He would stay on after midnight with me for a half hour. I would slip him vodka and some beer—nobody ever noticed the next day—and he would teach me some tunes and show me the chords on the fingerboard." Lutz held up his right hand. "If I had two fingers back maybe I could show you how to use them—I mean, how the fingers call up the chords."

Ursina said that nothing would give her more pleasure than to learn something about accordions. "My father hired an accordionist to play on his fiftieth birthday, but the trouble was, he started playing some czarist music."

Lutz looked over at the patient on his right, his bed eight inches removed. "That would not do," he whispered, his smile brighter than ever.

"Though I guess," Ursina smiled coquettishly, "you are not likely to grow back two fingers, Lutz."

"No," he said. "But I won't be hungry again, so why complain? And you—you are very young, I can see that, but you are already a skilled nurse. I wish you would look after me always, Miss Ursina."

"I promise, I will," she told him, leaning over to stroke the white hairs left on his head, and moving on to visit other patients, most of whom eagerly awaited their turn with "Babushka Nightingale." That was what the legless lieutenant who had studied at the university dubbed her one day, explaining to the wounded man on his right why he called her that, and leaving it for him to pass the word, until many of them were calling her Babushka Nakteengill.

———

Ursina knew that her uncle, Dr. Roman Eskimov, was soon to retire from his work in the urology department of the Moscow University Medical School. Neither she nor her mother knew what this would do to her aunt and uncle's living arrangements. A few weeks before Dr. Eskimov's retirement, he was informed by the Citizens' Housing Authority that he and his wife, being childless, would have to take leave of their two-bedroom apartment, spacious quarters to which he would no longer be entitled once he left his employment at the university. The alternative to moving to a smaller apartment was to take in an approved tenant. Dr. Eskimov filed an application on behalf of his sister-in-law, Simona Chadinov.

The letter Simona received from her sister one Saturday morning was full of news. The application to the housing officials had been approved; the two sisters would soon be reunited. And Uncle Roman had secured a place for Ursina to study in the urology department of the medical school to which he had been attached for forty-five years.

Ursina did not go to Ward 14 to say goodbye. She would not say goodbye to Lutz, because she knew she would cry, and she reasoned that to do such a thing would only add to his pains. She thought to consult with her mother about it, but decided against even doing that, because she knew that tears would flow from the mere telling of her problem of leaving her afflicted friends. They would all be dead soon, was the only comfort she could take.

CHAPTER 4

Ursina Chadinov lived for two years with her mother and the Eskimovs, then moved to the university dormitory. At age twenty-four she was granted her medical degree and took up her work at the university hospital. As her career progressed, she applied for an apartment. After the usual delay, she was assigned to one on Pozharsky Street, to be shared with another young woman, Rufina Pukhov, an economist and editor. Rufina, two years Ursina's junior, was trim and efficient in manner and in life. She and Ursina became fast friends, and genial sparring partners.

Rufina was nearly thirty-eight when she met and fell in love with an Englishman living in Moscow. Now, a year later, they had finally received the necessary permission to marry. Rufina would soon be leaving her roommate.

"You have never told me, Ursina, why you prefer to read

books in English." They were having tea, late in the afternoon, before going together to the ballet.

"Rufina, dear, there are lots of things I haven't told you. For instance, I am not going to give you the details on the patients I treated this morning."

"I don't want any such details. Well, maybe I would like to hear about some of them. Have they discovered a cure for erectile dysfunction?"

"Yes, but they won't publish it."

"Why?"

"The Cold War. Why do you ask?"

"What does erectile dysfunction have to do with the Cold War?"

"Ah, Rufina, you are so naïve."

"Me? I remind you I am affiliated with the Central Economics and Mathematics Institute."

"What do they know about the effects of erectile dysfunction?"

Rufina looked pained. She often did when conversing with Ursina. "The Institute is engaged in important research projects that touch down very heavily on the behavior of the bourgeois world."

"Does your Institute predict the birth rate in the enemy nations?"

"Of course."

"Well, can you not figure it out? The birth rate, which is a national concern, is influenced by erectile health."

Rufina decided not to play along. Ursina liked to tease, but she could carry it on longer than Rufina, sometimes, was inclined to do. So, "Never mind, Ursina, never mind. Are all your patients men?"

"Most of them. I have some female patients."

"What is *their* trouble?"

"Their lovers' erectile dysfunctions."

"Oh shut up, Ursina. I don't think I will encourage you to meet my fiancé. He is too delicate."

Ursina laughed. "Too delicate to do what? To work?"

"He does not . . . work, in the sense you are using the word. He does teach one seminar. Apart from that he is, well, retired."

"Retired from what? From work?"

"You have a way of twisting things around. Anyway, Andrei Fyodorovich doesn't talk about his former work."

"Oh, he too was a urologist?"

Rufina noisily closed her book. "Get back to the question I asked you. Why do you like reading in English?"

"Because Mark Twain does not read convincingly in Russian."

"Why not?"

" 'Dey's two gals flyin' 'bout you in yo' life. One uv 'em's light en t'other one is dark. One is rich en t'other is po'. You's gwyne to marry de po' one fust en de rich one by en by.' Is that enough for you, Rufina? Or shall I read more from *Tom Sawyer*?"

Rufina raised her hand in surrender. "Surely some Russian has tried translating Twain?"

"Yes. Dina Volokhonsky tried, and she failed. Maybe your Andrei will try his hand at translating Mark Twain?"

"I know of course that Mark Twain was an eloquent historian of the depravity of the American South." Rufina, the economist, thought something serious and productive should be said in this conversation with Ursina.

"Uh-huh."

"That is correct, isn't it?"

"No."

"How is it incorrect?"

"Mark Twain simply recorded what life was like. He was a portraitist, not an ideologue."

"Artists, we are amply informed, need to serve the truth."

"Mark Twain did that."

"How?"

"He spoke about young Negro Americans, and all of America listened, and learned."

"You can hardly say that. Mark Twain was when?"

"1835 to 1910."

"They did not have civil rights until . . . until they felt the pressure from us to treat people equally."

"Yes. Yes. They learned about human equality from Josef Stalin."

"Ursina!"

"Just teasing. Can your fiancé read American English? Or just English English?"

Rufina paused. "Yes. Yes, he knows American quite well."

"Well, ask him, dear. Ask him about Mark Twain."

"You ask him, dear. Andrei is very approachable."

CHAPTER 5

Ursina Chadinov looked down lasciviously at the telephone. A private telephone! After years of having to walk downstairs to the building concierge to make a call, or receive a call. "If that phone wanted to make love to me," she said to Rufina the first time she used it, "I would happily cooperate."

Rufina was also pleased. She felt herself entitled to a private phone, as an employee of the Economics Institute, but gave credit to Ursina for prevailing over the Soviet bureaucracy. "There are perquisites in being named professor of urology at the University of Moscow, on top of having published a book on urological research," Rufina acknowledged, fondling the telephone.

"Yes, dear Rufina. And one of those perquisites is the party you are giving for me on Wednesday. I am really looking forward to it."

"It's hardly a party. There'll be just six of us at dinner."

"I prefer to think of it as a party. And I will get to meet your mysterious fiancé, Andrei Fyodorovich Martins."

"Of course. Only please, Ursina, don't start teasing Andrei about his past. It's this simple: He does not talk about it.

"Now, we've invited two students he's especially taken with in his senior seminar. They are the Gromovs, Maxsim—Maks—and Irina. They are very attractive, and, by the way, you can speak with them in English—they are thoroughly schooled."

"Does Andrei Fyodorovich lecture to his seminar in English?"

"Yes, it is a part of the school discipline."

"What exactly does he teach, in his senior seminar?"

"That is another forbidden topic."

"I understand. Anyway, I'm to talk to Andrei in English. That is a part of *his* discipline."

"When he and I are alone together we use both languages. My English is quite advanced, as you well know. In fact, you have my permission to converse with me in English from now on, Ursina, if you wish."

"Can I use the language of Mark Twain?"

"Or switch back to the language of Aleksandr Pushkin. Suit yourself."

"What can I bring to the party?"

"Bring along a sedative, Ursina, something that will keep you non-argumentative for a couple of hours. Urologists use sedatives, don't they?"

"They certainly do when I am operating on them."

Ursina would bring, as her guest, Vladimir Kirov, a senior professor in the urology department. He had studied under

Ursina's uncle and had in turn taught Ursina at the medical school. She knew him as teacher, colleague, and devoted friend.

Kirov happily pursued studies in non-medical fields and was now taking courses in English literature at the university. He had introduced Ursina to works by Evelyn Waugh, Graham Greene, and Malcolm Muggeridge. "The first two are Roman Catholics, but even so, they write very well. Muggeridge was once an admirer of the Soviet Union, though he turned against us. But he is a very witty writer. Evelyn Waugh is a critic of manners, and Graham Greene writes mostly about the soul."

"The what?"

"The soul. If you said 'the soul of man,' you'd be talking about the noncorporeal side of man."

"You don't have to explain that, Volodya. For instance, you could say, 'Lenin caught the soul of Marxism,' couldn't you?"

Kirov chuckled, and confirmed the time of the party on Wednesday. "I'll come by in a cab at 1930."

Ursina had only once before visited Andrei's flat, shown it by Rufina one afternoon when he was away. Ursina had described it to Kirov. "It is on Uspensky Street, just off Pushkin Square. From the apartment there is a view to the west, east, and south. Rufina tells me that at sunset you can watch, from the kitchen window, the sunlight sliding down the spire of one of those hideous Stalin skyscrapers."

The one-legged doorman admitted them, and they walked up the narrow staircase adorned with colored prints of work by modern Russian artists.

Rufina was smart looking in early middle age. She wore a jabot blouse, a red rose pinned to one side, and greeted them at the door. They followed her to the little salon, which seemed at first to be simply a burgeoning library. And indeed it served as such—as a study for Andrei—and also as a makeshift dining room.

The dining table was covered with a white tablecloth. Two candles flanked a photograph of Ursina and Rufina, taken the day they both moved into the apartment on Pozharsky Street. Spread on the table were drinking glasses, what seemed a glass manufacturing company's total output. Ursina, teasingly, began to count them. "Rufina, did the czar lay on more glasses than you have done, at a party for, oh, a friendly count? Liqueur glasses, wine glasses, water glasses—Andrei, are Dr. Kirov and I, as practicing urologists, required also to drink water?"

Andrei, thirty-seven years older than his fiancée, his hair thick but completely gray, his shoulders square, was seated in an easy chair, a book open on his lap. He looked up, taking pains to participate in Ursina's jocular opening. "Ah, professor. Tell me. Is water a strain on the . . . system?"

Rufina stepped into the exchange. She said testily, "Too much vodka, Andrei Fyodorovich, is *certainly* a strain on the system. And you are not to use the wine glasses when pouring out vodka, or"—she laughed—"you will damage not only the body but also the Marxist cause. You will remember, I hope, that Comrade Khrushchev cautioned many years ago against the excessive use of vodka?"

"Yes, Rufina," Andrei stretched out his hand as he might have done to silence a student exhibiting his ignorance, "but he was talking about the peasantry. It is they who drink too much."

The hearty knock on the door interrupted the banter. Rufina went to the door and brought in the Gromovs.

Andrei rose from his easy chair. Those fat folk, Ursina thought, will need to enter the room one at a time. And, true, Maksim Gromov's girth was enormous, his wife's torso equally so. "Ah, Maksim, Irina, how nice to welcome you other than in a classroom setting. Have a drink of vodka before Rufina consumes it all."

They drank together and nibbled on the zakuski. Ursina turned to Maksim. "Tell me something you learned this week in class from Andrei Fyodorovich. Oh, I'm sorry—I forgot. I wasn't supposed to ask about what he teaches. If Rufina correctly describes the scene, we must assume it is very secret. Does it tell us, Andrei Fyodorovich, how we can overcome the West in agricultural production?"

Rufina shot a look of exasperation at Ursina. Andrei's face was suddenly rigid. He lit a Gauloise cigarette. And then, a mild reproach in his tone of voice, he said, "The Marxist revolution is not about how to make corn grow more plentifully than they evidently manage to do in . . . Iowa?" His patient smile now resumed, and he reached for his glass. Andrei liked to drink and smoke simultaneously, and frequently.

"Of course, of course. On the other hand," Ursina took a conspicuous bite of one of the zakuski, "is there anything grander than this smoked salmon? You're not going to try to trump that as a Soviet accomplishment, this salmon? With what? A peaceful revolution in Nicaragua?"

Rufina sighed resignedly. She turned to Maksim. "Maks, the way Ursina Dmitrievna is going, we won't get her to talk sense unless we start conversing about men's genital problems and getting it wrong. That's the only subject about which I assume she knows something."

"You want to talk about that?" Ursina laughed. "Well, there was this man called Adam, and this girl called Eve—"

"Oh shut up, Ursina, and have another drink," Andrei said.

"I'll gladly help you change the subject," said Kirov. "I will tell you about three British authors I have been reading. They are Evelyn Waugh and Graham Greene and Malcolm Muggeridge. Andrei Fyodorovich, you probably have heard of them."

"Actually, I have known all three."

Kirov was stunned to hear this. But he was confronted with the hard stone wall that encircled Andrei Fyodorovich Martins. All Kirov could get from his host was that he had "brushed up against" those British authors while studying in England as a very young man. But whereas Kirov, the elderly and soft-spoken scholar, was willing to retire from the fray, Ursina persisted. "Can't you tell us *anything* about these famous British writers, Andrei Fyodorovich? Like—did they fight in the Great Anti-Fascist War?"

"Yes. I think they were all . . . involved."

"Were they in favor of the war during the Stalin–Hitler pact?"

The reference brought silence. That episode in Soviet history, when Stalin had joined Adolf Hitler in a mutual security treaty, had stupefied Marxists and fellow travelers around the world. They had been taught that any concession to Hitler was a violation of the faith. The Stalin–Hitler pact was simply not mentioned.

Kirov spoke up, reproachfully. "The Soviet Union, Ursina,

was fighting for time, and had to make a truce with the devil."

Irina Gromov backed him up. "The anti-fascist constancy of the Soviet Union is a matter of record. We fought them, after all, in Spain."

"As a matter of fact," Kirov said, "Greene and Muggeridge were actively opposed to Franco. Not so much Waugh—he was a Catholic in his politics and of course Franco's fascists were Catholics."

"History obliges us," Andrei said, faltering a little in finding the Russian words, "to recognize Josef Stalin as a great war leader and sturdy champion of the revolution. But we are not obliged to applaud everything he did."

"And just now," Maksim, heretofore silent, observed, "Comrade Gorbachev has furthered the cause of peace by leading the American president to remove intermediate-range missiles from Europe."

"Yes," said Ursina. "Comrade Gorbachev is in favor of peace. Everywhere except Afghanistan."

Rufina's distress was no longer concealed. "We will not talk politics any more. This is a celebratory dinner. Celebrating Ursina's celebrated appointment as a professor and the great accomplishments of Soviet science. I present a toast: to Professor Ursina Chadinov and to—"

"Don't toast to an early end to men's problems. Vladimir and I would be out of business."

Everyone laughed, and with some relief, Rufina put on a new recording of Shostakovich's Tenth Symphony.

CHAPTER 6

Gus Windels, who had been living and working in Moscow
since reporting for duty in April, kept busy in the United
States diplomatic legation, as a public-affairs officer. His native fluency in Russian permitted him to scan the day's papers easily, and his political sophistication put developments
rapidly in their ideological place. This morning, the tall,
lanky, young American read the welcome news.

A Nobel Prize for Joseph Brodsky! *Good stuff!* Charlie
Wick—Wick was the director of the United States Information Agency in Washington, a keen cold warrior and a personal friend of President Reagan—would eat that up. He'll
have that *instead* of breakfast, Gus figured.

Inevitably, somebody—maybe Caspar Weinberger, defense secretary, or George Shultz, secretary of state—would
be cabling the ambassador asking how come the United

States Embassy in Moscow, with its nine hundred employees, hadn't got wind of this propaganda coup, a Nobel for a prime Soviet target.

Gus thought about it.

Joseph Brodsky, Leningrad Jew, superb poet and essayist. In 1964 they had arrested him and sent him to Gulag. He was there for eighteen months, until General Secretary Brezhnev—successor to Khrushchev—who had carted Brodsky away, decided that detaining the newsworthy young writer wasn't really worth the cultural uproar.

For all his experience with Soviet culture, Gus sometimes wondered in full voice about the sheer public-relations *stupidity* of the Kremlin. There were plenty of Russians they could more or less safely torture in Gulag. But Brodsky was (1) a young man (twenty-three), (2) a poet, (3) a Jew, who (4) wrote poetry in Russian and in English, if you please, and had an international fan club—"Everybody is asking, where is Brodsky?" someone had written in *Playboy*. So what does the dumb Soviet Union do? Charges him with the crime of "parasitism" and sends him to an Arctic labor camp!

The Soviet Union, eight million square miles, was not large enough to contain both the Kremlin and the poet, so the Communists finally deported him, as they would Solzhenitsyn a few years later.

Gus, baptized "Sergei" as an infant in the Ukraine twenty-nine years ago, had escaped, at age fourteen, with his mother. Why did his mother take the name "Windels" for herself and her son? "Because," Gus had once heard her say in broken English, that name—Win-dels—picked from the Manhattan telephone book, was "zee most un-Russian name I could find."

Gus and his mother had traveled to Iowa to join her

brother, who had got out of the Soviet Union several years before. Gus went to school there and was recruited by the Central Intelligence Agency.

His training was technical. He knew all the tricks—and on occasion used them. But for all his technical training he was, first, a Sovietologist. He served the U.S. Embassy openly in the press detachment, where he was occasionally consulted on the language of Soviet fulminations. He knew there would be huge resentment over the Nobel award to Brodsky. But there had been such a record of Soviet fiascos, the Kremlin might just be careful, this time around.

The Kremlin had forced Boris Pasternak to reject his Nobel Prize; Aleksandr Solzhenitsyn had declined to travel to Stockholm to collect *his* prize, for fear he would not be allowed to return; following which came the infinitely embarrassing Andrei Sakharov business. The great man of science, principal engineer of the Soviet hydrogen bomb, was not allowed to travel to Oslo to receive his Nobel Peace Prize—and *then* was sent to "internal exile" in Gorky.

The Kremlin is not looking for another battle with the Nobel committee, Gus calculated. There wasn't, after all, anything they could do to Brodsky himself—he had already been exiled as an enemy alien and lived safely abroad. And there was the other point: Every now and again the Nobel committee honored a Russian artist or scientist who was in good standing. The Kremlin liked it when that happened. Categorical denunciations of Nobels diluted the honor for such comrades.

Gus wrote out a note to the deputy chief of mission: "Soviets probably won't thunder over the Brodsky award. Maybe we shouldn't, either."

He got a call two hours later. "The ambassador agrees on Brodsky. We'll play it down. What he's most interested in— what everybody's most interested in—is the International Peace Forum coming up. Keep your eyes on it."

Gus Windels would do so, of course—he already had it in his sights. The peace forum was a Gorbachev initiative, scheduled to take place after Gorbachev's visit with President Reagan in December. The announced theme of the peace forum was to be "A Nonnuclear World for the Survival of Mankind."

Such a forum! Under such auspices!

Surely Pierre Trudeau of Canada would be there. And full-time Soviet apologist Armand Hammer. There would probably be some of the same U.S. celebrities (Norman Mailer, Gore Vidal) who had been assembled two decades earlier to promote Fidel Castro in Cuba. But Gus had heard that this time the Kremlin was going to try for some new blood.

Well, Soviet-backed public conferences always had tactical, as well as strategic, objectives. This time around, of course, the objective was to put pressure on the United States to slow down, perhaps even to abandon in the near future, Reagan's anti-missile program. Gus would be interested in what Ursina Chadinov had to say about the peace forum, when he met her at the Mussky restaurant that evening.

CHAPTER 7

The custom at Moscow University was to greet foreign students at a public assembly the first Monday of every month. "This custom is quite new," the public-affairs officer at the embassy had informed Gus Windels in April, when he arrived in Moscow. The departing press officer, after a four-year tour of duty, was being reassigned to Leningrad. He sat in the office he would turn over to Gus, a room bursting with newspapers and files; in his hand, a Coca-Cola with a straw. Gus had told him of the personal work he longed to complete—a history of the czar's secret police, the Okhrana.

"Up until two or three years ago," the departing officer said, "foreign students were all but physically blocked from Moscow U., unless they were coming in under ideological patronage. Every black African who could read and write and would cheer for democratic socialism was welcomed. Granted, they then had to learn Russian or English or German to make their way around the academic halls. But it's a little different now, the tone of the place. There are even people there who are interested in scholarship. Russia has plenty of geniuses, but they have to make their own way unless they are in ideological harness. What am I saying, Gus? That if you're going to start in on your research at Moscow U., you should attend one of their Monday open houses."

Gus did. He brought along a folder with research he had done at Georgetown. It included a suggested reading list of material published in Russian and housed at the Moscow University Library.

On that Monday he was one of thirty men and women, most of them in their twenties or thirties, occupying one tenth of the seats in the little auditorium. At one end of the stage a covered piano rested. The overhead lights seemed to peer down with an intensity suitable for an operating room; or else they were turned off, when a speaker was at the lectern, leaving the rest of the room in near total darkness. The headsets permitted listeners to hear what was being said in Russian, English, French, and German.

This Monday, to introduce newly arrived researchers to the hours and protocols and divisions of the mammoth university, there were four speakers. Two spoke in Russian, two in English. The first speaker was the chief librarian, an elderly woman with thick eyeglasses and anarchic gray hair, wearing black pants and a dark burgundy blouse. She spoke of the resources of the library, the hours it was accessible, and the credentials that needed to be presented by the individual researchers. The next two hosts spoke of the history of Moscow University, giving the names of some of its illustrious graduates.

The final speaker was a professor at the School of Medicine. Gus, who was looking down at his notepad when she began to speak, was struck first by her fluency in English. He looked up with curiosity at Professor Ursina Chadinov. She was a woman of commanding presence, perhaps five feet eight inches tall. Her light blond hair, swept back in a stylish French twist, heightened her brown eyes. She permitted herself a half smile at intervals, exhibiting a perfect set of teeth illuminated, almost glaringly, by the spotlight, which seemed especially focused on them.

She spoke of research being undertaken at the university in medicine, disease control, and general hygiene. Her tone of voice was pleasant if a bit imperious. One questioner, a Scandinavian by his appearance, asked flippantly if Professor Chadinov herself engaged only in research, or was she also a practicing medical doctor? She replied that if the questioner arrived at the hospital admissions desk with a certain order of complaint, he might be directed to her office.

So much for you, buster, Gus thought.

Gus was inventive. The next afternoon, before going to the stacks, he walked into the hospital and told the woman at the desk, "I have a certain complaint and have been told to report to Dr. Chadinov."

The woman asked his name. He gave a modified version of Windels that would be pronounceable in Russian.

The receptionist talked into the headset's microphone. "Mr. Vindellz is here for his appointment with Dr. Chadinov."

Gus raised his hand. "I didn't say I had an appointment—"

But the receptionist was talking on the phone. "Da . . . da . . . da . . ." She then turned to Gus, "You are to go to 912B; that is in the next building. The nurse there will direct you."

Gus rather enjoyed the daredevil aspect of it all, and a few minutes later was at 912B. He showed his identification card. The nurse, who spoke within earshot of two other nurses and a male orderly busy assembling medicines on a trolley, asked, "What is the nature of your complaint?"

What could he come up with? Gus Windels was tall and lithe. His face showed a trace of freckles leading to his full head of hair, in childhood almost certainly red, now a rusty blond. He could not suppress his cheerfulness. "Ma'am, if you do not mind, it's rather . . . personal."

She looked up at him with condescension. If Gus had been a little older, she'd have scolded him to the effect that one does not have "personal" problems in medicine. If he had been five years younger she'd have told him to act like a grown man and answer her question. But as it was, her expression turned motherly. "All right. Sit over there. You will be called."

A half hour later, an orderly told him to follow her.

He was led into a small office. Dr. Chadinov was seated, and nodded to Gus to sit down opposite.

Gus spoke his impeccable Russian. "Dr. Chadinov, I hope you will forgive me. But I heard you speak yesterday and I would dearly love it if you would let me take you to dinner."

She paused for a moment, looking concentratedly at her patient. Then, "I would be delighted to have dinner with you."

CHAPTER 8

At a few minutes to eight, Gus arrived at the Mussky restaurant and was taken to the table he had reserved for two. Making reservations at that restaurant was not easy to do. It required *blat*—the Russian word for influence, usually exercised in the form of bribes. Gus had *blat* at hand, and used it in talking with the headwaiter. He sat down and ordered a bottle of Russian wine. At eight fifteen, Professor Chadinov had not arrived. At eight thirty, Gus dejectedly concluded that the beautiful, dynamic, bilingual professor had had second thoughts about the date, or perhaps had never intended to keep it.

He lingered on for a moment, looking over at his third glass of wine and wondering whether to order a meal for himself, or take the metro back to his apartment, make a sandwich, and get on with the book on the Okhrana. Then she appeared. Accompanied by an older man, whom she introduced as "my dear old friend and colleague, Dr. Vladimir Spiridonovich Kirov. I knew you would be glad to meet him."

Gus suppressed his disappointment, and rose to greet the two doctors. He signaled to the waiter. "Professor Chadinov, is this wine," he pointed to the half-empty bottle, "all right?"

"It's all right if"—she went into English—"if you are unfamiliar with alternatives. I know of an alternative available at the same price. May I?"

The waiter brought the wine she asked for, and they were well into the next bottle before they paused in their conversation to order food.

Ursina addressed Gus familiarly, and appeared genuinely interested in everything he said.

Gus spoke about his mother's life in Kiev and of his early years at school there.

"Why did your mother leave? What year did she leave?"

Gus replied diplomatically. If the question had been asked a fortnight later, after two more visits with Ursina, he might have said, "Why on earth would she *not* have left the Soviet Union?" Tonight he said only that an uncle who had moved to the United States before the war had succeeded as a farmer in Iowa and had arranged to bring his sister and her fourteen-year-old son to live with him. "My father had died—well, we always assumed he had died. Mother didn't hear from him after he was taken away in 1960. When word came from my uncle, we felt we were very lucky."

"*Very lucky to leave the Soviet Union.*" She turned to her colleague. "Volodya, those are strange words to hear, are they not?"

Kirov came through with an inconclusive giggle. "Ursina,

you are always being provocative. Leaving the Soviet Union at age fourteen, Mister Windels—"

" 'Gus,' please."

"—our host was too young to feel the loss of his motherland."

"Exactly," said Gus. "I was just a dumb little boy insensitive to the loss I was sustaining by going to America."

Ursina looked him hard in the face. He had permitted himself just a trace of a smile, which she reciprocated.

But she gave the impression that attention needed now to be given to assessing the offerings lovingly described in the menu. There were piroshki, three kinds of herring and two of smoked sturgeon, blini, chicken and veal and lamb in various guises, baklava and ice cream. With the food and the wine, the diners cast off the blight of a tedious day, leaving them happy and distracted for a little while.

Ursina and Kirov wanted to know everything about Gus's life in Iowa.

"Was your uncle an overlord?"

"A what?"

"I mean, did he have many farmers who worked for him?"

"Yes. Well, he had a few. He was the owner of a medium-sized farm."

"Did his serfs earn a living wage?"

Kirov broke in. "Ursina, you are not an interrogator at the Lubyanka."

"What does Mr.—Gus—know of the Lubyanka?"

What is she up to? Gus wondered. The Lubyanka was celebrated in book after book about the Soviet Union as the headquarters in Moscow of the KGB, the Soviet Gestapo. Half the Russians who were brought into that massive stone building ended up on trains bound for Gulag. The other half were cremated, after the bullet in the head.

"Dr. Ursina, everybody in the Western world knows about the Lubyanka." Gus felt he could get away with saying that much, leaving unsaid what it was about the Lubyanka that had been written by such as Arthur Koestler and Aleksandr Solzhenitsyn.

"But, Dr. Ursina" (she had acquiesced in this form of address, stopping short of asking to be called merely "Ursina," even though the elderly Dr. Kirov had asked to be called "Vladimir"), "you know, because I told you, that I am with the press office of the United States Embassy. We are briefed on all the important landmarks of your country."

"*My* country?"

Gus smiled. "All right, I was born here, too. My ex-country."

It was a long evening, and not lacking in warmth, even though Ursina from time to time edged politics into the discussion. She asked if Gus intended to be present at the upcoming International Peace Forum, scheduled for early the following year. "I suppose you will be there to spy on it."

Gus laughed. "President Reagan also hopes for a world without nuclear weapons."

"Why then is he sponsoring an anti-missile missile program?"

"That," said Gus cautiously, "is for the purpose of . . . *destroying* nuclear weapons transported by missiles."

Ursina began to answer, but cut her reply off and took another tack. "I suppose I must not ask what exactly you do in the press office."

"You are free to do so. And am I free to ask what you do in the medical world, besides welcoming so graciously visitors to your university?"

"Dr. Kirov and I are practicing urologists."

"I see. Well," he raised his glass, "let's drink to your success in *that* field!"

"And not in other fields of my interest?"

"That," said Gus, "would require some thought."

Vladimir Kirov had gone to the men's room, and Gus was counting out bills for the waiter. Ursina took a card from her purse and wrote down a telephone number. "Perhaps we can give it some thought at a future meeting?"

Pocketing the card, Gus smiled broadly. "We must give these matters a great deal of thought."

CHAPTER 9

Konstantin Chernenko, at age seventy-two, could not be expected to live forever, but he acted as if he intended to do exactly that. On February 13, 1984, when Chernenko was named general secretary, Nikolai Dmitriev was confident that Chernenko would nominate him as successor. Dmitriev had been friends with Chernenko for a long time and was twenty years his junior.

The idea was that when, in due course, Dmitriev became general secretary, he would immediately name General Leonid Baranov as chief of staff. The choice of Baranov, Dmitriev reasoned, would be welcomed by the military court. There was, granted, the problem of his age—Baranov was seventy-six—but his standing with the Politburo was solid. He had weathered all the changes in government from the death of Stalin to the present. "If he could get on with Beria—with Bulganin—with Khrushchev—with Brezhnev—with Andropov," one colleague had observed, "why he could probably have got along with both Stalin and Hitler simultaneously."

In fact, over the twenty-two-month duration of the Hitler–Stalin pact, Baranov was able to boast that young though he was in August 1939—a lieutenant colonel at age thirty-one—he had been at Foreign Minister Molotov's side during the negotiations in Moscow leading to the pact between Hitler and Stalin. That chapter in his life was forever forgotten after the Nazis marched into Russia in June of 1941, but Baranov continued to rise in the military order under the patronage of Politburo member Konstantin Chernenko.

Chernenko was an odd duck. When he decided to let a policy decision be known, he would call in not the Presidium, nor the Central Committee, nor the chiefs of staff, but Nika. Nika had been his personal secretary for thirty-five years. She was a woman born to serve. Her only idiosyncrasy was her obstinate concealment of her surname. She was Nika—just that, Nika—in every situation. "Does the KGB know your last name?" the new payroll sergeant asked her, coming in to fill out the roster.

She managed a quick smile. "Oh, I wouldn't reveal any secrets, Sergeant. You can absolutely trust me." She got away with it.

But General Baranov did not forgive her for failing to call to the attention of the dying premier that he had an important undischarged obligation: to name Dmitriev as his successor. And what happened, of course, in the absence of any testamentary word from Chernenko, was a political dogfight, in which one Mikhail Gorbachev prevailed.

General Baranov had had an agenda. He had communicated parts of it to Premier Chernenko, especially his conviction that the Soviet occupation of Afghanistan should be called off. It was costing too much, in lives, money, and international favor.

There were the hot young military men—there are such in almost every situation—who wished to pursue the military objective with, Baranov argued, the kind of undiscriminating tenacity Hitler had shown even when his fascist war was clearly doomed. There was no prospect that the Afghan adventure would actually doom the Soviet Union, but the high cost of it threatened other state enterprises, including a badly needed reform of the administrative structure. Nikolai Dmitriev, discreetly committed to the same reforms, was sidelined under the new Gorbachev regime.

"Those who lose out in high-powered competition in politics," General Baranov said to Oleg Pavlov, his son-in-law and closest aide, "are almost always destined to be sidelined in life. There is a large apartment house at Sukharevsky 298 with small apartments in it. One of them was occupied during the last years of his life by Nikita Khrushchev, another was occupied by Vyacheslav Molotov. I do not want to end my days there."

The general struggled to bring the whole scene into focus. The government was weak, after two years under Mikhail Gorbachev. The Afghan war had stalled, but Gorbachev still resisted bringing it to a close. The general staff—and who should know this better than Leonid Baranov, the senior general in active service?—was demoralized.

It was late in the evening, after many drinks shared with Pavlov, who had the rank of captain. General Baranov talked about how different the prospects would be for a healthy Soviet Union if Dmitriev had been selected as general secretary.

Captain Pavlov spoke now with an odd abruptness in his tone. "General, is a coup d'état proscribed by Marxist . . . thought?"

The general paused with vodka glass in hand instead of emptying it down his throat, as he had done many times during the long evening.

In measured tones, though there was a slight slur in his speech, he said that the purpose always was to advance the revolution. "If this can be done by deposing the ruler—the wrong ruler—would Lenin have approved of such a movement? Lenin was careful to supervise his own succession. Perhaps you will say, Oleg, that he was not careful enough, because although he warned privately about Stalin, it was Stalin who took command."

"General"—Pavlov always thus addressed his father-in-law—"we have never spoken about the plot last year against Comrade Gorbachev. You should know that Ivan Pletnev, a boyhood friend of mine, is the brother of one of the conspirators in that plot."

"Was he himself involved in it?"

"Absolutely not. He was in Afghanistan at the time. But when the plot failed and they had his brother in custody, the KGB summoned him from the front and . . . interrogated him vigorously. Too vigorously."

"What do you mean by that?"

"He is crippled, living at home with his mother. He speaks to me with great candor. He tells me that the plot, which almost succeeded, depended heavily on the Americans. If, with Gorbachev out of the way, the Americans proceeded to recognize the government of his successor, everything would fall into place."

"How did he learn all this, if he was off in Afghanistan?"

"Viktor, Ivan's brother, confided in his oldest friend, a woman called Galina. They grew up as close as sister and brother. And after Viktor's death she confided in Ivan."

"Was she also questioned by the KGB?"

"Yes. There was brutality, but—nothing crippling."

"How does one get in touch with her?"

Pavlov swallowed another drink. "She is a lady of the night."

General Baranov took that in calmly, as he might have taken in the news that one of his regiments had been destroyed. "Can you take me to her?"

"General, I can do that, yes. When?"

"Tonight."

Pavlov looked down at his watch. "It is just past midnight. I suggest you send your driver home, and come discreetly with me in my car."

Twenty minutes later, Pavlov's old Volga sedan pulled up to the curb in the lonely street north of Rozhdestvensky Boulevard. The woman at the desk was not there. Pavlov led the general upstairs to room 48. He knocked several times, but there was no answer.

"Let's leave," the general said, turning away.

In the car, they did not speak. But shortly before reaching his imposing house, the general turned to Pavlov. "I will think about this whole thing. Think about the advisability of . . . visiting with the girl. I will let you know my thinking."

"Yes, General."

CHAPTER 10

When Gus next met with Ursina, this time at the Preskov, she arrived alone—walking from the metro, he concluded. She sat down without any affected salutation. She said simply, "Well, it's nice to see you, Gus. You need not call me Dr. Ursina, even though this time I am unchaperoned. At least, not until you appear on my operating table." She babbled on as Gus poured out the wine she had ordered at their earlier dinner.

They talked at first about the initiative of Gorbachev to end the testing of nuclear weapons. "Your government has been rather ambivalent on the point."

"The Reagan people," Gus said, "are looking out for any clause in a new treaty that would limit pursuit of our Star Wars program."

"Yes, and of course the language of the ABM Treaty is under discussion. Your people are promoting the position that Star Wars experimentation can proceed without violating the treaty."

"Unless the explosions take place in the atmosphere."

"Oh goodness. When will it end?"

"I don't know. But Ursina, should it concern us?"

"Obviously it concerns us, young idiot." She began now speaking in English, and Gus replied in English. They moved in and out of the two languages, according as idiomatic references lent themselves better to one or the other language.

After the first course, he asked her whether she would care to spend the night with him. "You are a dazzling lady."

"Well, you are not a dazzling man. You are by my standards a child. Though a well-spoken child. And I rather like your face. I am a little surprised that such a face could have been generated in the Ukraine. Are you certain your parents were Ukrainians?"

Gus laughed. "I'm sure a Soviet historian doing faithful duty to his boss could find a way of proving that I was actually born and bred in Iowa."

"Our scientists can be very ingenious."

"Yes. Like Lysenko. He could prove anything that your scientific commissions wanted proved."

"For instance, that when you were growing up, whether in the Ukraine or in Iowa, you were taught to be respectful in the company of . . . middle-aged ladies?"

"Oh, shit. Forget Lysenko. I'm not sure any phony scientists got in the way of your specialty."

"No. There is no party line on the subject of male urological problems. . . . You know, Gus—maybe you have not lived here long enough to run into it: The official Russians are great prudes. You cannot read pornography here."

"But there is no difficulty in Moscow—I am told—in finding prostitutes."

"Well done, Mr. Gus. No difficulty—as you tell it. We are left to infer that you never inquired personally into the subject."

Gus thought to say, and did, "Well, there was the one occasion, it was very late at night—"

"I hope you were protected."

"Well, at one level I was protected."

"What other levels are there? What are you talking about? I forgot to ask, are you CIA?"

Gus laughed, and poured her some more wine. "You have asked me a lot of questions. I begin by saying you are intelligent enough to know that if I *was* a member of the CIA, I would not admit it."

"Unless it was necessary in order to seduce me."

"Ursina, you have a bad habit of trumping every point I make. I am using plain English—*trumping every point*. Do you understand?"

"Of course. I have played bridge."

"Well, I'll tell you what. If you sleep with me I will tell you that I am a member of the CIA and will report on every detail of the evening."

"I suppose I could use you to advance my research, too." She smiled and kissed him lightly on the cheek.

CHAPTER 11

At regular intervals, during his visits to the university library, Gus did a special kind of research. He spent a lot of time at the library, collecting data for his book on the Okhrana. But once every week he would call up Volume III of the *Encyclopaedia Britannica* (1911 edition). Inside the front cover were the signatures of every library patron who had consulted that volume of the encyclopedia (it was forbidden to remove it from the library). He would scan these looking for the code— the name of Galina Sokolov. When her name appeared, that was the signal, and he would initiate a meeting with her by calling in at the brothel and paying for a half hour with her, putting down forty rubles on the counter. The clerk, a heavily made-up elderly woman, would check upstairs on the intercom connection without removing her cigarette from her mouth. Galina was—or was not—available.

Galina—short, blonde, with sleepy hazel eyes beneath her bangs—conceived of herself, depending on the patron, as a ravishing sexual object, or a warm den mother, or a sophisticated salon matriarch.

She collected political gossip. Her tips weren't always reliable. She trafficked mostly in rumors, but some of these, Gus, whose meetings with her satisfied several of his appetites, listened to with assiduous interest. She had once reminisced to Gus about General Secretary Chernenko, who had been one of her clients. Already an old man when he succeeded Yuri Andropov in 1984, he had told Galina he was going to inform the Presidium of his recommendation for a successor within a few weeks. Whether he had actually done so she did not know. Chernenko fell seriously ill one week after his last encounter with Galina, and died two months later.

On this visit, Gus was surprised when Galina spoke with some familiarity about "the plot last year to assassinate Comrade Gorbachev." Few people knew more about that plot than Gus Windels, who, posing as the son of Blackford Oakes, had traveled to Moscow with Oakes to foil it. Yet Galina spoke knowingly of the plot. She managed to give it an erotic dimension, going on about it even when they were deeply entwined. Now, her formal duties done, she lit a cigarette and returned to the subject with very special information.

That the attempt a year ago had been made, she said, was widely known by the cognoscenti, though the plot was never officially acknowledged. The insiders, Galina told Gus, knew that a bomb had actually exploded in Gorbachev's desk, killing an aide. Galina now told Gus that one of the assassins, caught, tortured, and executed, had a brother. And he, seeking revenge, was determined to make a fresh attempt on

Gorbachev's life. To that end, he had lined up support from a disaffected general.

"Who?"

"I don't know. But the brother—he told me that the general hopes to find financing for the next attempt."

"Financing from whom?"

"Gus. I do not know. From the Americans, one imagines. It is Americans who usually finance things. Perhaps the American Central Intelligence."

"Galina, you are in touch with the brother?"

"I have been in intimate touch with him."

"You can find him, then?"

"No. We don't have a code system. That's only for you. And somebody else who is special. But the brother comes back quite often."

"Why would he tell *you* about a plot against Gorbachev?"

"Because the general told him to tell me."

"Why?"

"I guess, wanting to use me to set up a meeting with an American official. The brother knows I have U.S. contacts."

Gus took a deep breath. He mustn't just say Americans-don't-do-that-kind-of-thing. And he wanted as much information as he could get. "Is the brother . . . talking about a day? Soon?"

"He said that was for the general to decide. Oh. The most important thing. Really, the reason I went to the library to give you the signal to come. The brother knows you and I are friends. He said that perhaps you could enlist the aid of a 'Mr. Singleton.'"

Gus dug his nails into the palms of his hands. He raced though his memory. When he came to Moscow last October

it was as Jerry Singleton, son of Harry Singleton, allegedly in search of a Ukrainian aunt. No one in the Kremlin knew that the Singletons had other reasons to be in Moscow.

"I never heard of a Mr. Singleton," Gus told Galina. But her intercom was buzzing.

"Yes," she said. "Send him up in five minutes."

CHAPTER 12

The rules were formal. CIA activity in a foreign country had
to be disclosed to the U.S. ambassador in that country. But
formal rules sometimes bump into presidential prerogatives.
The moment had come when Gus Windels had to face the
problem, in total privacy with the ambassador.

They went together into the embassy's so-called bubble
room—the capsule with glass enclosure designed to block
eavesdropping of any kind. Jack Matlock was a historian, a
learned student of Soviet life and politics. Gus Windels had
rehearsed what to tell him, what to hold back.

"Sir, you probably know Blackford Oakes? CIA?"

"Yes, sure I know him, though I haven't spent any time
with him. What's he up to? Not coming over here, I hope."

"Yes sir, he is. He's on a presidential mission."

Ambassador Matlock peered over his glasses. "What is
the mission?"

The answer to that question Gus had rehearsed over a protected telephone line with the director. "Mr. Oakes wants to investigate a rumor of special interest to the president."

Matlock's expression was wry. "Presumably of no special interest to me, merely the ambassador. Such a rumor as would cause the president to send his own man to check?"

"Sir, it's nothing more than a rumor, and Mr. Oakes wants to play it that way."

"Well, it must be a mission of some importance, bringing in the former head of the covert-operations division of the CIA. Bringing him here, as we both know, is against security rules. But the president can override such rules. He is presumably engaged at this moment in overriding them by your failure to disclose to me more exactly what Oakes—what the president is looking for. What kind of cover is Mr. Oakes using?"

"He will be here, sir, as a kind of book agent or promoter, with ties to the USIA. The USIA is routinely committed to the exchange of cultural information, and, you of course know, '88 is the year for a special exhibit—once every two years. It's on your calendar to be there physically at the opening. The USIA exhibit will open in June. In Gorky. It's Oakes's assignment to involve himself thoroughly in the Gorky exhibit and to try to persuade Gosizdat to publish a few U.S. titles."

"Getting Gosizdat to open up on foreign books takes a while. It took Soviet publishers twelve years before they published Philby's book."

"Yes, sir. But that was a unique operation. Kim Philby is the crown jewel of Soviet intelligence operations."

Jack Matlock tightened his lips. "Thank God one can think of Philby as unique. If there were more Philbys, maybe one of them would work his way to becoming national security adviser." Matlock reflected on Philby's remarkable career. He was a clandestine Communist agent who managed to get himself appointed head of counter-Soviet intelligence in Great Britain. He did a tour of duty in Washington and betrayed a dozen clandestine operations and who knows how many human beings. "I never got over that: a Communist agent working his way into the job of looking out for Communist agents! I don't suppose Oakes is coming over to sell Gosizdat on publishing more books about the successes of Soviet spies in the West."

"No. But we *can* take advantage of Gorbachev's easing up on the reading rules. Remember the fuss at the eighth congress of the Union of Writers? Well, the battles between the reformers and the gatekeepers of orthodoxy aren't over. Those people are sore as hell that *Novy Mir* is publishing Pasternak's *Doctor Zhivago*. Mr. Oakes has that very much in mind. His idea will be to get publishers to release a few books written in English and promote them in connection with the Gorky cultural exhibit."

"Like what books?"

"Well, one of them is the *Encyclopaedia Britannica,* which is now a U.S. publication. Also, the Great Books, which is fifty-plus volumes right there. Another is *The Federalist Papers*—"

"That's one of the quote unquote Great Books."

Son of a bitch Matlock knows everything. "Yes, of course. But the point is, we're not asking them to okay books by Whittaker Chambers or Eugene Lyons or Max Eastman. Or, for that matter, speeches by President Reagan." Gus returned Matlock's smile. "I think Blackford Oakes is going to tread carefully."

"Will he need an office, or just a hotel room?"

"We're getting a couple of rooms at the Metropol Hotel. There are a dozen suites there rented and lived in by 'businessmen.' He told me he wants to get around, be where the culture mavens gather."

"Does he speak Russian?"

"Some. Not enough to get very far. That's an important point, sir, because he wants me to work with him again."

Matlock paused. "Well, that's okay. We can detach you for special duty on the Gorky exhibit. I hope he does not want to see me."

"No, sir. He wants very much not to see you."

The ambassador got up. "Okay, Windels. You've gone through the necessary motions. I don't need to tell you to be careful. Try to do things so they don't end up kicking me out of the country. To be U.S. ambassador to the Soviet Union in 1987 and be kicked out of the country! That would be torture for a historian."

"I see what you mean, sir."

CHAPTER 13

In preparing for this trip to Moscow, Blackford Oakes elected to become "Henry Doubleday."

The assignment was very different from the one of a year ago. Then, the planned assassination of Gorbachev was set for a few days ahead. This time, such a plot was not by any means set, it was gestating. Blackford had told the director he would be away perhaps for several weeks. "It's your call," Bill Webster had replied. Blackford's seniority shielded him from bureaucratic interference, and having given up the post of chief of covert operations, he had no managerial responsibilities.

The facilities of the agency, on the other hand, were entirely at his disposal. So he went to the shed and checked in with Andrew. They were contemporaries, and Blackford had, over the years, relied on this close-mouthed, bald-headed specialist in disguises and identification paraphernalia.

"Andrew, if anybody in Moscow knows anything at all about U.S. book-publishing history, they'll know the name Doubleday. If anybody approaches me and says, 'Are you a Doubleday?' I can answer, 'Well, in a way.'" He winked. "'I'm named Doubleday, but I'm not *a* Doubleday.'"

Gus Windels had, of course, diplomatic immunity. And the KGB had not taken note of his phony mission of the year before, looking for a lost "aunt." But Blackford needed cover. There were CIA in the Soviet Union, and KGB in the United States. Their mobility—and sometimes their safety—depended on not being noticed. It was for this reason that the most valuable Soviet agents in the West were natives of the countries they worked in. It was so, too, in the Soviet Union: U.S. assets were mostly Russian-born. But Americans in the Soviet Union, doing covert duty for Washington, needed plausible cover. Thanks to Andrew, Oakes would have this.

Andrew went to work preparing his documents. Meanwhile, two letters went out to counterparts at the Soviet end of the planned cultural exhibit. Preliminary letters from Henry Doubleday, advising that he would soon be on the scene, and giving a preview of the books he hoped might be made available to Soviet students and readers—which meant getting clearance for them from the censors.

Not a bad idea to plead for more books in connection with the scheduled two-nation exhibits. These were a part of a decades-old agreement, reached by President Eisenhower and Premier Khrushchev in 1958, with the exalted title, "Agreement between the United States of America and the Union of Soviet Socialist Republics on Exchanges in the Cultural, Technical, and Educational Fields." The first exhibit, in Moscow, had been the scene of the legendary "kitchen debate" between

Richard Nixon and Nikita Khrushchev. Nixon, the young vice president, seemed overpowered by the massive presence of the Soviet premier. But Nixon had been a debater in college, and a strenuous advocate in his days as congressman and senator. When Khrushchev made reference to the great achievements of the Soviet economy, Nixon replied by showing off kitchen equipment—refrigerators, toasters, blenders—that was routine in the United States, mouth-watering to Soviet citizens.

The exhibits were to be open for three months, the one in Russia devised by Americans, the one in the United States devised by Soviets. They were conceived as giving expression to life and culture in the two countries. "I'm glad I don't have to design the USSR's exhibit," Blackford said to Andrew. "What will they come up with? The ballet and missile-producing factories? Never mind, that's their problem."

The United States leaned heavily on the universal appetite for American cars and movies and popular music. The exhibit at Gorky would show off eight 1988-model cars, including the flashy Chevrolet Camaro and the solid new Plymouth Reliant. There would be a snowland of refrigerators and freezers, long tables of word processors and tape recorders, stacks of music CDs and movies on videotape—and libraries of books. That was the division of the exhibit Henry Doubleday would be paying special attention to.

From the Russian desk he got a listing of U.S. books that had been approved for circulation in the Soviet Union. The Communists, the covering CIA memo said, were especially concerned to forbid any book that dealt with internal USSR quarrels. There was an ethnic division among the cultural advisers to the Kremlin—Great Russians vs. Georgians, Central

Asians, and so on. There was also division over Gorbachev's glasnost, his declared policy of openness. Some were enthusiastic about the general secretary's reforms, some cautious, some actively opposed. On the matter of what books to promote, some called for a return to "classic Russian writers," others to "proletarian populism."

Blackford looked over the long memo, then put it down. He booked the clear phone line for a call to Gus.

"What made you think I'd still be in the office, Dad?"

It was endlessly amusing to Gus—and, actually, also to Blackford—to hark back, when in private, to the father–son relationship they had feigned the first time they worked together.

"Gus, I'm going to steer clear of the glasnost maelstrom, but here's something I need advice about. The people I'll be dealing with on the Gorky exhibit—which way do they lean? Toward glasnost, or against? I'm preparing a pitch, and that would be useful to know."

"I'll dig into that."

Gus agreed that Blackford would do best to concentrate on Western masterworks of composition, "like Hemingway," or collections, "like the Great Books." They talked about other American authors. Gus had a list of individual books that had been vetoed in the past. "I'll send those to you on the wire. Wouldn't be a bad idea to tell the Gorky people I'll be following you around while you're in Moscow."

Using USIA facilities, Blackford sent letters to the U.S. head of the Gorky exhibit and to his counterpart in the Soviet cultural-affairs office. The letters advised these officials that Mr. Gus Windels of the U.S. Embassy, who was fluent in Russian, had been detached to assist him with the exhibit, and that he, Henry Doubleday, would be using as his office a suite at the Metropol Hotel, and would receive mail and messages there. He hoped to arrive in the next few days, he said, and to stay in touch with the operation until after the exhibit was opened in June.

A few days later Henry Doubleday arrived at the Sheremetevo Airport.

The activity there had begun to reflect the more open policies of glasnost and perestroika. It was twice as busy, Blackford Oakes reflected, as just one year ago. He had brought with him two crates of books, and he supervised, unhurriedly, the unloading of these, carefully labeling them for the official exhibit, before he got into a cab to go to the Metropol. The next, snowy morning, he met for breakfast with the U.S. head of the Gorky exhibit and his Soviet counterpart. They discoursed at some length on the subject of the exhibit, staying away from the heat of political concern over cultural relations. He would go the following day, he told them, to Gorky, traveling by rail with his assistant from the embassy, Mr. Windels.

There was plenty of time to talk during the three-hour train ride over sparsely populated farmlands. The railroad car was of European design ("These cars were designed in Germany, built in France, and transported to Russia by the Nazis," Gus informed him). Arrived in Gorky, they spent hours surveying the buildings in which U.S. technology would be featured and then the movie auditorium. The USIA guide took them to the area being prepared for American books. "It's here, Dad, that you'll be displaying *The Federalist Papers* and inciting the counterrevolution."

"Quiet, Gus." Blackford looked about. He measured some distances within the U.S. quarters by taking his yard-long steps, while Gus smoked a cigarette.

Back on the train that afternoon, Blackford asked about friction at the Politburo level. "Is the division between Dmitriev and Gorbachev completely healed? What *about* Dmitriev? And what have you pulled together on 'the general'? We're talking about Leonid Baranov, we have to assume. The single bit of hard evidence we have of the whore's credibility is her use of the name Singleton. Since our talk on Monday, what have you been able to find out about how many of our friends were in on the Singleton episode?"

"I've run," Gus Windels said, frowning deeply, "into the solidest stone wall I've ever butted up against." He tried to lean back in the unyielding railroad seat, finally lifting his hips and stretching out his legs. "Let's go over the story. Yeah, we know it, but doing it this way, I think, we can lay it out like a computer folder, see how it looks. To us—and to them.

"Two American characters come to Moscow, Harry Singleton—that's you, Dad—and Jerry Singleton, that's me, your son. They are pretending to be here to look for an old Ukrainian aunt, thought long dead, but there was that sign of life in a letter to her sister that arrived just before—Mom's death. So the Singletons, father and son, are determined to discover whether Aunt Avrani is alive, and, if she is, to arrange to give her a little material comfort.

"But actually—" Gus stretched open his arms as if addressing not a solitary colleague, but a tearful wake of mourners. "But actually"—Gus spoke now in a stage whisper—"Dad's mission is to communicate with his old antagonist, the retired spy Boris Bolgin, to instruct him that he has to abort the plot to assassinate Gorbachev.

"Any corrections?"

"Go on, Gus."

"I will. Maybe my real vocation is for the theater.

"Anyway, the senior Singleton contacts the KGB defector, who is conniving in the assassination of the premier, and says: *Boris, you can't do that!* The United States would not like it at all. And if you don't break up the conspiracy, Harry Singleton, acting for the president of the United States, will.

"So what happens? The bomb goes off and kills not Gorby, but an aide. The KGB swoop down and get one of the four conspirators. Now—pay rapt attention, Dad—*none of the conspirators knew you were in town under the name Singleton.* So how did Galina get to talk to me about 'Mr. Singleton'?"

Blackford looked over from his seat, opposite. "You forgot a little detail."

"Oh well, er—"

"Oh no you don't. You wanted to play Laurence Olivier. Well, I can do that, too. What you left out is that young Jerry Singleton, although he had been told not to take any chances, couldn't refrain from accompanying a young lady from the embassy home to her apartment and screwing her just in time for the KGB to come in, photograph him, and haul his ass off to jail. They were looking for drugs—they said—and they didn't hold you for very long. But they had plenty of time to stare at your passport, and to record the name."

"Which was Singleton," Gus nodded, soberly.

"Which was Singleton."

"All right. But how did an American guy called Singleton, shacking up with an American girl, held overnight on drug suspicion, get to be known by Galina, a prostitute, as involved in an operation to assassinate Gorbachev? An operation in which, as we both know, the only role the U.S. *did* play was to get there and try to abort the whole thing."

Blackford said he could not come up with an answer to the question. None of the assassins had brushed up against either of the Singletons. The senior Singleton had returned to duty in Washington. Gus, the junior Singleton, had also returned, but was quickly reassigned to Moscow under his own name. His superior had consulted the Moscow embassy and learned that Gus did not appear to have been listed on any active Soviet ledgers as persona non grata. If he was later identified, he would simply be recalled, pursuant to Moscow–Washington standard practice when spies were detected under diplomatic cover.

So how might Galina's friend have known there was an American called Singleton in the picture?

"Odd stuff. Almost"—Gus hesitated—"unbelievable."

"Did you study any logic at the University of Iowa?"

"Well, sort of."

"We have here a prime example of a posteriori reasoning. (1) We know that Galina's friend mentioned the name 'Singleton.' (2) We reason back to the conclusion: that somebody gave him the name. Who?"

"What if his brother, the conspirator . . ."—Gus's hand was over his head—"what if he tailed you, Black, coming away from your meeting with Boris?"

Blackford paused. He spoke as if to himself. "And then passed on the name to his brother, who passed it on to the prostitute . . ."

"Maybe he thought Boris *had* called in a U.S. contact—Singleton—who would relay to Washington that the scheduled assassination was by anti-Communists."

"Yes. We will need to track the conspirator's brother to

the general. But our own investigations give us some idea on the matter of the likelihood of a coup. There is an anti-Gorbachev faction in the Politburo. But Gorbachev strikes me as very much in command."

"Well, he isn't, actually, Dad. There is a lot of opposition to his whole perestroika approach. A lot of people up there in the high world he inhabits think he is an ideological wimp."

"Do we think that?"

"I don't. But maybe you will."

They arrived back in Moscow ready for a little distraction. They would have it at the cocktail party Gus had planned for that evening, in a private room at the Metropol.

CHAPTER 14

Gus had composed his invitation list with care and in consultation with Artur Ivanov, a self-important deputy minister of culture who liked to be involved in any social function in connection with any enterprise, cultural or even anti-cultural. Comrade Ivanov was in charge of special arrangements for the Gorky exhibit.

Once upon a time, Ivanov was a writer. He had published, at age thirty, a novel so slavishly sycophantic that (it was widely reported) Stalin himself had specified Ivanov's selection as a member of the State Committee on Publishing.

A novel praising all aspects of life in the Soviet Union in 1952, plus membership in the state committee, wasn't quite enough to keep Ivanov in the higher echelons of literary life in Moscow. But he could not be ignored, even by writers who felt contempt for him. What Ivanov lacked in literary imagination, he made up for in artful bureaucratic improvisation.

He had climbed the ladder of the Writers' Union and served it now as vice chairman. His colleagues had little use for him as an interpreter of Soviet life, but enormously esteemed his ability to catalyze bureaucratic preferences. One hundred Moscow men of letters were obliged to Artur Filippovich for this or the other special grant or favorable notice or university preferment or permission to travel. It would be he, nominally, who would have the critical vote on which foreign books could be displayed in Gorky.

"He's an old fraud," Gus had briefed Blackford before the guests arrived, "but perfectly pleasant in social situations. Every now and again, if there are Soviets in the room and an American is within earshot, he'll think it prudent to enter a chauvinist wisecrack. Ideological boilerplate. Tuppence in the collection plate."

"Is he curious? What does he know about me? Just the description you sent out? . . . Book agent . . . consultant to the New York Public Library . . . associated with the USIA?"

"He's not going to ask you what were you doing when JFK was killed. Not that kind of detailed curiosity. No, he'll just coast on the Gorky business, and you're well up on that."

"Tell me about Ursina Chadinov."

"Well," Gus said, turning his head slightly. "She's a local star in the intellectual set. A practicing physician, a professor at Moscow University, author of a book on—urology, actually."

"Can we get the English-language rights to that one?"

"Don't sell this lady short. She is also as fluent in English as you are, and just as beautiful as you . . . used to be. Come to think of it, I guess I get my good looks from you, Dad!"

Gus turned his head sharply at the sound of a door opening, but it was only the waiter. "And, of course, she's active in the Scientists' and Scholars' Union."

"So be nice to her?"

"Yeah. Be nice to her. We've got a few other natives who are quietly friendly to the U.S. There's the Nikitins, husband and wife, Yevgeny and Antonina. They're true cultural grit. He plays the piano, she, the violin, and they do joint musical appearances. Both of them teach, and they're members of the Musicians' Union. There's a new edition of *Grove's* coming out, and they'll want to talk about putting that book—all twenty volumes—on the list of books to be authorized, even though it's a Brit publication, not one of ours."

"Gus, a delicate question I hadn't given any thought to: Have you got a specific allowance from the USIA to pay for outings like this one?"

"Oh sure. And Ivanov is almost certain to give a reciprocal cocktail party. Nothing lavish. The Commies are extravagant only on the military; everything else is penny-pinch. But they are also pretty hospitable. And, somehow, the money materializes."

"How are your guests in English?"

"Ivanov speaks it pretty well. So do Eduard and Sofia Konstantin—they lecture at the foreign-service school, and they've traveled abroad. The Nikitins speak it a bit. And as I said, Ursina is fluent. I don't have to tell you, these things have a way of working out, common sympathies. This is glasnost time, hang it all out. You got some body language worked up to communicate the true meaning of *The Federalist Papers*?"

The doorbell rang.

CHAPTER 15

Gus signaled to the waiter, hired help for the cocktail hour, motioning him to the door. Pyotr opened it for Deputy Minister Ivanov, whose raincoat Pyotr took, asking what refreshment he'd prefer. Pyotr nodded energetically when Ivanov mentioned champagne, his eyes surveying the rest of the room to order his social priorities.

Gus introduced the minister to "Mr. Henry Doubleday, our guest of honor, here to do what he can to make our Gorky exhibit truly successful." Blackford looked at the short, portly bureaucrat with the decorations peeking over his breast pocket. Acknowledging the guest, Blackford apologized for his ineptitude in Russian.

Ivanov shrugged his shoulders. "I am glad to speak in English except that you must not . . . ah . . . make records of my mistakes. I am a writer, not"—he looked over at Gus with manifest condescension—"a translator."

Blackford smiled, of course. "And most important"—he would begin to ply his professional line—"we speak to one another in books. I am ever so pleased that the Culture Ministry is as enthusiastic as we at USIA over the *fifteenth* U.S.–Soviet cultural exhibit coming up in June. It is an honor to have your enthusiastic patronage."

Ivanov nodded and sipped at his champagne, and Pyotr opened the door to other guests. It was the Nikitins, the musicians. They asked for soda water—"Yevgeny and I have to perform later in the evening," Antonina said with a smile, shaking Blackford's hand, "so it is too *early* to celebrate. I hope that before you leave Moscow, we will have an opportunity to play for you?" Bits and pieces of that thought were delivered in pidgin English and Russian, with Gus's assistance, and Blackford nodded his way through it and said, "I very much hope so."

Yevgeny wasted no time. As other guests, some Russian, some foreign, arrived, he stuck with Harry Doubleday. "Our English is not perfect, but our devotion to *The Grove Dictionary of Music* is—total. One would make a great effort to learn English for two reasons: Shakespeare, and *Grove's*." Blackford agreed. Agreeing was easy. He'd put off the claims of Ernest Hemingway.

"There is the problem of . . . price," Nikitin continued. "Do you by any chance, Mr. Doubleday, know Harold Macmillan?"

Blackford was caught off guard. "*Know* Harold Macmillan? You mean, the prime minister? The chancellor of Oxford?"

"Well, yes. But I meant the Harold Macmillan who is the president of Macmillan Publishing, which is the publisher of *Grove's*."

"Comrade Nikitin, Macmillan is on his deathbed!"

"Perhaps, then, this is an opportune time to get Macmillan Publishing to release *Grove's*? If the terms were right, I'm sure we could reproduce the twenty volumes here."

Blackford was letting himself get in too deep in publishing particulars. He was glad to be interrupted, this time not by Pyotr but by Gus Windels.

"Harry, may I introduce Professor Ursina Chadinov? Mr. Henry Doubleday."

Blackford lowered his head to hear through the hubbub. The glare from an awkwardly placed lamp forced him to blink, in order to take her in. She was a startling figure, tall and slender, her fair hair loosely swept back. Her pearls exactly matched her teeth in her smile of greeting, her inquisitive eyes fastening with some interest on Gus's guest of honor.

"You are here, Mr. Doubleday," she addressed him, "to get us to read more books in English. Well, I would not object to that."

Blackford bowed his head with a half smile. "I am informed there is nothing in the *Oxford English Dictionary* that would surprise you."

"A gallantry, of course," she accepted the glass of wine from the waiter, "and I do not conceal my knowledge of your language. But how many Russians do you believe would interest themselves in your compendious Oxford dictionary?"

"Professor Chadinov, the Oxford dictionary is not something I presume to represent. I am an American, here to stimulate the readership of American-published books. On the matter of the Oxford dictionary, the *OED* as it is called, compendious is exactly the word to describe it. The new edition will have, like *Grove's*, twenty volumes, and will integrate the entries from the old supplementary volumes with the rest of the dictionary."

"The Russians, you obviously know, since you inhabit the world of books, are a profoundly literate people. I do not use the word 'literate' in the purely demographic sense. A people who are formally illiterate can still be profoundly literate, living as some societies in the past have done, by oral rather than visual perceptions."

"Well, Professor, if you mean do I know that the Russians are profoundly sensitive to language, the answer is yes, I am aware of that. It is in Russia, I would guess, that there is the highest per-capita consumption of poetry. Though I'm not sure whether this includes China. There, of course, the poetry of Mao Tse-tung is vastly popular." He permitted himself the slightest trace of a smile, and watched to see if she would reciprocate it. She did not, though the light in her eyes told him she had registered the crack. He went on, "We of the USIA are anxious to introduce more students of the Russian language to the marvels of our own language."

"Excuse me. You are an official of the United States Information Agency?"

"No, Professor—"

"Call me Ursina."

Blackford felt a movement, absolutely distinctive, in his loins. He was suddenly a college boy, ignited by a girl. Did he overreact? What he said was, "Ursina . . . Ursina, this is a stellar moment for me. I am Harry."

There was a clinking sound—Gus tapping his glass with a ballpoint pen. Eyes turned to the host. "Everybody who is not seated, kindly find a seat. Take your glasses with you— Pyotr will keep them filled."

Gus Windels went on for a while on the theme of the United States' interest in making available to Soviet scholars whatever material might be useful to them in their work. He was careful to make his way around unguarded expressions hailing a free press, or routine praise for the idea of the un-inhibited circulation of books. After all, Gus reminded him-self, he was speaking in the center of Moscow, where even Solzhenitsyn's last novels had not been published. He trod on no ground that was disputed, or that would arouse ideolog-ical resistance. "The efforts of the USIA in the scheduled cul-tural exhibit in Gorky are aimed simply at making available desired critical and historical material," etc. etc. etc.

Blackford turned his eyes to Ursina Chadinov, seated alongside. She was not quite listening. Her eyes did not turn from Gus, but her head was in slight, constant motion, as if concerned to permit the eyes to perform their civic duties, while expressing progressive impatience with the text she heard being recited.

"Do you have any questions that I or Mr. Doubleday could try to answer?"

Blackford leaned over and whispered to Ursina. "I have a most urgent question. Can you free yourself to have dinner with me?"

She turned her head, while Gus began an answer to a question from Comrade Ivanov. She gave the slightest nod, followed by a smile of mischievous pleasure.

They talked like old friends at the restaurant she led him to, candle-lit, the mirrors old, and appropriately smoky. It was clearly a favorite of men and women of the university. The conversations were nearly all in Russian, though the couple at the table immediately behind the one assigned to Ursina and Blackford was a font of endless French, from both the vigorous young woman and the elderly man.

Ursina sat, and the waiter asked, "The usual?"

"Do you trust me?" she asked. "—Harry?"

"Not entirely, but yes, in the matter of wine."

"Some day, before I die, I want some person, male or female, who is given to drink the wine I select, to say, 'I don't like it.' "

"I promise to try to dislike it."

"Do you speak French?"

"Not really. Just the kind of French one can't escape running into, if . . ." His hesitation momentarily unnerved him. "If you've, you know, been around."

"Well, I want to know about your background, where you've been around. To show you I'm prepared to do as much: My father was a civil servant, he died when I was twelve, I grew up in Leningrad, then I went to medical school in Moscow, and I have been quite successful—but you know that. Oh yes, I am a member of the Communist Party. I don't suppose you can match *that,* can you?"

"Well, no. I was never a member of the Party. And I have disagreed with Soviet policies over the years—"

"So have I."

"Well, I guess it's easier, where I come from, to express these disagreements."

"You haven't told me anything about yourself that is interesting. Everybody in America is anti-Communist, so what makes you so special that I changed other plans in order to have dinner with you?"

"Maybe the fascination I feel for you."

The wine came, and the menu. She managed to talk even while going over it and expressing her preferences. "The lyulya kebab is quite good, also the ham, and the shashlik. You were going to tell me how you picked up French."

"I was going to tell you that my French is only just good enough to get me through French-speaking restaurants. Are there such things in Moscow?"

"No. Here and there are peons who speak French."

"*What* did you call them?"

"Peons."

"An odd word. You mean peon as in the kind of person who works for slavemasters?"

"Roughly. Are you going to make an ideological point? All right. I'll call them serfs."

"French-speaking serfs working in Moscow restaurants."

"You are being provocative."

"I didn't mean to be. Were you ever married?"

"No. Were you?"

"Yes. My wife died five months ago."

"Children?"

"No. A stepson. My wife was married before. Her husband was shot by a Cuban Communist."

"That's too bad."

"I thought it so, yes."

"But then you married her and adopted the son?"

"That's right. How is it you are not married?"

"Maybe I know too much about men's insides. You were told—or were you not?—that I am a urologist?"

"Are you telling me that urologists are turned off by men?"

"Nothing of the sort. I brought the matter up thinking you might be wondering about it."

"Well I wasn't, though I did wonder that you weren't married. You're not a lesbian, are you?"

Her laugh was wholehearted. "No. Lesbians and homosexuals are disapproved of by the Communist state. I am . . . quite faithful to the Communist state."

"What does that actually mean? That you don't conspire against it? That you wouldn't engage in a plot to . . . assassinate a Soviet leader?"

"It means that I keep my private views private. For instance, from you."

The banter went on, and two bottles of wine were now empty. Blackford reminded himself, every little while, that he was to answer to the name of "Harry." That wasn't difficult for him. Years of field work had subjected him before to living under assumed names. "Are you interested in what Harry Doubleday is in Moscow to do?"

"Not really. The usual business, cultural exchange, and you specialize in books. I am aware of the New York publishing firm Doubleday. Are you one of them? One of the Doubleday family?"

"No, actually. A lot of people ask me that question."

"Not everybody asks you that question. The headwaiter hasn't asked you that question."

"If he were French-speaking perhaps he would."

"Vous êtes de la famille Doubleday?"

Again he laughed, marveling at her expressive eyes.

They had been at the restaurant for almost three hours when Ursina said, "I will have to be getting back to my apartment. I brought you here because we are close to a metro station."

"Where shall we meet for dinner tomorrow?"

"Tomorrow I will be in Sevastopol."

Blackford drew a deep breath. "Then I'll have to find a restaurant in Sevastopol."

"Sevastopol, dear Harry, is one thousand kilometers away."

"How are you getting there?"

"I am a part of a medical group."

"Well, I am quite ill. Can you look after me?"

Her smile was tender. "If you come to Sevastopol, yes, I will treat you."

"Where?"

"My group is booked at the Omega Sanatorium."

"I have always wanted to visit Sevastopol."

He flagged a cab and took her home, and kissed her goodnight.

He reached Gus at just after midnight.

"What brings this call on? Shall we converse in Swahili, or do you just intend a little midnight chat to keep me from going to sleep too early?"

"Gus, I've got to knock off for three or four days. I think there's no problem here, certainly nothing Gorky-related. On the other front, are you anticipating any moves in the next few days?"

"Well, boss. Let me think. No—though if our young friend should visit his professional . . . masseuse . . . like, say, tomorrow, she might get some information we've been trying to get."

"Yes, but whatever he tells her wouldn't trigger action by us, that I can see."

"No. Where you going, Dad?"

"Actually, I could use a little clerical help here. I want to get to Sevastopol."

"Sevastopol? Looking after your health?"

"Yes, in a way. Gus, this is very important to me. I want to get there tomorrow."

"Well, why not? You connect to Sevastopol via Kiev. Do you know where you're staying?"

"I've been looking at the new tourist guide. I want to book at the Sevastopol Hotel."

"Let me see what I can do. Do you mind when you leave?"

"No."

"We're talking a couple of hours to Kiev, one more to Sevastopol."

"I'm in your hands. Can I expect to hear from you by ten?"

"Maybe earlier. I can use the embassy travel office."

"Thanks."

"Okay, Dad."

CHAPTER 16

He knew it would be warmer than the icy cold of Moscow, but was surprised to find the air almost balmy. Well, that's what the Crimean peninsula offered—warm air, saltwater bathing, wines, and health. A cab took him to the Sevastopol Hotel, completely rebuilt, he quickly learned, from the wreck of an eight-month siege which, in 1942, ended with Nazi occupation of the entire peninsula, recaptured by the Soviets two years later. He looked down at the local map exhibited at the desk. He found himself trembling with excitement: The Omega Sanatorium was a mere twenty minutes' walk from the hotel, vindicating the guidebook he had devoured last night. He would have a swim, no less, and then walk over to the Omega.

The Black Sea water was brisk, but he swam vigorously, and warmed himself in a few minutes. The lifeguard was reading the morning paper, seated on his platform, bullhorn at hand. But there were no children to call out orders to. That would come later in the season, Blackford reckoned. Swimming in December was for the stoics, though the sun, when he emerged from the water, felt comfortably warm.

In his room, he napped for a half hour. He would set out at five. What would Ursina Chadinov be doing at five? What would she be teaching? He read in the hotel guidebook that the Omega Sanatorium was equipped for electrotherapy, arrafin and ozokerit applications, medical baths, and oil inhalations, all of this in a carefully controlled indoor climate. These therapeutic methods were especially useful for treatment of lung diseases, including asthma, and nervous, cardio-vascular, and locomotor diseases. Where does urology come in? He would make it a point not to ask.

Meanwhile, what to wear?

When in doubt in northern latitudes, a blazer and gray flannel pants. In southern latitudes, khaki pants—and, again, a blazer. He took along a knapsack. A history of the Crimea, a novel by P. D. James, and a Russian dictionary. At a shop in the airport he had found perfume. Sally had liked Chanel No. 5. He would not buy that. These would not be moments in which he would welcome any reminder of Sally.

The late afternoon was brilliantly clear, and the warmth hung on. He walked with a view of the sea, by a grove of freshly planted trees, a vineyard on the opposite side of the road. There was a receptionist at the desk, who served also as a telephone operator. Fat, with hair untended, she was not a prime exhibit of the health Omega was concerned to promote. He wished, he said, to speak with Professor Chadinov.

"She is with the Moscow University seminar?"

"Yes."

"There are no telephones in the rooms. I will get word to her; you can wait here. What is your name?"

"My name is Vorontsov." That was a little risky, Count Mikhail Vorontsov having, in the nineteenth century, descended on the Crimean coast with his huge wealth, building a palace that stayed on through cycles of war and rebellion as a landmark. Ursina would get it right away; the receptionist would probably not have expressed skepticism if he had given his name as Stalin.

She was wearing a white pantsuit trimmed in yellow, darker than her hair, though not by much.

"Last night I thought miraculously you'd come. Miracles do happen." He kissed her lightly on the forehead as she spoke. "Though we do not believe in miracles, do we?"

"What do you mean 'we,' Paleface?"

Walking with her toward the terrace on the sea, he explained the joke. General Custer on the battlefield, lowering his field glasses and addressing his Indian aide, expresses his alarm: "We're surrounded by Indians." To which the aide replies: "What do you mean 'we,' Paleface?"

"What's 'Paleface'?"

He sat her down by the little table. "That's the joke. 'Paleface' was used in basic Indian vernacular to refer to a white person."

"I see." She laughed. "He was conveniently drawing attention to the fact that he was himself an Indian."

"Correct! And not correct that 'we' don't believe in miracles. I am . . . living a miracle right now."

They thought it over and decided that comfortable though the Omega Sanatorium was, they would have more privacy at the Sevastopol Hotel. "Shall I get a cab?"

"No. I'd enjoy walking. I will go upstairs and find a sweater."

Blackford sensed how the evening had to end.

Three hours later Blackford lay on his bed, the yellow light from the little picture lamp hanging opposite only just reaching her eyes, closed, her breasts softly shaping the sheet that stretched toward Harry Doubleday. But the light didn't reach his sex and the long, light fingers that enveloped it. His lips came together only enough to say her name. She responded by a further caress. His joy was unbounded, miraculous.

She taught a seminar at nine, participated in one at eleven, felt a collegial obligation to share lunch with her associates at twelve thirty. "And after that, we are all on vacation."

At two thirty, he drove up in the rented car. Their tour of southern Crimea would begin at Alupka, at the Vorontsov Palace. "My great-great-grandfather's," Blackford said, his face contorted into gravity. She laughed and said she was pleased that the Bolsheviks hadn't executed all the grandchildren. Two hours later they would marvel, as they took tea in the palace teahouse, at the great garden, and at the library and the art that had made their way through the Crimean War, the Revolution, the White Army holdout, and the Nazi occupation. "And the egalitarian frenzies."

"There were frenzies, as you say, Harry. But the fact that

this palace survives in such splendid shape is a tribute to the care for the patrimony exhibited by the Soviet state. Granted, the original owners were dispossessed. But what that means is that *I* can visit the Vorontsov Palace. Otherwise, only you and other Vorontsovs would have access to it. Harry, have you ever been in Leningrad? If not you must go there, and see the reconstructed palaces, done over twenty years with such meticulous attention, putting together what the Nazis all but destroyed."

"I have read about Leningrad. Will you escort me around the palaces? Your native soil?"

They drove past the Swallows' Nest. Staring up at the fanciful medieval castle, perched on the cliff towering over the sea, Blackford expressed surprise that William Randolph Hearst hadn't just bought the whole thing and transported it to San Simeon.

Ursina was not up on Hearst, and he explained to her the lengths to which the great acquisitor had gone in his efforts to bring the treasures of the world to his property in California. "San Simeon is on 250,000 acres—about 100,000 hectares—of land." Looking down at his guidebook, Blackford noted that the Swallows' Nest, which had achieved symbolic status in the Crimea, had been built in 1911–1912. "That's just ten years before Hearst began the San Simeon enterprise. So, really, Hearst and Baron Schneigel, the builder of this, were contemporaries!"

They drove on to Yalta, and walked hand in hand along the huge natural amphitheater surrounded by the mountain ridge that protected the seashore from cold northern winds. Another fashionable resort of the nineteenth century. They sat gratefully, after so much walking, opposite the white Livadia Palace, intended as a residence for the last Russian czar.

There was a string quartet playing "the kind of music I guess the czar would have expected in his palace."

"Yes. Harry, we must listen to a lot of music together."

"You generate music . . . But I am sounding as young as I feel."

"Do you know, the Crimea is asking for a kind of autonomy. They won't get it. The Ukraine would object first, then Moscow. And when Moscow objects, it is 'Objection sustained.' "

"Has Moscow ever got in your own way? I mean, other than the . . . privations of life in . . . Communist countries?"

"I know what you are saying about privations. I remember the celebration when Rufina—she's my roommate—and I got our own telephone. But of course the whole Communist idea is the commonweal. Well, you know all that. Have they got in my way specifically? Yes. And I burn up when my mind goes on to it. It is the barriers that prevent the circulation of research material and also of researchers who want to exchange information. My own book would have been completed two years earlier if I had had access to what I wanted. It is a standing complaint of the intellectual community."

"Though unvoiced?"

"Yes." She was silent for a moment. "Largely unvoiced. The result of generations of suppression. One complaint too many—and it becomes Gulag time, a suspicion of infidelity to the Party. I have a little journal I have not shown to anyone. I have there the times I have tried to get some material, or tried to communicate with some scientist abroad, or get some useful books, and run into state censorship."

"I hope you will not risk exposure of your journal."

"I think it safe. And the most sensitive parts of it are in a kind of code that would not be readily detectable as code.

Harry, who pays your way? Your expenses? Your extravagances? Do you *have* extravagances? Well, I know you do, because I can smell the perfume I have on. Does USIA keep you
in prosperous condition? Or do you have a private fortune?"

"I don't have a private fortune. I have thirty years of sav-
ings. Not much, but—I guess, by Communist standards, ex-
tortionately large."

"Do you hate Communism?"

Blackford contracted his stomach, and then said it. "Yes."

"I like the directness of your language."

"Here is more directness. Will you marry me?"

CHAPTER 17

That Rufina would finally be marrying Andrei was convenient all the way around. The wedding had been held off for what seemed ages because passport numbers needed to be recorded on marriage licenses, and Andrei's Soviet passport needed reissuing. There were delays, infuriating delays. But such was life in the Soviet Union, and Andrei was a complicated petitioner.

Pending the marriage and the formal move to Andrei's apartment on Uspensky Street, Rufina spent most nights with Andrei. This had the advantage of permitting Blackford and Ursina to pursue their own romance at the apartment on Pozharsky Street. But most nights, however late, Blackford would return to his hotel suite. Doing so avoided questions from his USIA contacts that he would rather not answer.

It was not always convenient, leaving Ursina late at night.

Usually he found a cab, sometimes he could not, and in late December there was the cold to cope with, and often the snow.

It was a twenty-minute hike, but sometimes he found himself glad when no cab showed up. Then he could walk, unmolested, through empty streets in that fabled city from whose fortresses terrible despots had done so much to hurt so many.

He reflected on some of the victims he had known and worked with personally, and occasionally helped. He thought back on his thirty-six years in the secret service of his country and how diligently he and others had worked to frustrate the enemy, so productively engaged, for so long, in its myriad enterprises, including death for millions, misery for other millions, laboring always to penetrate the defenses of the Western world, whether by actual or hypothetical weapons, or by electronic stealth. Or, with a terrible record of success, by the seduction of individual Westerners. Klaus Fuchs was illustrious in that roster. Fuchs had learned in New Mexico how to construct an atom bomb, and provided a steady stream of reports on the secrets of this ultimate weapon to the agents of Josef Stalin.

But Oakes was seized one night by a quite different concern. What was it about Ursina Chadinov?

He did not know, knowing only that he could not endure the prospect of life without her, or even the thought of life without her. There would be awful disruptions in constructing a new life with this Russian dynamo, who was twenty years younger than he, but he was moved now with a singleness of purpose that had moved him at other times in his life, toward ends to which he knew he had to yield. Sally, his love for so many years, would have been, if she were still alive, the main victim of this emotional compulsion. Sally. The obstinate, academic, intellectually brilliant adjunct professor at the University of Mexico, who had railed always against Blackford's life in the CIA.

The CIA—another casualty? Who knows? He couldn't say. When would the agency feel the particular loss of the services of Blackford Oakes? Surely he would complete his present mission. Already he surmised that it was remote, the threat of the assassination of Gorbachev in a coup. There was no coup in the offing, so far as he could tell. There was practical work to be done, but an important part of that work would be done in a week or two, as the effort went forward to track down the crippled brother of the failed conspirator, and to illuminate the mysterious talk about . . . the general.

So much to do. But every evening, for a part of the evening, he would be in the company, and in the arms, of Ursina, which was what mattered.

There was never any doubt in Ursina Chadinov's mind that she would be invited to the wedding celebration. The actual wedding, of course, would take place at a government office, but then the reception would be held at Andrei's apartment, which would now be officially shared with his new wife, Rufina. What Ursina wasn't altogether sure about was whether the invitation would extend to Harry Doubleday.

She and Rufina had become best friends, in the years they had shared the Pozharsky Street apartment. Ursina was as independent and self-contained a friend as Rufina had ever experienced, but her full life—professional and personal—had never kept her from active and genuine interest in Rufina's life and travails. Ursina respected the work her apartment mate did for the Central Economics and Mathematics Institute, and she would occasionally actually ask Rufina to explain some of the statistical problems in which she specialized. Rufina kept nothing from her.

Ursina, for her part, was always ready to talk about the work she was doing, both theoretical and clinical. But for all that she sometimes seemed to be harboring no secrets whatsoever, the identity of her clients (patients! No Soviet doctor had "clients"!) could not have been got from her under torture.

Her induction as a professor contracted the list of patients she could treat. These were mostly men who had bladder problems. She would explore the vital organs herself—"Funny, many of the men are appalled at first that they should be examined by a woman. It is important in such circumstances for them to know that I have, well, an illustrious reputation as a urologist." Rufina suspected that Ursina rather enjoyed the embarrassment she visited upon male patients. "What remains a problem is the occasional young man who comes in for help with his sexual life. Especially when I discover, as I do every now and again, that the young man's problem is that he has no real interest in the other sex."

One day Rufina gave her curiosity a long leash. "Does that mean sometimes that you have to tell them they are actually homosexuals?"

"I have to gauge that question individually. If I think there'd be psychological damage, I attempt to avoid it. Not easy to do when, under certain observable stimuli, there is arousal."

Had she contributed a piece of scholarly medical knowledge, attributable to her own research?

"Not absolutely my own. I would have to share credit with Vladimir Kirov, my beloved friend and patron, even as my uncle was *his* patron. We collaborated in the design of a catheter that is now widely used."

"The Chadinov–Kirov catheter!" Rufina laughed. "I sound as if I were teasing you. I do not intend to do that. What do you do for women?"

"My specialty there is incontinence. There are many women who suffer from it, mostly older women."

"Well," said Rufina, "I am going to suffer from it if I don't get relief soon." She rose and went into the bathroom.

That was a problem in the Pozharsky Street apartment. There was a single sink, toilet, and shower for both occupants. And up until two years ago the male tenant in the adjacent apartment also shared the bathroom with them. At least now they had it to themselves.

Over the years both women had entertained male visitors, requiring privacy. There was only the single entrance to their suite. When the visitor entered the apartment, he would find himself in the living room, with sofa and coffee table. The bathroom door opened immediately to the right of the entrance door. On the other side of the room was the door leading to the bedroom, which the two women had to share. Ursina, early in their joint occupancy, devised a clothesline. It rested, invisible, behind the window curtain, but could be quickly pulled out, attaching to a hook. Then a sheet would be hung over it, isolating the bedroom/bathroom end of the apartment, and permitting whichever of the occupants was entertaining the guest to use the living room. It was functional but cumbersome, and Rufina was pleased when her romantic life started being enacted at Andrei's. And now that she would be moving in with Andrei completely, Blackford could come and go even without the clothesline in place.

That luxury would last until the housing commissar imposed a fresh person to share the apartment. Ursina let herself fantasize—the first night when, clothesline tucked out of sight, she celebrated her privacy with Blackford—that somehow, something could be done to maintain a single apartment. It would not be easy. The marriage license Rufina had now got required a strict reporting of which space in a municipal apartment, previously taken, would now be available.

But things take time, Ursina thought. What she sensed as timeless was her love for this romantic sixty-year-old American, who seemed to know everything, and who certainly did not need any professional attention from Dr. Chadinov when asserting his manhood, in their long embraces, night after night.

CHAPTER 18

Nikolai Dmitriev enjoyed his dacha and was grateful to his late friend, Konstantin Chernenko, for giving it to him. Kuntsevo had a very special history. It was there that Josef Stalin finally died on March 5, 1953, after lying insensate for four days, attended by frightened doctors and courtiers.

For three years after that fateful day, the abandoned dacha, twenty minutes from Moscow, was under military supervision. It was thought, generally, that it would one day be made a national memorial site. But when Khrushchev delivered his historic speech to the 20th Congress in 1956, denouncing Stalin and his works, Kuntsevo began a long life of studied neglect. A small posting of military police maintained watch at the gatehouse at the beginning of the long roadway that led to the dacha. No one was permitted on the property, and no one of any importance was designated to look after it in any custodial sense. It was eerily reminiscent of Tsarskoe Selo, the palace inhabited by Nicholas and Alexandra before they were taken to Siberia to be shot.

Kuntsevo sat there until Konstantin Chernenko decided to do something about it. On being named general secretary, he had begun to act on a number of private resolutions he had stored up, one of them to pull the dacha out of limbo. It would not do to attempt, after thirty years, to create a memorial site associated with Stalin, but it would be sheer waste to demolish so carefully constructed and capacious a country house. The best way to demystify Kuntsevo was to award it to a Soviet official.

This was one of several items Chernenko planned to discuss at a private dinner meeting with Nikolai Dmitriev, his most trusted friend in the Politburo. General Baranov had spent much anxious time on the matter of possible arms talks with President Ronald Reagan and was eager to take up the question with the new general secretary. Before meeting with Baranov, Chernenko wanted Dmitriev's advice on attendant political problems.

They had a genial dinner, with wine, discussing matters on Chernenko's agenda. After twenty minutes on Star Wars, Chernenko ticked off that topic on his notepad. "Now, Kolya, I propose that action be taken on the matter of Stalin's dacha at Kuntsevo. I think that it should be reoccupied, and I propose that you should make it your own."

Dmitriev knew well the old associations of his senior political friend, the general secretary. Chernenko, now seventy-two, had been forty-one years old when Josef Stalin died. As was so with many members of the Politburo, he had had close associations with Stalin. Dmitriev therefore greeted this news with caution.

He began—of course—by expressing his gratitude that such a—he thought better than to call it an "honor," which would risk passing by insouciantly the demythologization of Stalin. And so he expressed gratitude for such "deference as turning over to him so splendid a . . . property."

"You will need a great deal of work done on it before it is habitable. I have therefore designated it a historical 'site' but intend to keep it that way only until the workmen are finished repairing the house and the lawn and surrounding woods—were you ever there, Kolya?"

"No, Kostya, I never was."

"Well I was. Twice. In fact the second time, in February, was only one month before . . . the monster"—Dmitriev was glad to hear him use the word—"died. They will be arguing into the next millennium whether the doctors in attendance gave him adequate advice, the wrong advice, or perhaps killed him. Anyway, it is, as you say, a splendid property, and it is now—yours."

Dmitriev bowed his head, to suggest his gratitude.

"We move now to the matter of President Reagan's re-election. We should consider replacing our ambassador. Yes. And"—he looked down at his notes—"we need to find an . . . asymmetrical means of responding to the CIA's arming of the rebels in Afghanistan."

Dmitriev took notes. *Good man, Konstantin Ustinovich,* he thought. But would he go on to advise the Politburo to name Dmitriev as his successor?

CHAPTER 19

Vice Chairman Dmitriev hadn't visited privately with his old friend General Leonid Baranov for several months. On a cold day in January, Dmitriev decided to give Baranov a tour of Kuntsevo. They got about first in an army jeep, the vice chairman at the wheel. The acreage was small, by czarist, or for that matter post-czarist, standards, not much spacier than an eighteen-hole golf course. "When *he* was here," Dmitriev explained, "the security was like that of a penitentiary, with electrical grids and guards posted at regular intervals. All traces of such, you will notice, Leonya, have been removed. I make do with just the two men at the gatehouse. To be sure, we have ample electronic communication."

"If you had been named general secretary, would you have used this as your official dacha?"

"I don't mind telling you I gave that some thought. And

decided—I would not, I would move to another dacha. In that sense, the ghost of Stalin does not sleep. If, on my ascendancy, the world had turned its attention to Kuntsevo and gone on and on on the subject of *him*, I would not have welcomed that."

"Understood. And of course you know that I myself would have welcomed your election."

The jeep pulled into the big shed alongside the main building. Dmitriev, springing from the jeep, signaled to the general, who moved more sedately, to follow him. "We'll perhaps talk about some of the implications of my having been passed by for general secretary. At dinner. Meanwhile, a quick tour. Here," he opened the door into a heavy room, a squat felt-lined table, heavy bookcases, a projector and screen, eight chairs, one of them especially prominent, with traces of gilt at the crest rail. "That is where *he* sat . . . He drank a lot, but when he met here with his people—were you ever before in this room, Leonya?"

The general shook his head. "I knew that there was an inner sanctum, but never got this far."

"I was saying, he customarily convened his visitors at two in the morning. I was talking about his drinking. He drank a lot but never at such meetings as he held here. He encouraged his court to drink. Some of them went to the bathroom down the hall needing actually to throw up, but they mostly had to return, drink more. Molotov was a special target when detected going regularly out to vomit. When Stalin wanted to stay sober, he was served a flavored sparkling water.

"With a tip of the hat to history, I have arranged for our own dinner to be served here, after you bathe. Shall we meet in the salon, just outside, at—"

"Two A.M.?" Baranov laughed.

Dmitriev managed a smile. "At eight P.M."

Several hours later, with coffee, cigars, and liqueur on the table, Dmitriev, well along in nostalgia, reaffirmed the special relationship he felt with his guest. "You, Leonya, were commander of the Frunze Academy when I received my commission as a second lieutenant. And in the thirty-five years that have gone by, I have always relied on you for important strategic advice."

"Is strategic advice what we need to explore this weekend?" Leonid Baranov asked.

Dmitriev replied warily. "Yes. Advice on the strategic challenges faced by our motherland. But not—I prefer not—about contingent measures to be taken if things do not go right. The army remains securely in your hands.

"But let us recapitulate. The general secretary is finally showing some sense on Afghanistan. He has permitted the president we set up there to declare that all Soviet troops will withdraw from Afghanistan in twelve months. At last there is an end in sight to this lesion on our country's morale.

"But Comrade Gorbachev's domestic policies! Perestroika and glasnost are doing to morale in Soviet society what Afghanistan is doing to the military. If he continues on this road, it is impossible to foresee the consequences.

"Quickly, then, my illustrious general and friend: The enemy is, always, the United States. Our leader has proposed a treaty that would prohibit nuclear testing. It is obvious what Comrade Gorbachev has in mind, and here we back him wholeheartedly: Any diplomatic contrivance whatever that succeeds in discouraging active U.S. work on an anti-missile system is welcome."

"But what is by no means plain," the old warrior broke in, "is what to do if the United States refuses to derail its anti-missile program."

"Yes," Dmitriev agreed, "by no means plain. There is no way we can spend more on the scientific-military enterprise. We have ten thousand Russian scientists working on anti-missile development already.

"The general secretary understands that, too. But he has now met for the third time with the United States president. He seems to be altogether too close to this bourgeois war-monger. Who knows what agreement he will sign with him next?

"Leonya," Dmitriev paused, and stared down into his brandy. "There is one central problem. And it is a human problem."

Dmitriev had not seated himself in the principal chair at the dining table. It was there, opposite. Stalin's chair. Empty.

Looking over at it, Vice Chairman Nikolai Dmitriev said, "*He* would have known what to do."

Dmitriev and his guest left the table.

Major Uliev, his earphones on, waited a minute in the hidden trailer. Then he signaled to the technician at his side. "That's enough. We have what we want." *He* would have known what to do! Indeed. But Comrade Gorbachev, when he hears this tape, will also know what to do.

CHAPTER 20

Ursina was delighted but not surprised when Rufina told her that not only was she expected at the wedding celebration, "but also your beloved American publisher."

It was cold that Sunday afternoon, but brilliantly sunny, and Ursina proposed to Blackford that en route to the apartment house on Uspensky Street they should walk through Pushkin Square, which she admired in part because of its beauty, in part because it celebrated "the greatest Russian ever. Pushkin," she said, "discovered the Russian soul."

As they approached the stout apartment building with the ornate entrance, Blackford asked, "Who else is invited? Or do you know?"

"Rufina didn't give me a list. There would not, in that apartment, be more than eight or ten, I should think. She knows we're going on to the ballet later, so she won't expect us to stay long. The last time I was there they invited two students of Andrei's, the Gromovs, Maksim and Irina. Two very large middle-aged Russians. I don't know what Andrei teaches them. He speaks not at all—*ever*—about anything to do with his own life. Oh—" she stopped to correct herself. Blackford admired the sunshine on the fur around the blue hat she wore, concealing most of her hair. "Oh, yes, he did reveal that night I was there that, however perfunctorily, he had crossed paths with three British authors. Evelyn Waugh, Graham Greene, and Malcolm Muggeridge."

"That would be good to talk about at the reception, right?"

"No, I don't think so. I remember asking for some details of his friendship, or exchanges, with those people, and getting nowhere."

"Well, I'll give it a try."

They climbed the two sets of stairs. Rufina was at the door. Ursina hugged her and handed her the little package, wrapped and tied with yellow ribbon. It was a half kilo of the caviar she knew Rufina especially liked, but could seldom afford to buy.

"Well, darling, this does make it a celebration," said Rufina in a delighted tone. "That, and of course Andrei's passport coming through, finally. It is odd, after all these months together, that we get officially married only today because we had to wait for Andrei's passport to be renewed. As if that mattered! But come come come in. The Gromovs—you remember them?—are here already, and also the registrar Morosov and his wife, Lidya, who sings. That's all! Andrei has been practicing his toast in Russian—like his marriage proposal, which he did in Russian—and is really quite nervous about it. Imagine!"

They walked through the hallway into the salon/dining

room, where the guests milled about. Rufina led Blackford to her husband. "Andrei, you can speak in English all you want with Ursina's special friend."

Blackford smiled and extended his hand, and managed to say in the Russian language, "My congratulations, Comrade Andrei, and may you both have a long and happy life."

Andrei acknowledged the greeting and spoke back in his own Russian. Blackford was able to discern the words, to the effect that he and Rufina were very grateful to Ursina, and he was pleased to meet Ursina's good friend and—he lapsed into English—"companion. You are, Mr. Doubleday, from the United States?"

Glasses of wine were pressed into Blackford's hand by Ursina and into Andrei's hand by Rufina.

"Yes. New York. But also Washington. I do occasional service for the United States Information Agency. In fact, I'm here to help plan for the cultural-exchange exhibit in Gorky. And—as a freelance agent—to urge the circulation of some books in the English language."

"Which books?"

"Above all, your—the great *Encyclopaedia Britannica.* And, from America, the Great Books series. We have a list of individual books, of course, but we have found from the Russians who pass through the USIA library at the embassy that there is considerable interest in primary historical documents. For instance, *The Federalist Papers.*"

Andrei lifted his shoulders, and pulled out a pack of cigarettes. "Yes, I can imagine that there is such curiosity. There is also interest, I would imagine—I have never myself been to that particular library—in other U.S. documents. Perhaps the Emancipation Proclamation? The Sherman Antitrust Act?"

He struggled, against the breeze coming in from the window, to light his cigarette, but he did not want to put down his glass.

"Let me light it for you, Comrade Andrei." Blackford leaned forward and took the match box. Odd, this syllabus of U.S. historical documents his host found interesting. Was there an animus there?

"Thank you, dear boy," said Andrei, before turning to the Gromovs, who spoke to him in a slow, labored Russian, while eating zakuski hungrily.

Blackford's eyes lit on the overflowing bookcase nearby— where could Andrei fit a single new book? Blackford spotted the three-volume set of Solzhenitsyn's *Gulag Archipelago*. Prohibited in the Soviet Union. Perhaps Rufina—or Andrei— had got special permission. At knee level to one side there were ten or twelve identical paperback books lying on top of one another. Blackford struggled to make out the Russian lettering on the spines.

But the formal festivities were beginning, and Blackford edged back to the celebration. Rufina was speaking in Russian, and soon everyone applauded, not easy to do with wine glass in hand. Then Lidya began to sing a song. Blackford watched her, mouth open wide, eyes closed. Everyone was quiet. But Blackford Oakes's mind was racing. He looked hard at his host when the spoon, tapping on the glass pitcher, signaled to the company that Andrei Fyodorovich Martins would now make a toast.

"This is a joyous occasion," he said speaking the language slowly, yet with some assurance. He had of course memorized the Russian words. "I have been a friend of Rufina for some time, and now I am happy to be recognized as

her husband, united son and daughter of the Revolution."
There was applause again.

Blackford lifted his eyes and stared at Andrei as the company applauded him.

He was looking—he suddenly knew, with total clarity of vision—at Harold Adrian Russell Philby.

Kim Philby.

The most illustrious spy of the Cold War.

The realization triggered his professional training. He smiled at Philby, bit into a zakuska, drank his wine, and chatted quietly with the songstress. He must betray no emotion, no sign of recognition.

They had been there two hours when Ursina signaled to him to end the visit. Ursina, one arm around Rufina, leaned over and gave Andrei a little maternal kiss on his broad forehead. Blackford extended his hand to Rufina. He maneuvered so as to submit to the pressure of other departing guests who edged him toward the entrance door, so that he was left able only to nod, with a smile, at Philby, as he reached for Ursina's overcoat, and his own. If his host had been standing on the platform of a gallows, Blackford Oakes would happily have pulled the trap.

CHAPTER 21

Harold Adrian Russell Philby hadn't expected special treatment from the Soviets when he defected formally in 1963. Yet those early years were a little nervous for him. He was an important figure in the spy world. He had, after all, served as the head of Section IX of MI6, the British CIA—Section IX, responsible for monitoring Soviet espionage. And he had been first secretary to the British ambassador in Washington in 1949, assigned to work with the FBI and the CIA in detecting and countering Soviet espionage. While in Washington, he had permitted his old friend Guy Burgess to be his house guest, an uncharacteristically incautious thing to do inasmuch as Burgess was now under direct suspicion of being a Soviet agent.

In a matter of months, Burgess and his collaborator Donald Maclean had slipped away to France and points east, narrowly evading a tightening noose. Inasmuch as only Philby knew that detention threatened if they remained in the West, he presumably had warned them. The question was raised directly: Was Kim Philby himself a loyalty risk? His colleagues looked into the matter, and questioned him. Philby of course asserted his innocence, though he did not make a public protestation of it, dismissing the whole fuss as more of the tawdry business of McCarthyism, the inflammation begotten by Senator Joe McCarthy, who about that time was raising a storm nationally on the question of allegedly lax loyalty and security practices in the U.S. State Department.

But suspicions lingered, and in 1955 a Labour Member of Parliament openly accused Philby of being the "third man." Foreign Secretary Harold Macmillan called for a white paper on the subject, and when it was completed, Macmillan, the leading Conservative voice in England, uttered the most famous exoneration in the postwar history of espionage, advising his colleagues in Parliament that there was "no reason to conclude that Mr. Philby has at any time betrayed the interests of his country."

Even so, there was a lot of smoke left swirling about the corridors of MI5 and MI6, and when Philby, who had already left govenment service, announced that he was going to practice journalism in Beirut, a part of the world where he had lived and worked in the 1930s, there was a general sense of relief in security circles. Philby wrote for *The Economist*, *The Observer*, and *The New Republic* from Lebanon, and spent time with his third wife traveling in the Middle East, which he knew so well from earlier days.

But then George Blake was caught, with his hands very very deep in Soviet espionage. He was tried and convicted (but escaped from prison). Information gathered from the Blake experience led directly and unmistakably to Harold Adrian Russell Philby, and this time MI6 was not going to let him go. Philby sensed that his time was up and one day disappeared from sight in Beirut, leaving, among others, a thoroughly perplexed wife. A few weeks later he surfaced in Moscow, where the Kremlin announced exultantly that he had been given political asylum. His life in Moscow began with, no less, a three-year-long debriefing by Soviet intelligence.

The Soviet Union conferred honors on him, including the Red Banner Order. But his life was tightly restricted. Successive case officers would meet with him, day after day. He was not officially permitted outside his apartment building without an escort. His quarters were bugged (he simply took this for granted, and his suspicions were later verified), his mail, incoming and outgoing, surveilled.

There was irony in the whole business, Philby later confessed to a friend. "The fact of the matter is," he said with something bordering on amusement, "the Soviets aren't *one hundred percent* certain that I am faithful!" Perhaps he was a double agent, dispatched by MI6 to penetrate the innermost Soviet circles. If that had been so, the ironic poetry would have been unmatched.

The Kremlin's edgy suspiciousness continued, Philby would report in his uproariously successful memoirs, *My Silent War.* The book was published in Great Britain and America in 1968. As evidence of the Kremlin's suspicions, the memoirs were not published in the Russian language until 1980. The KGB was still harboring that little sliver of doubt.

Philby had decided to confront it head on. He wrote in *My Silent War,* "In early manhood I became an accredited member of the Soviet intelligence service. I can therefore claim to have been a Soviet intelligence officer for some thirty-odd years, and will no doubt remain one until death or senile decay forces my retirement."

There was a madcap aspect to Philby's memoirs. A Cambridge boy is recruited for British intelligence. *He is actually a secret Soviet agent.* He goes to Washington to help detect and counteract Soviet espionage. *In Washington he is made head man in coordinating activity with the FBI and the CIA.* There are questions raised about his loyalties. *He is formally exonerated by Harold Macmillan.*

For a while, after the book appeared, there were calls from journalists wanting to interview Philby in Moscow. But he granted no interviews. He would not have been permitted to give any even if he had wished to do so.

So he lived quietly, reading and writing. Eventually he was given his senior seminar to teach. And every now and then the KGB called on him to give his opinion on one or another ongoing investigation. The government stipend was adequate, and occasionally it was even increased. Little ironies continued. Royalties from his book, published in seven languages, in ten countries, were remitted to him, with the quiet approval of Soviet authorities. But not in Moscow. That would have been recidivist capitalist practice. He picked them up in Vienna. Philby would travel there, from time to time, and live grandly for a week or so.

The reviewers of his book were not all of them indulgent. It had been an inconceivable stroke of luck for his publishers that the influential man of letters Graham Greene should have consented to write an introduction to the memoirs. Greene had been a personal friend of the spy—and technically, during the war, a subordinate of Philby's in MI6. Several other factors prompted Graham Greene's patronage. The memoirs were captivatingly written. That appealed to Greene. And they made mordant comments on American icons. Writing the introduction was, for Greene, one more chapter in the lifelong book in which he tried to find a philosophical star fixed enough to warrant full-time servitude. Philby had found his own star, and lived on, reading and writing, teaching, and, occasionally, serving his ideals yet again.

CHAPTER 22

Ursina didn't dwell at any length on the wedding or its celebrants. She felt pressed to be on time for the ballet at the Bolshoi Theater. She led Blackford deftly to the metro station, where he admired yet again the famous mosaics. One stop later they were within two blocks of the theater. Hand in hand they walked up the stairs and gave up their coats to the clerk in the hallway. The great stage was soon alive with the lithe figures of a Russia which, thought Blackford, had been mostly allowed to sleep through the whole Communist enterprise, though of course three of the country's major stars and several lesser ones had defected to the West.

His thoughts went astray and Tchaikovsky could not engage him completely. *Kim Philby!* Well, why not? Everybody knew that Philby lived in Moscow. He had to live *somewhere*. That he was now married to Ursina's closest friend was a coincidence, hardly affecting national policy. Whatever Blackford's enchantment with Ursina, sitting beside him, her face rapt in the music, there was no reason to break the rule of his profession, which was: *Do not tell anybody anything that touches on security if it is possible to stay silent.* This was not easy to do, to remain silent about the man whose cigarette he had lit a couple of hours earlier. Philby, Soviet agent, had pretty well completed his assignments, Blackford thought it safe to assume. But Philby had become, in publishing his memoirs and scorning the West, an aggressor on another front, a public front. Lines written by Lord Birkenhead in his review of Philby's book for the *Daily Telegraph* were permanently in Blackford's memory. "We shall never know how many agents were killed or tortured as a result of Philby's work as a double agent and how many operations failed. He is now safe in Russia and we must, alas, abandon any wistful dream of seeing this little carrion gibbeted."

Might he himself have been identified by Philby? Inconceivable. Except for a few snapshots by intimate friends, Blackford Oakes's photograph had not been taken, so far as he knew, since his wedding, twenty years earlier. Yet it might have been snapped by Soviet security agents at any of a half dozen encounters he had had in thirty years' work. It was therefore not *absolutely* inconceivable that Philby might have suspicions about "Harry Doubleday" of the USIA. He needed to talk it over with Gus.

He did this the following morning. They met at a café near the embassy, the Café Atelier, where they had twice before conferred.

"Does our gang know where Kim Philby lives?" Blackford opened the conversation. "Because I do."

"He moves around a lot. But I think we have it. In case we don't, write his address out here."

"Gus, I am a product of the old school. I don't write out such things. I speak them. He lives at Uspensky 78. You can memorize that."

Gus nodded and went on. "On our own front, I've got big news. Dmitriev. He was arrested yesterday morning at his dacha, Kuntsevo. It's a pretty dry report, what they've released." He took the copy of *Pravda* from his briefcase and read aloud: "'Politburo Vice Chairman Nikolai Dmitriev was brought to the Lubyanka on January 10 for questioning. His duties have devolved to the Assistant Deputy Minister.' That's all."

"Gus, I assume you've been able to get more about him than just that?"

"Yes. Dmitriev was weekending, as usual, at his dacha. His house guest was General Leonid Baranov."

"Oh my God. It's like old times."

"I'm thinking, Dad. I wonder if you shouldn't get the hell out of here."

They talked.

This would be a high moment of danger, if a plot was actually being contemplated by those two Soviet figures. The need to depose Gorbachev, in the eyes of the general, would surely be heightened by this move against his pal Dmitriev, yes. On the other hand, any conspiracy's prospects for success were surely reduced by the arrest of the principal political rival of Gorbachev.

Blackford decided to stay in Russia at least until they had Galina's promised report. She expected a visit from Ivan, her client and informant, brother of the executed conspirator, Viktor. He could avenge Viktor only by carrying through the plot in which Viktor had failed. "He is certain to come by in the next few days," Galina had assured Gus.

When Blackford joined Ursina it was late in the evening. She had been called to a surgical operation, canceling by message their dinner date. "Come to Pozharsky Street at 2100. I will certainly be back, and will serve you some soup and wine." It was signed, on her stationery from the Department of Urology, "The ballbreaker."

She was not there when he rang, so he ferreted out the key from its hiding place near the bathroom at the east end of the hall. He entered and sat down to read the paperback book he carried. Moments later Ursina came through the door. They kissed, holding each other tightly. He thought her pale in complexion. She removed her babushka and shook out her hair. "The operation was long. And not successful."

She would give him more details, he knew, if she felt like it. He would not ask for them.

She didn't. She pulled a bottle from the closet and handed it over to Blackford to open. "It's sherry. It's not cold. One day when they promote me to president of the university they will give me a refrigerator. Harry, is it so that in America *everybody* has a refrigerator?"

"Yes. Almost everybody."

"You mean, convicts are not allowed their own refrigerators?"

Blackford laughed. "Put it this way, that's roughly it. Only convicts are excluded."

She took her glass and went to the stove. She pulled out a kettle and opened a can of soup.

"Harry, you have heard about Comrade Dmitriev?"

"Yes. He was pulled in, I read."

She paused. "Harry, what *exactly* does 'pulled in' mean?"

"That's the first time you've ever asked for any leads in English." He explained the meaning of the expression.

She listened. "Here you do not 'pull in' Politburo members if you have any intention of restoring them to their former offices. Taking Dmitriev to the Lubyanka! The word goes out immediately. That word is that the general secretary will not tolerate any serious political opposition."

Blackford proceeded cautiously. "Why is that surprising, Ursina? The general secretary's predecessor did not permit serious opposition. Nor did his—going back to—"

"You are going to say, going back to the beginning of the Revolution?"

"Well, I wasn't going to say it in just that way. But yes, darling. Going back to Lenin."

"Your system is different."

"Yes. It is very different. We don't . . . we don't pull in political opponents."

"Has it ever occurred to you that this apartment might be bugged?"

It had in fact occurred to Blackford. What he did not tell her was that he was professionally equipped to detect hidden microphones, and that he had swept the apartment when helping Rufina move out.

"I think that where I live and work, at the Metropol, there is most likely surveillance. But I don't think there is any here. Did you see that President Reagan protested the number of bugs found in the American Embassy?"

"Yes. Harry, I have to suppose that *your* people bug *us*. What insanity."

"Yes. But Lenin, who started it, was yours, not ours. The secretary of the army in the United States was quoted in the thirties, when listening devices were proposed, as saying, 'Gentlemen do not read other gentlemen's mail.'" That brought laughter, which was welcome.

She let him pour her another glass and then went back to the stove. From the breadbox alongside she took a loaf of bread and cut off a few slices, putting them on the table. She brought out ham and cheese and eating utensils. "Sit down there, I'll bring the soup."

Instead, she dimmed the light and kissed him avidly, working a hand under his belt. Between kisses she said it was reassuring that she would . . . never . . . need to operate on . . . Harry, "my Harry."

A half hour later the soup was reheated. Ursina said she was now hungry.

"Did the exercise stimulate your appetite?" he asked, his face resolutely serious.

"Harry," she said. "You must know something." She poured the soup with one hand, holding the other hand to his. "I am pregnant."

Blackford rose to his feet, backing up against the wall. What question could he put to her? What biological doubts could possibly exist, in the mind of a medical doctor?

He said only, "This is what you must have wanted, dear, dear Ursina."

She nodded, and then there were tears.

CHAPTER 23

Galina agreed to report to Ivan Pletnev that she was in touch with the "appropriate link."

Gus had told her: "Tell him right away that you have somebody who can listen to his story, but can under *no circumstances* provide American help for any plots against the government."

"Then why would he want to see you, my little Gus?" Galina raised her shapely legs and touched her toes down on the mirror that reflected her voluptuous figure.

Gus took a minute to think. Blackford's instructions were that Gus should press for a personal interview with Pletnev. But he had to give a reason for needing to see him, since Pletnev was being told that any prospect of U.S. cooperation was excluded. Galina relieved him of the quandary by whispering, "He is in fact coming tonight. Now, we must play by some rules. Even *we* have some rules. He will come, he will talk with me, perhaps we will make love together. Then, only then, can I tell him someone is waiting for him at the Rialto."

It was at the Rialto that Galina sometimes dined with her clients. It was essentially a bar-buffet. There was always something there to grab and eat, and the bar was never dry.

"What time is he coming?"

"He comes late. Let's say he gets to you at a quarter to midnight. Put the front page of *Pravda* by you, as an identification. Where it can be seen."

"If he doesn't show up?"

"If he is not there by a quarter after the hour, come to me, and I will help you to drown your sorrows."

Gus conferred once again with Blackford at the Café Atelier. Blackford asked if there was more on the fate of Dmitriev. The answer was no. "All the spookier, not a single mention of him in *Pravda* since last Monday. It begins to look like one of the Stalin routine eliminations, though I doubt they'd execute Dmitriev."

"Unless he was cahooting with the Pletnev kid."

"That's true. In that case, we'd wonder how long before they bring in General Baranov."

"The general has a fervent following in the armed services, doesn't he?"

Gus nodded. "And if I ever get to lay eyes on the Pletnev brother, it will be tonight." He raised his hand in response to the raised hand of Blackford. "I told her, I told her. Told her to lay it right out to Pletnev: zero U.S. complicity. And she isn't sure that Ivan Pletnev will agree to see me."

"We have one final way to deal with this mess."

"What you were prepared to do with the people a year ago?"

Blackford nodded his head.

"I know what you went through then, Dad. Betraying folks who've leaned on us is bad stuff, bad stuff. But"—he reached for a break in the clouds—"back then we were dealing with four young idealists who were anti-Communist, yes, but who could have touched off a national convulsion. This time, if we're dealing with anybody at all, it seems to be an insiders' fight, a jilted vice chairman and an ambitious general."

"With considerable implications, if we can guess what General Baranov is exercised about. Like the future of the reforms Gorbachev has started."

They arranged to meet the next day, after what Gus hoped would be a productive visit with Ivan.

At the Rialto, Gus, his red-blond hair tousled over his forehead, gave the impression that he was smoking, drinking, and reading simultaneously. The beer was at his right, the morning's *Pravda* alongside, the lit cigarette, from which he drew absentmindedly, in his left hand. A phonograph was playing accordion music, and customers were filing by the buffet and returning to chairs and tables in the larger room. A few minutes after midnight, Gus heard the words, "I am Ivan."

His visitor was tall, thin, bearded. He wore glasses and a heavy overcoat that could instantly be recognized as standard issue for Russian soldiers. Gus motioned him to sit opposite.

"I am Eric. Do you want to go to the buffet, or will you want only . . . drink?"

"Yes, I will go to the buffet. And I'll take vodka."

When Ivan came back with his tray, Gus said to him, "Galina has told me that you were . . . badly treated."

"At least I can walk. My brother also was tortured. And when they got tired of that, they shot him. They had him in a cell at the Lubyanka and brought me there, after the torture. They—I say 'they.' My handling was done always by Captain Lukin. In the many hours we spent together, I was able to piece together what it was all about, and what they were looking for."

"Lukin told you what the charges were against Viktor?"

"Not exactly, but I figured it out. There was—obviously—a conspiracy to assassinate Gorbachev. I don't know how many were involved, but Lukin mentioned several names in our . . . conversations. I knew nobody he mentioned, except for Viktor, my older brother."

He drank from his glass. "Yes, Viktor was one of the plotters. I was actually with him. For almost an hour. It wasn't easy for him to speak. He had someone even better than Captain Lukin taking care of him. If I could have pleaded guilty there and then, in order to save Viktor, I would have done so with a full heart. But I knew nothing, nothing at all, about the plot on the general secretary. The interrogators decided, finally, that they could get nothing further from me and left me with Viktor, who was shot after I left."

"Was he able to talk? You could understand him?"

"It was hard to make out what he was saying to me, but he wanted to tell me something. He used the word 'betray' and the word 'Singleton.'"

Though Ivan garbled the American name, Gus knew instantly what the syllables he spoke added up to.

"But that was all I could make out. I wanted to tell him that I would pledge to take up his cause, to do what I could to assassinate the tyrant. I didn't, of course, actually say it. There was obviously a bug in the cell. They'd have stood me up against the wall with Viktor, except I had trouble standing, and he couldn't stand at all."

Gus looked at him. He was drinking rapidly, and biting into bread, ham, and cheese with evident relish.

"Look, Ivan, I do not want to hear anything about any plot you are engaged in. I am here because your friend Galina informed us that a man she called 'the general' was plotting against Gorbachev and wondered about contingent American aid. Our interest is in communicating to him that under no circumstances would such aid be available."

"Are you telling me, Eric, that the United States was not involved in the events of a year ago?"

Gus betrayed for only a moment that he was having difficulties. He fudged. "My government was absolutely not involved in the plot of a year ago."

"Are you a lawyer?" Even the complexion that went with his red hair didn't disguise the blush on the face of Gus Windels. "You were not involved in engineering my brother's attempted coup, but I have good reason to believe that you were involved in trying to stop it."

"Where did you get that idea?"

"From the general. He was informed by a senior KGB man, a longtime friend, whose first name is—was—Boris. I have got it from the general that this Boris called Viktor—my brother—the day of the attempt and said he believed the

Americans were interposing in the planned operation. Boris spoke first to Viktor, then to the general, and then he shot himself. He told the general that he had warned Viktor, *'Look out for Singleton.'*

"The general had access to KGB records. After I left the Lubyanka, he called the KGB and asked for any tape they had on my visit there with Viktor. He noticed, immediately, the name 'Singleton,' the name he had heard from Boris."

Gus downed his beer.

"The general sought me out. General Baranov is a patriot. For that reason I told him that my brother's cause still had champions. He replied that no such enterprise could ever succeed, and asked me what I knew about Singleton.

"I drink too much. I told that story to Galina. And now you are here. To do what? To call the KGB to arrest me? To keep me from parachuting down on the general secretary with my machine gun?"

It was at this hour too late even for Galina.

Gus took special care, when walking to the metro station. He could discern no one following him.

CHAPTER 24

Blackford had reconciled himself, while in Moscow, to reduced communications facilities. He wanted greatly to learn whether Gus had met with the elusive Ivan, and if so, what had come of it. But he would not know until the following day.

He had spent the afternoon visiting Artur Ivanov and listening to Soviet complaints against the United States. Some of these he thought in fact reasonable. Why, for the third cycle in a row, should the U.S. exhibit open before its Soviet counterpart? . . . Some demands, of course, were simply unacceptable, like the proposed veto over the list of American books and videotapes to be brought to Gorky. It was one thing to acknowledge Soviet authority over *distribution* of books in the Soviet Union, another to defer to the Soviets when within the U.S. exhibit.

Blackford promised, on his return to Washington, to relay Comrade Ivanov's suggestions and complaints to the Director of the USIA. For the one-thousandth time since his career began as a CIA agent trained to study Communism, Blackford wondered how the Soviet Union could economically afford what it sponsored. The ballet, let alone moon flights. Over the years he had regularly consulted, as had most of his senior colleagues in the agency, published reports that addressed the Soviet economic scene. These were strangely conflicting. Estimates of the money being spent by the military and by the weapons-development branch of the Union of Soviet Socialist Republics varied irresponsibly, Blackford had long thought. Dr. Nervitz of the University of Ohio assessed 32 percent of GDP going to the military and paramilitary, but Dr. Swiller of Stanford said the proper figure would be nearer to 45 percent. You could run a world through that discrepancy, Blackford thought. Meanwhile Reagan was spending— Blackford picked up his *World Almanac*—only 6.7 percent of U.S. GDP on defense. *And our Ron is a hawk!*

Blackford wondered what a USIA clerk in the embassy would say, if asked over the telephone by a journalist to validate one side or the other on the question of Soviet defense spending. "We will have to refer that question to Washington, sir."

He looked out the window. Snow again. Always there were pedestrians with heavy overcoats—their Cossack hats held down by scarves—and autos and trucks, never numerous, by U.S. standards, slogging through one more winter in Moscow. How did such driven people find time to produce such literature, and would the artists ever recover from the ideological repressions?

But Moscow, for the Russians, was everything. The heart of the nation, their everlasting pride. Already they were engaged in a venture to guard the city against missile attack: Star Wars for Moscow, *anything* to protect this city. It had been a source of infinite amusement for most of the world, and of near-hysterical alarm for the custodians of Moscow, when a nineteen-year-old amateur pilot from Germany gaily landed his two-seat Cessna in Red Square. *In Red Square!* The utter audacity of it! The—*unthinkability* of it! For comparison, one had to call up the thirty-year-old Londoner who a few years before had managed to make his way right into the queen's bedroom while she was having breakfast in bed, launching into a conversation about world affairs with the benumbed monarch.

The CIA estimated that the Soviet Union had ten thousand scientists working full time to develop an anti-missile missile. President Reagan had succeeded in getting Congress to come up with $3.9 billion for the U.S. program. The contrast in the intensity of the effort of the Soviet Union and that of the United States was enormous. But the figures were not widely known, and President Reagan did not stress them.

Blackford knew that the CIA was attempting, quietly, to get the word out on the extravagance of the Soviet effort to pre-empt a U.S. anti-missile missile. The great Andrei Sakharov had traveled to Washington only two months earlier to receive a joint award with top U.S. atomic scientist Edward Teller. They both accepted a freedom award at a splashy dinner given by the Ethics and Public Policy Center at the Hilton Hotel. The focus of the event was the historic meeting, for the first time, of the father of the Soviet hydrogen bomb and his counterpart in America. A discreet arrangement had been made to slip into Sakharov's briefcase reports, written in the Russian language, on the Soviets' heated Manhattan Project–style program for developing anti-missile technology.

"I'll tell you something," a CIA colleague had remarked to Blackford a few days before the event. "I am betting that Sakharov does not *know* what the Kremlin is allocating to missile defense. Remember, he's been holed up in Gorky, completely out of touch with his former colleagues. My idea is to have someone make available to him, at that Washington dinner, photostats of actual Soviet publications. A careful reading of that"—he pointed to a sheaf of photostats—"would give anyone, let alone a scientist, some idea of the effort they're putting into a program which they regularly denounce as (1) unworkable, (2) a violation of the ABM treaty, and (3) an invitation to another arms race. Sakharov would be intellectually embarrassed to make statements like the one yesterday in Massachusetts, denouncing the Reagan program as 'a Maginot Line in space,' if he knew what his own people were up to."

The photostats were put into a large envelope, ready to convey to Sakharov. A little bedtime reading.

The two august scientists bumped into each other by accident in the hotel elevator, bound for the special room in which, with interpreters, they would converse privately before the gala event. Teller was dressed in black tie, Sakharov in a business suit. Both carried folders with the speeches they would be delivering. Edward Teller always looked a little conspiracy-bent, with his unruly hair and his suspicious smile. Sakharov was resolutely genial, but edgy if his interpreter strayed more than six inches away from him.

Dr. Andrei Sakharov and Dr. Edward Teller meet before the Shelby Cullom Davis award dinner.

The assembly was well aware of Sakharov's heroic resistance to Soviet censorship. He had received a Nobel Prize in 1975, but, in 1980, his criticisms of Soviet repression resulted in internal exile, at the demand of Brezhnev. He was sent off to Gorky, where he endured gross material privations. He had emerged from exile only a few months before the party in Washington, a city he had never seen, whose destruction was absolutely plausible, by means of the weapons he had invented.

In their exhilaration, Blackford and Ursina hadn't spent time on the implications of her news. *Their* news, Blackford corrected himself.

In the years with Sally, he had never sired a child. When she left him to marry a Mexican lawyer, after ten years of the inconclusive romance that had begun when they were both at Yale, he had reflected morosely on her refusal to marry him and have children so long as he was—he remembered Sally's words—"engaged in man-killing activity around the globe." The pain was especially keen a year later, when she bore a son to Antonio Morales. Antonito was born, but his father was dead, assassinated by a Castro agent while on a mission of great concern to U.S. intelligence. Sally then agreed to marry Blackford, and he acquired a stepson whom he loved dearly. But there could be no more children, after the operation that accompanied the birth of Antonito.

Professor Sally Partridge Morales Oakes had declared to Blackford that as long as he continued with the CIA, she would continue to live in the Morales family estate in Mexico City. She would raise her son there, and would go on teaching English literature at the university. Blackford would join them on breaks from his own work, bringing her and Antonito to Merriwell, in Virginia, for summers.

It had been so many years since any thought of raising a child of his own had even crossed his mind. Now, with that prospect ahead, he felt an excitement he had to suppose was novel for men of his age. But the thought of retiring from his work, living with Ursina, reconstituting her professional life in America, and raising their child gave him a thrill especially exhilarating, he reflected, precisely because of his age. At sixty-two, he was walking into pleasures he had long since thought forfeit to a childless marriage, a widower's bleak prospects, and a certain professional fatigue. They would have to talk about every aspect of life together, plan carefully, look after—especially—her safety, devise the means of bringing her away from the Soviet Union, time his own withdrawal from the agency. Talk about everything. . . . They'd do that, talk about everything.

He paused at the dollar shop on Kozitsky Street. Dollar shops were the piquant arrangement by which the Communist regime took in foreign currency, the little silver rain that collected from tourists, diplomats, businessmen, and black-market operators, in exchange for Western cigarettes, special foods, and sundry other items not available to mere citizens of the Union of Soviet Socialist Republics with access only to their own currency. It was a kind of commercial Jim Crow, separating ordinary citizens from the nomenklatura. Blackford paid for a bottle of champagne and two hundred grams of caviar with a twenty-dollar bill.

Once again Ursina was late, but she shrugged off her weariness quickly on laying eyes first on the father of the child in her womb, then on the champagne and caviar. They decided to enjoy these right away, intending a proper dinner later at the Metropol Hotel.

Soon after opening the bottle, Ursina turned serious. "Let's explore the alternatives—and please, Harry, let me get through them without interruption. Remember, my training is scientific, and therefore I am instructed by the scientific method. Yours is—what *is* your formal training, Harry?"

"Well, I went to Yale. And I am—thanks very much for assuming exclusive scientific credentials—an engineer by training. The kind who builds bridges and skyscrapers—"

"And intercontinental missiles?"

"Well, maybe. Though you're edging there into nuclear science, which leaves me out."

"Never mind. Obviously we don't need to be scientists to know that we could abort the child."

Blackford's face drained of color.

She looked away from him. "I am reciting alternatives, not making recommendations.

"I could bear the child in Moscow and send him or her to be raised elsewhere. I have a childless married cousin." She turned and faced him again, but looked to one side when she resumed talking.

"Or I could bear the child and raise him myself. This is not easy to do, but our bounteous Communist society has provisions." She paused.

"Going on with the alternatives: We could marry and raise the child.

"We could raise the child in Russia. Or we could raise the child in the United States. Harry?" Ursina's tears interrupted her. "Harry, could we just agree to think about these things, and put off trying to answer the questions?" He gave her his hand. "To spend time on those questions," she spoke now saucily, the champagne glass in hand, "would get in the way of our love life."

CHAPTER 25

Philby's KGB case officer checked in every day. There usually wasn't much conversation. But there was at least the single question formally put to him every day: Did he have plans to go out? If so, the KGB provided a bodyguard, walking discreetly behind him.

The Uspensky Street flat was the third assigned to Philby since his arrival in Moscow in 1963. It was very much his favorite, and in his walks about the city, he had a pleasant time of it. He knew he was never alone. He was watched wherever he walked, and when he went by cab he was followed by an unmarked car. The reason given for this—when Rufina, impatient, pressed him—was that the authorities could not take any risk of foreign assassins. "There are people," he told her, "who, in the judgment of my handlers, want to kill me as an important enemy asset, or just to avenge themselves."

For revenge? Yes, that would be understandable, Philby once said directly to a Soviet case officer he liked. It was infinitely annoying that the KGB changed regularly the case officers assigned to him. Even if he had come to know fairly well his incumbent case officer, he would discover that the man had been replaced only when a successor drily introduced himself. No mention was ever made of the officer relieved, and no word was ever heard from him or about him.

Rufina found this harder to take than Philby did, but then, she was younger. Though hardly accustomed to freedom of action, she was dismayed that she now had less of it than she had had before she married him. But she knew they had to live by the rules. Philby routinely cooperated with the case officer on duty, and with higher handlers in the KGB, and this morning his case officer, whom he knew only as Oleg, told him that his presence was requested by Colonel Bykov at headquarters.

Why? What did they want from him? He never turned them down, but they hadn't overtaxed him. Philby knew better than to ask Oleg if he knew the reason for the summons.

As Philby dressed to go out—boots, overcoat, hat, gloves—he thought back to his first visit to the Lubyanka, only eleven years earlier. Philby, the most celebrated secret-service officer in the world, had been in Moscow fourteen years before he was invited to set foot in the Lubyanka, the yellow citadel of the KGB. From that fortress, occupying a city block, his own life had been governed for his twenty-five years as a secret agent. He remembered reflecting, on that first visit, that here in this building were housed the men and women who gave him orders back then, and still did.

A car was waiting to drive him the thirty blocks to Dzer-zhinsky Square 1. Comrade Feliks Dzerzhinsky was a blooded Polish revolutionary who had survived six arrests before the day came when he would actually have a hand in helping Vladimir Ilyich Lenin achieve his goal. On December 20, 1917, two months after Lenin achieved power, Dzerzhinsky interrupted his ongoing execution of disagreeable people to found an organization well adapted to further the security interests of the state, and to fend off hostile foreign interventions. That organization was the Cheka, which succeeded the czar's Okhrana and, over the years, evolved into Stalin's powerful and terrifying NKVD. Post-Stalin, it became the KGB, the initials deriving from Komitet Gosudarstvenno Bezopasnosti, the Committee for State Security.

Dzerzhinsky died young (age forty-nine), in 1926, just two years after Lenin, but Stalin already had the power he needed, not only to chart the future of the USSR, but to elevate Dzerzhinsky to the national pantheon.

Kim Philby once remarked about his colleague in subversion, Guy Burgess, that he was incapable of dissolving into a crowd. Intelligence agents are trained to be inconspicuous, but Philby did not have that skill in dissimulation when among Russians. In almost every situation he stood out. He was tall, his gray hair moderately long, his cheekbones high, his attitude at once compliant and independent. The most he could do was dress other than as a British don or banker. He wore a Western-style suit, and a fedora like Khrushchev's.

The effort to disguise his singularity was, in one respect, simply abandoned. In 1963 the KGB had assigned him the Russian name Andrei Fyodorovich Fyodorov. But this quickly proved an impossible impediment to workaday life. The first time he used his new name was at a dentist's.

"What's your name?" the nurse asked.

Philby attempted to pronounce "Fyodorov" athwart his conventional stutter.

What emerged brought merriment. The nurse remarked with some impatience, "Who would take *you* for a Russian?"

His handler quietly noted the episode, and the next day Andrei Fyodorovich was invited to select a new surname. He chose "Martins," more appropriate, more pronounceable. A new passport was issued. *Andrei Fyodorovich Martins.* It recorded that Martins was Latvian, born in New York, December 20, 1917. Comrade Martins was left with the problem of answering a question directed at him in Latvian when he found himself at a hotel in Riga. He knew not one word of the language identified in his passport as his native tongue. That was a problem. But there were always problems, Kim Philby had reminded himself.

On that first visit to the Lubyanka he was greeted by a uniformed officer who had been waiting in the ground-floor hallway. He was taken to the third floor and led into an office with three desks, occupied by two women and a man. And through that, to what he took to be the head office.

His host, almost bald but with the face of a forty-year-old clerk, arose and extended his hand. "You may call me Colonel Bykov." He spoke using basic English, here and there egged on by an interpreter. Bykov came quickly to the point. The KGB wished Comrade Andrei Fyodorovich to deliver a lecture to three hundred top KGB agents.

Philby replied in English, speaking slowly. He had never denied a request by his superiors in the KGB, he said. What especially did the colonel wish him to speak about?

"We have given that some thought. There is no one more experienced than you in our great profession, in the service of so great a cause. We would expect you to give time to recounting your own experiences. I read your book—in English." Philby was tempted to ask the colonel why the authorities had taken so long to bring out a Russian-language edition of that book. But that would have been special pleading; to be avoided. "You became interested in Communist doctrine at age seventeen, resolved at age nineteen to lead an active life on behalf of the Party. You began your long and remarkable career."

Philby nodded, managing something of an appreciative smile. "You would not expect me to talk about any matters I believe to be still confidential, surely?"

"You would certainly be free to mention any subject already treated in your book. We detected no . . . serious . . . indiscretions there, and no security lapses. I think it would be interesting to our agents to hear your personal experiences. What is the best conduct for an apprehended, or suspected, agent? We of course have lectures on the subject, but it would be more refreshing if it came from you."

Again Philby nodded. "Yes, comrade, yes." He had resolved to be entirely compliant, but he decided against suppressing one question obviously on his mind. "Colonel Bykov, you will perhaps understand my next question, under the circumstances. I have been here fourteen years without being asked to address so distinguished an assembly. Is it contemplated that this should be an annual assignment?"

The colonel looked up and, in Russian, spoke to the interpreter, who quickly gave the colonel's reply. "An annual lecture, meaning the same text as you will use this time at Yasenevo, you are asking?"

"I simply wondered whether this lecture represents a new regimen in my services for you."

"That is a question we would wish to weigh after hearing your lecture." Colonel Bykov was speaking rapidly now, in Russian immediately interpreted. "To which we very much look forward. If you are left wondering why you were not called upon before, I can only answer that it is always possible that one director of our agency is better than another at taking advantage of unique opportunities." He smiled. And stood up.

"Your case officer will keep you informed. Meanwhile, if there is anything you are . . . wishing for . . . which we can provide, you have only to advise us."

Philby stood, shook hands again, nodded at the interpreter, and followed his guide out of the office.

His case officer was waiting for him in front of the building. The sun was very bright. As if to shield his eyes from it, Kim Philby turned to stare up at the great stone building and its prominent front entrance. Those who entered by the other great door, around the corner from Dzerzhinsky Square, were mostly never seen again. Philby wondered whether any of his case officers of the past few years had been led through that door. What might have been their offense? Some omission in overseeing Andrei Fyodorovich Martins?

Well, that was life. He was certainly not going to let himself get tied up on any such question, not at this stage in his career.

CHAPTER 26

The telephone rang before 8 A.M. It was Gus. He spoke in general terms about the cultural-exchange program in Gorky and managed to pass on the code that specified where they would meet and when. Café Atelier, nine fifteen.

Gus was already there in the booth. He told the story of his meeting with Ivan Pletnev. "I thought of going back to Galina and telling her Pletnev was a little wacko and she should forget the whole thing—just forget him, forget the general, forget the plot, forget everything.

"But I was just plain too tired. It was after two. Meanwhile—hear this—a bulletin from Party headquarters I saw before coming here: General Leonid Baranov has been removed as Commander, Warsaw Pact Forces, to become superintendent of the Frunze Military Academy—their West Point. That's better than going to Gulag, but it's a demotion, pure and simple. Gorbachev is on to something, or else he pried something out of Dmitriev."

Blackford took a pen from his pocket and made little nicks on the table napkin.

"Okay, here's what we've got, Gus. What exactly the Kremlin is up to, we can't say. We know Pletnev wants revenge, but we don't know whether there was a high-level overthrow plot that went any further than a hypothesis. We do know that the main players in the plot that came to our attention have been pulled out: Dmitriev and Baranov. If the demotion of General Baranov is going to touch off a general revolt by the military loyal to him, it will probably happen quickly. Whatever happens, there is no reason for any suspicion of U.S. involvement."

"But listen, Black." Gus's blue Ukrainian/Iowan eyes were wide with curiosity and suspicion. "There are links floating around. General Baranov *did* talk to Ivan Pletnev. He *did* tell Pletnev what he knew about 'Singleton,' the name Boris had disclosed to both him and Viktor. Security records, patiently pursued, will reveal that Mr. Harry Singleton—you—and his son Jerry—me—arrived in Moscow three days before the bomb went off in Gorbachev's desk. The records will reveal that one of those Singletons was in bed with an American girl—"

"You."

"Yeah, okay, me. And that they pulled him in on suspicion of dope. The U.S. ambassador fired a lot of volleys and they let the kid out, and he and his father left the country.

"Now. Maybe they want to de-ball Dmitriev and Baranov just over intramural disputes. But maybe they're *suspected of plotting*. And since Baranov was a member of the commission that investigated the October plot, maybe they're wondering what ever happened to those Americans, the Singletons, who flew into Moscow and out, at either end of the attempted assassination."

"Sure, Gus. But it does help a little that the reason we were in Moscow was to *abort* the assassination. Boris knew that, and got that message through to Viktor. The USSR isn't going to concoct a false story this time around. They might as well accuse Reagan of it. Now here's what's going to happen."

Gus listened and made a note or two.

From his suite at the Metropol, Blackford called the hospital and got through to Ursina. He felt a tension in her voice, but she didn't let him probe. "What are you calling about, Harry?"

"I have to go back"—the change in the tone of his voice communicated to her that his language was Aesopian—"to report on developments in the cultural exhibit. I have reservations for Washington, the Tuesday Pan Am flight. I don't know the exact day that I'll be back, but—it will be very soon, Ursina."

"I see. All right. I see. . . . Harry?"

"Yes?"

"The culture minister wants a copy of my welcoming remarks for the opening of the peace conference tonight."

"That's not surprising."

"Well, there is a problem. Because what I propose to say is very very surprising."

Blackford wasn't alarmed. They had talked in Sevastopol about Ursina's small but prominent part in the ceremonies launching the International Peace Forum.

"You're a leading woman medical researcher and author. You're representing the Scientists' and Scholars' Union. You are welcoming to Moscow prominent visitors who are here at the invitation of the general secretary. So?" He stopped, and suddenly wondered. Was Ursina thinking to choose this moment to profess her ideological doubts? "Ursina Chadinov! I must talk to you about it. Do you have your script?"

"Yes, but I have not given . . . them . . . a copy of it."

"When can I see it?"

"You will have to come to the hospital. Meet me at the cafeteria at twelve forty-five. Sixth floor."

He looked at his watch. He would set out in twenty minutes. The telephone rang. He was confirmed out on Pan American to New York, connecting with Washington, arriving at 2115.

The telephone rang again. It was Gus. "Artur Ivanov, the deputy minister, wants to see you, says it's important. Says 5 P.M. would be good. Now, Black, I haven't told anybody you're leaving tomorrow, or for how long. Is this trip off the record? I mean, if the USIA guys call wanting to see you?"

"Tell them I've been called home for a few days. And I'll see Ivanov this afternoon."

Ursina was wearing her hospital dress. Blackford thought that it left her with the profile of an astronaut. But she smiled, illuminating her entire body. She nodded and sat down at the nearest table.

"I'm not hungry. You go over to the counter and pick out whatever you want. Here is a chit." His profile, unlike those of most others in line, was not encumbered by an amorphous cotton uniform. She studied it as Blackford filed away toward the buffet counter. She loved it. She loved it even more when he had no clothes on at all. Harry's physique, she thought, showed how Soviet men just didn't make it, when they reached middle age. That is, once they were a few years away from Olympic fitness. Harry was still beautiful.

He was back now with stewed fruit, a roll, and a hunk of country cheese. "Well, dear Ursina, what do you have in mind for tonight to advance the theme of the conference, which is . . ."

"'A Nonnuclear World for the Survival of Mankind.'"

"So can I see what you're—what you want to say?"

"Only after you finish your lunch. I don't want you wasting away in *my* hospital." She chatted on, her usual self now, it seemed.

He had already eaten half the cheese, and he put his spoon now into the stewed fruit. "Was this a pear once?"

"A very sick pear. It died before it could receive treatment." She smiled, the coquette, and handed him two pages of text. "We're not supposed to take more than 2.5 minutes each. There are twelve welcomers. They—we—give the welcomes representing the writers, artists, scientists, the professions. Then Gorbachev speaks. He tends to speak for a long time. I have heard him. A very long time. But I am distracting you."

Blackford read hurriedly. He reached the third paragraph. "Uh-oh."

It was a plainspoken criticism of repressive Soviet practices blocking foreign news, research, and literature.

Blackford pursed his lips. "What will the culture minister say to this? Ursina, he will certainly object to this paragraph."

"Probably. I don't know. Do you think I should just eliminate it?"

"Yes! Nobody at this conference is eager for criticism of the Soviet regime, the sponsor of the conference."

"I'll think about it. Rufina called this morning. She plans to be there. She asked if it was all right to bring Andrei. You are coming, of course, Harry?"

"I very much want to, at least for your part of the program. But I've got a meeting with Ivanov about the Gorky exhibit, and I don't know whether I will be done in time."

"Harry. The Gorky exhibit is four months away. The peace conference is *now*. I would think you'd want to be there. I mean, I would want you to be there. Some of the introducers and Culture Ministry people will be speaking in English. And they'll have the interpreters working full time. I will leave a ticket at the box office in your name."

"Where will you be seated?"

"Well, onstage, until after my talk. When the intermission comes, before the general secretary speaks, I'll sneak down and sit by Rufina and you."

"Will you be required to stay for Mr. Gorbachev's address?"

"If I'm no longer onstage, maybe I can—"

"Plead a surgical appointment?"

"Yes! So. After I have spoken, you get up, shake hands with Rufina and Andrei, and go out and wait by the ticket office. I will work my way there. I will have to make an excuse later to Rufina. But she has lived with me, she knows about medical emergencies."

"Then the next time I see you will be at the Great Kremlin Palace, at seven o'clock."

"Harry. I will be a little nervous. Are you one of those Christians who say prayers?"

"As a matter of fact, I am."

"Will you say one for me?"

He promised, and wafted her a kiss.

CHAPTER 27

Culture Minister Roman Belov had instructed his staff to bring to his personal attention every detail of the program for the International Peace Forum. It was very important to the general secretary that the forum should go well, and it was Belov's job to see to it that this cosmopolitan exposure of the Gorbachev government should serve its purposes.

The general secretary had been three years in power and had traveled and conferred with world leaders. But this international forum would place him in close contact with people other than world leaders. Moreover, it was not to be entirely routine. It would not be like the pro-Communist conventions the Kremlin had had a hand in a dozen times, in Paris, Rome, Frankfurt, New York. The participants here were individually invited, selected with some care, and some of them came from outside the ranks of regular Communist apologists and Moscow-firsters. What Gorbachev really wanted was a public step forward, aimed at the consolidation of sentiment among liberal internationalists against the U.S. program for an anti-missile missile.

The list included some of the usual people, but this could not very well be avoided. There was no way to ignore Armand Hammer, old warhorse pro-Soviet industrialist, so go ahead and invite him—he accepted immediately. The same for American writers Norman Mailer and Gore Vidal, and British iconoclast Graham Greene. The Soviet ambassador to Ottawa personally called on Pierre Trudeau, recently retired prime minister of Canada, to urge him to attend. He was pleased by the invitation and accepted without demur.

However, Culture Minister Belov thought it especially important to invite some new faces from cultural redoubts in England and America. He succeeded in getting American actors Gregory Peck and Kris Kristofferson, and Peter Ustinov of Great Britain. Belov reached out for Professor John Kenneth Galbraith, who was wary of cooptation by Soviet-front enterprises, but whose attention was easily attracted to any gathering that deplored military expenses. Egon Bahr, the West German Social Democratic leader, was an important political catch.

A total of seven hundred people accepted. Quarters were found for them in two hotels. Minister Belov was eager to give participants every opportunity to speak and to contribute and to express their concern for a world without nuclear weapons. He drew up a schedule with a carefully worked-out distribution of time and attention to Russian, Italian, French, British, and American speakers. The major address, of course, would come on opening night, from Comrade Gorbachev. He would be introduced at about eight thirty, after the intermission. This would follow the twelve special Soviet hosts, allotted two and a half minutes each to say their piece, welcoming the delegates on behalf of their professions.

Roman Belov had an immediate problem. Just after four in the afternoon, the opening-night program clerk called. "Comrade Belov, I need to consult with you. Professor Chadinov is in my office—you will remember she is one of the welcomers scheduled for tonight? She has filed the text of her proposed remarks."

Ursina, seated in the clerk's office, could hear what he was saying, and clearly he intended that she should do so. "I have read the text and find it . . . unacceptable. . . . Yes, I have it right here. Professor Chadinov is in my office. . . . Yes it is brief, within the allotted six hundred words. . . . Yes, I will bring it right up."

He turned to Ursina. "Kindly wait here, Professor."

She felt her head flushing. Had she made a terrible mistake? How would she explain it all to Harry? What would he say about her deception at lunch, where she had shown him a different text? Harry was her sea of tranquillity. She had wanted to avoid any unpleasant disruption—keep the storm away, if she could.

"Yes," she said, "I will wait."

Minister Belov, with his carefully trimmed moustache, his specially made eyeglasses, his anxious desire to show off his knowledge of three foreign languages, was trained to listen patiently to different points of view. Indeed his patience was a qualification for his role as organizer of this conference. The clerk remained standing in front of the desk as the minister read. Belov put down the second page and stood up, utterly aghast. Whatever his training, he could not remain seated after reading what he had read. "Boris Danilovich, this woman will of course not appear tonight. *Exactly who is she?*"

Boris reminded the minister who Ursina Chadinov was and what her qualifications were. He thought to add, "And you specifically approved her selection," but quickly thought better of it. Instead he said, "The program committee nominated her. Perhaps because she is an author, a woman, and she speaks perfect English. In fact I had thought of asking her to give her speech in English."

"I'm surprised she didn't plan to give it using torches and smoke signals. Such anti-revolutionary, primitive . . . paleolithic talk has not been heard in the Great Kremlin Palace—ever. Ever, Boris Danilovich, ever."

"What shall I do, Comrade Roman Ivanovich?"

The Minister of Culture did not want scandal. *Under no circumstances,* any risk of scandal. But the woman would of course have to be kept away from the rostrum. "Tell her, Boris Danilovich, that her speech has been canceled as—inappropriate. And that after the conference is over, I will summon her to my office. To discuss her situation."

The word was relayed to Ursina.

Her voice quaked just slightly. She said, "What reason is going to be given? What will Comrade Belov say from the stage? My name is on the program. I know that, because I have seen it."

"What problems there are, Professor, are ours to take care of. We will do so. You are cautioned not to release the text of your subversive speech to anyone. Your future is to be decided upon after you have met with the minister."

He turned, and motioned her to the door.

When she reached her apartment, she closed the door behind her and sat down. She thought it wise to put her head down between her knees and let the blood revive her. Was pregnancy heightening her lightheadedness? The telephone rang, but she didn't answer it. She had read in one of her furtive books, by an English ex-Communist, that whenever the KGB called, the practice was just to keep on ringing for as long as four or five minutes. The heat of the caller who will not take no for an answer. She was relieved when the telephone clicked off after four rings. Yet she was exhilarated by the thrill of what she had done. Her declaration. Her affirmation. Her personal contribution to the churning faith she had denied for so many years. Never mind the imprudence of it, would Harry be proud of her?

She shook her head as if to wake herself. The telephone call! It might have been the hospital. She had told them she would be away a part of the afternoon. She picked up the phone and rang the number for the ninth floor. All calls to and from the hospital traveled through the switchboards on individual floors. "No, Dr. Chadinov, no calls to your number from here this afternoon." She put down the phone and wondered suddenly how she should dress for tonight.

Perhaps she simply shouldn't show up.

But there was the problem of Rufina and Andrei—and

Harry. Harry was to occupy one of her four seats if he could get there in time for the welcoming speeches. If not, he would meet her outside the auditorium, at the ticket office.

Would they say anything from the stage about her absence from the roster? She was to have been the sixth welcomer on the program. After speaker number five, would they go directly to number seven?

She decided against the modish green silk dress she had picked out for what she had described to Harry as "my debut at the Great Kremlin Palace." She pulled out instead the brown pantsuit she wore for more formal meetings at the university. It was what she was wearing when Harry first laid eyes on her.

She looked at her watch.

Timing was important. Relieved of duty, she was free to sit anywhere, but she didn't want to take her assigned seat before the program actually began. If she did, Rufina would be startled at her absence from the stage and would question her.

What she would do was take her aisle seat, but only after the program had begun. She would whisper to Rufina that her speech had been canceled—and pass her the envelope.

At the hospital, before lunch, she had made three copies of the two-page document. One copy, Minister Belov had. A second, Rufina, her closest friend and confidante, would have. The third she kept for Harry.

She looked at her watch. The festivities would begin at seven. Arriving a few minutes before seven, she would take a spare seat. She had noted which were the seats—N113, N114—allotted to Rufina and Andrei. When the curtain parted and the minister of culture approached the lectern, then she would walk over and sit down next to Rufina.

CHAPTER 28

Ursina wished she hadn't had to wear a coat to the Great Kremlin Palace. The checking of coats was obligatory, and she didn't want to run the risk of having to wait in line to leave. But she reminded herself that she would be leaving during the intermission. Only a few others would also be leaving. A little creeping liberty. During the reign of Stalin, to leave the hall before he spoke would have been inconceivable, interpretable as an act of infidelity, mutiny, treason.

So, after deliberation, she decided it would be safe to go ahead and wear the coat so necessary to getting about in Moscow in January, especially since the Great Kremlin Palace was several minutes' walk from the metro. She most anxiously hoped she would not run into Rufina in the gilded corridors with their large French mirrors. If she did, she would say hastily that she was on her way backstage.

The hall of the Great Palace was filled with flowers, brought from the Caucasus. The National Symphony was performing excerpts from Tchaikovsky. The leading figures among the cosmopolitan delegates were seated in, or heading toward, the front central section of the hall, clearly set off with wide red sashes.

The orchestra played on, and there was the beginning of an official stir. Ursina looked at her watch. It was seven minutes past seven. The lights dimmed slightly. She walked up the aisle and over to the passageway leading down on the left.

The music ended. A spotlight focused on the minister of culture. He welcomed the special guests, pausing after the mention of each name to give time for applause. The orchestra played snatches from their respective national anthems. Then Roman Belov introduced the first of the official welcomers.

When he spoke, his words were instantly interpreted into English by an unseen voice, and the screen behind him gave his greetings in French and in German. The fifth welcoming speaker was Dr. Lindbergh Titov, middle-aged, bald, energetic in step, who had often been mentioned as a Nobel Prize candidate for his work on radioactivity and his seminal book on Hiroshima and its victims.

Blackford had entered the Kremlin Palace using the ticket Ursina had left for him. He arrived just before Belov started to speak, and sought out an empty seat in the rear. He had put it simply in his own mind: He would not take a seat next to that cocksucker Philby. Ursina need not know that. She would guess that he was in the audience somewhere, in time to hear her speak.

According to the program, it was Ursina's turn to come to the lectern.

But the minister was introducing the seventh speaker, Alisa Vorobev of the Lawyers' Union. Blackford brought his program down below his knees, to give him reading light from the tiny bulb at seat level. He wanted to check again the page listing the welcoming speakers. He could make out—number six, Dr. Ursina Chadinov.

What was going on?

He would wait until the next speaker was announced. Perhaps there had been just that slipup, with Ursina coming not sixth, but eighth. But introduced now was Osip Grigorev, the poet, on behalf of the Writers' Union. And there had been no explanation from the master of ceremonies. Not a mention of Ursina. Blackford's impulse was to spring from his seat and go to the ticket office outside to see if she was there waiting for him.

But he'd have been disruptively conspicuous, rising in the dark and climbing his way past the couple seated to his left. He would have to wait.

Oh, the agony of having to listen to number nine . . . number ten . . . number eleven . . . number twelve. In his mind it was all just a blur of Russian and of metronomic English interpretation. He prayed that when the twelfth welcomer finished, the culture minister would instantly announce the intermission, the lights would go on, and Blackford could sprint up the aisle to the ticket window to find Ursina.

The intermission was finally announced, and he bounded past the seated couple and reached the ticket window in moments. The bulbs behind the crystal sconces brightened. A dozen men were lighting up cigarettes. He looked about anxiously for Ursina, and noticed then a knot of celebrants gathered at the other end of the hall, around another ticket window, under the sign, FOR TODAY'S EVENT. Ursina was there, her overcoat on. She looked up at him. "Let us leave, Harry. Follow me."

They found a cab in the cold, and she gave her address on Pozharsky Street. He held her hand. She was shivering. She spoke not a word. They made their way through the door and climbed up the stairs to apartment 2B. He saw her hand trembling and took the door key from her, opened the door, and turned on the light.

"What shall I get you?"

"I think, vodka." He sat beside her. She would not release his hand. He let her say it as she chose.

"I was there. I was in the seat next to Rufina and Andrei. But I didn't arrive until after the program had started. I didn't want to have to talk to her, but I did want to give her something. All I did was lean over—this was after the first welcomer had begun his talk—and say, 'Rufina, I will not be speaking after all. I will tell you about it later. But I want you to have this. It's just two pages. Put it in your purse, and don't show it to anybody.' I wanted her to have a copy."

"A copy of what?"

"My speech. My intended speech."

"Ursina. You mean, the speech I read at lunch? They wouldn't allow you to give it?"

"No. It was another speech. It was one I didn't dare to show you, didn't want to show you."

"Tell me what happened, exactly." She told him.

———

They lay in bed, having resolved to defer further talk about the problem.

They said nothing for a half hour.

Blackford's mind was working, groping for useful elements of the story. It wouldn't do, clearly, to ask her just the obvious questions about her furtive work on the talk and her purpose in writing it. So he said, "You know, my darling, I have to leave at noon tomorrow. I will be back in Moscow as soon as it can possibly be arranged."

He edged out of the bed and put on his trousers.

"You are in a hell of a pickle, Ursina. But they too have problems. That whole thing tonight, the whole conference, has also to do with displaying the new face of the Soviet regime. To take direct brutal action against you, given your contacts at the university and elsewhere, they surely don't want. If it had been five years ago, let alone fifty years ago under Stalin, you would not have left the office of the minister of culture under your own power. You would be right now in the Lubyanka."

She said nothing, staring into space.

"That doesn't mean that they aren't going to investigate you thoroughly. Who has influenced you? What have you been reading? Who've you been seeing? Hell, you know all that."

She lay back on her pillow. Blackford's passion rose up again. He lay down alongside her and again she took his hand. After an interval she said, "You haven't asked me why I wrote that little speech."

"No. I haven't."

"You remember last night we sat here and discussed what the alternatives were for the future? Of the child, and of you and me?"

"Yes, Ursina, I remember."

"Well, I decided which of the alternatives I would choose."

"Yes?"

"To leave Russia, and to go and live in America with you. And with our baby."

It was after three in the morning when Blackford attempted sleep. He felt a need to communicate in a special way his joy from her. He would not be seeing her again before flying off. He had whispered to her what he intended to do. Arriving at his hotel suite, he went to his desk and wrote out an amendment to his last will and testament, bequeathing one half of his estate to Ursina and their child. He would have Gus witness it tomorrow. It was not to go to Ursina. No document would be safe from scrutiny at the Pozharsky Street apartment. But, with this letter written, it was unlikely that anyone could move to deny his role as father of the child.

BOOK TWO

CHAPTER 29

There were just the two of them. They were served a simple dinner. She sat at the table, he, to one side on a sofa close enough to allow him to reach over to his plate on the table. He was reading a book, she, a magazine. He sipped from his glass of wine, but put it down hastily to allow himself to laugh. His glasses were well down his nose; his thumb held open the paperback.

"You've got to hear this. But I won't say anything to give the plot away."

"You can't read and eat your dessert at the same time. Apple cobbler takes two hands. Come on, honey. What is it about?"

Ronald Reagan folded the page and put the book down on the coffee table. "It's Graham Greene. *Our*—" he grabbed the book to remind himself of the title—"*Our Man in Havana*. It's the craziest plot I've ever read, and the funniest. This middle-aged Brit who lives in Havana is at his usual bar and starts talking with a younger Brit, just come in from London. Our guy is just a little loony. He's been in Cuba ten years, a tiny business selling vacuum cleaners. The young guy starts to talk to him and pretty soon, after two or three drinks, says there is a great need for the Brits to beef up their intelligence service in Cuba, talks about how London needs to be warned in case the Reds take over.

"No. No coffee, thanks.

"Well, the older Brit says sure, he'll cooperate, but these things take money. The young guy says *of course* these things take money. We need, for instance, somebody in Cienfuegos to keep an eye on what's going on there. The older guy says, I have a little outlet in Cienfuegos and I know just the guy to line up."

Reagan's eyes were rounded in mirth.

"So this whole thing goes on—I haven't finished the book—and MI6 is pouring money in there to our guy, who makes up funny reports. What's about to happen is that a professional guy from Britain is coming in, and, to save money, he'll board with our guy. Why couldn't Graham Greene just write comic novels?"

Nancy nodded. "I saw his name in the story on the conference going on in Moscow."

"Oh sure. Graham Greene will fall in with that whole peacenik set, and Gorbachev will play to them. *You* know I was pushing for the treaty we signed in December, and I'm pushing for confirmation right now in the Senate—while that gang gasses on about how the U.S. is engaged in a new arms race."

"Jesse Helms is opposing the treaty."

"Jesse would oppose a treaty with the Soviets banning

poison ivy. But Jesse's on our side, and he can be useful—though George Shultz doesn't think so."

Nancy Reagan raised her hand. "But does Jesse have a point?—about the Soviet Union, under the treaty, having to junk intermediate-range missiles? Only, Jesse maintains, there's no way for us to verify that they're *actually* doing so."

"That's always a problem, and Jesse had a nice line on that point."

"If it's a nice line, I'll bet you've memorized it."

He laughed. "As a matter of fact, I have. Jesse said, 'Old Soviet warheads never die, they are just retargeted on the United States.' That's in part true, but—listen, Nancy. We can junk our intermediate nuclear weapons in Europe, and anything the Soviet Union started up we could wham them just as decisively with our submarine fleet. Did you see that Klaus Fuchs died?"

Yes, she had seen that, Nancy said.

"He managed to get the atom bomb to Stalin years ahead. Our guys got on to him, too late of course, but we did track down the Rosenbergs. They fried.

"No more cobbler, thanks. But it's really good."

"What about George Bush! Beating Jack Kemp in Michigan yesterday."

"My guess is George will get the nomination."

"Is Bob Dole a factor?"

"Well yes, he's a factor. But I'm still guessing it will be George."

"Well, a lot of people will say: If Ronald Reagan picked George Bush for two terms as vice president, he's got to be—the next best man."

Reagan blew her a kiss. Then, picking up the novel, "You've really got to read this book. Makes you almost forgive Graham Greene."

CHAPTER 30

On night two, after the festivities at the Great Kremlin Palace, Graham Greene would leave the International Peace Forum for an evening with Kim Philby. Forum participants were not easy to reach by telephone, so Philby had sent him a note. Greene replied in writing that he was leaving the Cosmos Hotel, in which he had been assigned a room. "It has terrible cockroaches scuttling in all directions, and very dodgy characters," Greene wrote.

"I have made my way to the Sovietsky," he continued. "It is grander, but also full of petty crooks. I will expect you at the end of the proceedings on Tuesday, and will happily go with you to Uspensky Street."

It had been an afternoon and evening of high antics and political passion. Beginning in late afternoon, there had been a concert of many delights, as Gus Windels reported in a confidential memo to file. These included "folk songs and poetry and the American actor Kris Kristofferson urging everyone to eschew whiskey and women for sober thoughts on God, war, and peace, all taken in by an audience including the likes of Yoko Ono in white mink, and Gregory Peck."

Graham Greene never objected to late evenings, though Rufina reminded him, some time after midnight, that Kim Philby did not have the same stamina. Having said this, she said she would retire, leaving her husband and his guest with food and drink. Earlier she had asked Andrei not to discuss with Greene the explosive matter of Ursina's extraordinary behavior the night before. "I myself," she said, "would not want to participate in critical conversation involving my best friend, and my country."

Philby didn't exactly promise her that Ursina's behavior would not be a subject of conversation, but at least Rufina would be spared it. At her own desk in the bedroom, Rufina wrote in her journal, "The Graham Greene sitting opposite me tonight was nothing like the Greene I had imagined. I was captivated straightway. The man who wrote the foreword to Kim's book was nice, delicate, soft-spoken, with the clear, naïve eyes of a child. As we chatted he was attentively interested in what I had to say, reacting to my little jokes in an unforced way, with a pleasant chuckle."

She opened the door of the bedroom sufficiently to view again her husband and his famous guest, talking in the corner of the study. She could not hear what they were saying. She returned to her journal to write, "He and Kim have several subtle characteristics in common: inquisitive, piercing blue eyes, and directness and sincerity, combined with a British reserve. But the similarities are not just skin deep.

They have a lot else in common, notably a strong sense of fair play: Their sympathies were always on the side of those who were striving for freedom."

Everything going on in the world was interesting to Kim Philby and Graham Greene. "It's fine that the Soviet people finally got around to publishing your book—"

"*Our* book," Philby interrupted.

"You are nice to say that. I have never been apologetic about writing the preface to My Silent War, though there are passages in it I deplore. No. Passages in it I regret."

"Well, Graham, we aren't here to review a twenty-year-old book."

"No. We are here to review a two-day-old conference. I said in my speech this afternoon, which I assume you heard, that I see us as fighting—Roman Catholics and Communists together—against the U.S.-backed death squads in El Salvador, against the U.S.-backed Contras in Nicaragua, against the U.S.-backed General Pinochet in Chile."

"That was a weighty toast you made to Gorbachev."

Greene smiled and reached into his pocket. "I won't read out the whole of the toast you've already heard, only the last sentence, which is scandalous enough certainly to be emphasized by the press." He fiddled with pages. " 'I even have a dream, Mr. General Secretary, that perhaps one day before I die, I shall know that there is an ambassador of the Soviet Union giving good advice at the Vatican.' "

"You are what, Graham, eighty-three?"

"Yes. Time goes by. I was only thirty-nine when you were my superior officer in the directory."

"I'm surprised I didn't order you to enlist in Soviet intelligence!"

The two friends were quick to acknowledge the irony. Philby refilled their glasses and lit another Gauloise.

"You are best, as a great novelist, in seeing life through individual human beings. Rufina didn't want me to talk about it, and I would not in her presence. It has to do with that clerical disruption yesterday, so slight you might not even have noticed it."

"You mean the missing speaker at the complimentary session?"

"Yes. She is Ursina Chadinov, professor of medicine, practicing urologist, and best friend of my wife. She was here in the apartment for our wedding reception."

Graham Greene was instantly taken by the story. He lived by his interest in human stories.

"Well, Graham, this may disappoint you, but Ursina is not a practicing Catholic."

Greene laughed. And, with heavy sarcasm, "I have known some people of interest who are not practicing Catholics."

"Ursina grew up in Leningrad, the daughter of a civil servant. He died when she was young. She did volunteer work in a hospital and decided she wished to be a doctor. This was made possible by an uncle, a professor of urology here at the university."

"I take it urology runs in the family."

Philby laughed. "As a matter of fact, her mentor at the university, a student of her uncle's, is *also* a urologist. But shall I get on with it, Graham?"

"Of course. No more acidulous interruptions. What was it that actually happened?"

"Well, Ursina has been living with an American, some sort of emissary from the United States Information Agency here to prepare for the cultural-exchange exhibit down the road—June, I think. Rufina used to share an apartment with Ursina and saw the American often—in fact, he too came here to our wedding reception, escorting Ursina."

"What has the evil American done this time? Did he by any chance set someone in the Lubyanka free?"

Kim Philby's mouth tightened a bit. "Are we going to discuss things like that?"

"I doubt you'd want to, Kim. You might have to write another book."

Philby decided to ignore him. "Well, it is an affair of great passion. Then yesterday, quite late in the afternoon, she arrives, as she has been instructed to do, at the office of the culture minister to give a copy of her text to the clerk. He reads it and is understandably astonished. Goes upstairs, shows it to Roman Belov—he's the minister of culture, old-line—he reads it and says, 'Of course, not one sentence of this will be read to the assembly.'"

"What in the name of heaven had she written?"

Philby got up, paused to fill their glasses, walked to his desk, and reached deep into the back of a drawer. He pulled out the two pages, clipped together, and handed them over to Greene.

"Should I read it now?"

"Yes. It's short. And in any event, I could not permit you to leave with it."

Greene put on his glasses and moved his chair closer to the light.

After a minute or two he put the text down. "This is a cri de coeur, if ever I saw one."

"A cry of the heart? Well, it may be that, Graham. And I can see you already reaching down for an emotional, psychological, philosophical, theological explanation for it all. Meanwhile, it is also outright treachery."

"You are against treachery these days, Kim?"

Philby did not even pretend to smile. "The very idea. Thinking to make such a statement to seven hundred visitors to the Soviet Union here to promote peace."

"Kim, Kim. They are here to promote the general secretary's program. Which is what *I* am here to promote. Everyone has to be actively engaged in saving the world, with that terrible man in the White House."

"Well, Ursina certainly did not, in those two pages, attempt to forward the cause of world peace we are talking about."

"There has got to be a personal explanation. There always is, Kim. Maybe you are an exception, going into the arms of mother Marx at Cambridge at age nineteen."

"I don't mind exploring that possibility, that there is a personal explanation for her behavior. It was I who brought up the subject of her American lover."

"Tell me more about him."

"I wish I could. When he was here briefly for the wedding toasts I remember he looked very inquisitively at my library over there. But why shouldn't he? Everybody's personal library is interesting."

"Yours is well stocked with books on the political scene, I assume."

"Yes. And I have a dozen copies of my own book, the paperback edition."

"Did your American—what is his name?"

"Doubleday. Harry Doubleday. He does consulting work

for the USIA—I told you that, I think—and is specifically promoting books in English for circulation in the Soviet Union."

"Is he . . . physically interesting? Sexy?"

"He is, I'd say, sixty-sexy. He does look like a physically well-endowed American movie star, reaching that age. He endeavored to speak a few words of Russian, and his eyes showed an amusement with his verbal miscalculations."

"What will become of her, Kim? You're not just going to take her out and shoot her, are you? Impoverish the urological resources of your great country?"

Once more Philby was not amused. "Nothing will happen, of course, while the conference is in session. She has been told to report to the minister of culture as soon as it is over."

"Then what?"

"I do not inquire into these matters. That should not surprise you. I am not even told what happens to my own case officers when they suddenly disappear."

"If I were a novelist," Graham Greene said, tipping his glass to his lips, "I would look into this American and his hypnotic powers."

CHAPTER 31

Blackford pulled from his pocket the key to his house in Virginia, the house in the countryside, in a village called Merriwell. It was past eleven at night. He didn't want to wake Josefina, and didn't have to. She knew he would be coming. Not at what hour, though, so she had not stayed up to let him in. He fitted his key into the lock and flashed on the light. Walking into the hall he was surprised by a red ribbon hanging from the chandelier, holding an envelope marked, ATTENTION: B. OAKES, SPY.

He tore the envelope open. "Papabile," the note began.

Blackford's face was wreathed in pleasure. The note was from his stepson, Tony. Don Antonio Morales. Tony was twenty-three years old and had grown up in Mexico and in Virginia, in this house, with his mother, the late Sally Oakes. Professor Sally Oakes. Blackford's heart raced with anticipation. He hadn't seen Tony since the funeral in Mexico, a full six months back. He was tempted to spring upstairs to his room, but paused to read the note.

"Papabile." The name had been contrived by the four-year-old boy struggling to understand the difference between his real father, who was dead, and this father, and Tony had used it ever since. "It didn't take much to get Josefina to let me into your house! On the other hand, I guess she didn't find me very suspicious. Maybe because she's known me since I was, what? three, four days old? So: My illustrious employers, Morales y Morales, decided I should spend a graduate semester at Georgetown Law School on American–Mexican law, so I'm here to find out about enrolling next term. But—scratch that. Es todo por ahora. I am dead for lack of sleep. Acapulco–Mexico–Miami–Washington. See you tomorrow. Much love, tu hijastro, Tony."

Blackford looked in the silver bowl where Josefina had placed assorted mail. Anthony Trust had been conscripted to come in once every week to look over the mail. Anything that might be in any way special, Trust, Blackford's oldest friend, was authorized to open. If Trust read anything he thought Blackford would want to know about immediately, he'd précis it, and get it to Gus on the secure line.

There hadn't been much traffic of this sort. A couple of deaths, including one of Black's professors at Yale. A god-daughter telling him of her First Communion. Events Blackford would want to know about, even if they didn't require him to react in any way. Magazines were on the shelf over the radiator, unless they were more than one month old, such being thrown out. Blackford had there, to look at, two issues of *National Review,* four of *The New Yorker,* one of *Commentary.* He picked up a couple of them and that morning's

Washington Post, and lugged his heavy suitcase up the stairs to his bedroom.

He flopped down on the bed he had shared for twenty-two years with Sally, and thought for the very first time of the symbolic infidelity, lying there, the father of a five-week-old child who would bear his name, which Antonio Morales did not. His eyes moistened as he thought of Sally. He had been so deeply grieved when the aneurysm struck her in Mexico City, twenty-six hours before her death in La Madera hospital. He had mourned her truly. But he would not deny to himself that his passion for Ursina now overwhelmed any other thoughts.

Antonio Morales was a worldly twenty-three-year-old, alive with energy and curiosity; for understandable reasons, proudly Mexican. He had never known his own father, but grew up quickly learning that his name—passed down from his grandfather, who had founded the law firm—was respected in Mexico.

Tony had inherited from his father the villa in Coyoacán, in the heart of residential Mexico City, as also a trust fund that provided for its upkeep and, of course, for his mother. He attended school in Mexico City until he was twelve and was brought then to live in Virginia, attending St. Albans School. But he knew, and his Papabile had never by any hint stood in the way, that Mexico was his adult destination. His mother, sensitive to the pressure of her Mexican in-laws, reaffirmed that he would be attending college and law school in Mexico.

Blackford's absences from his hearth were sometimes for periods as long as two or three months. Somehow, though, the Morales/Oakes, Coyoacán/Virginia family unit remained functional, healthy, and happy. The sudden death of Sally precipitated a turn of mind. The old lady, Great-Aunt Morales, opined that, with Sally dead, there was no longer a binding tie to the United States.

"Papabile is a strong tie," Tony had observed at the family meeting that took place following the funeral: great-aunt, two uncles, an aunt, a half dozen cousins. Blackford had absented himself from that meeting, sensitive to the fact that in this family discussion his voice would be subordinate, and even, in a sense, alien.

But the formal end to Tony's tie to Virginia hadn't induced personal alienation at any level. Tony knew that he was welcome, any time, to visit with his stepfather, and just now he had done so without giving any notice at all.

Blackford slept well, but not for long. He was already through with his breakfast when Tony came down, his face alight with the pleasure of seeing his stepfather again.

"Don't tell me where you've been, Papabile. Let me guess. You have been in the . . . enemy country! My lips are sealed. Just nod. That way the bug won't pick us up."

"You sound like your mother."

"I know. I heard her often enough berating . . . teasing you."

"Your mother had to put up with a great deal."

"So do I, missing her, and also, the household staff, and her friends. They come around still, but of course it isn't the same. But then nothing is ever the same."

Was this the moment to tell him about Ursina? No. He would put that off. "You are going to attend Georgetown Law School?"

"Not quite. I am going to take some courses they offer, geared to Latin American law and American–Mexican precedents."

"You will of course live in Merriwell."

"I knew you'd say that, Papabile. But I think it would be better in an apartment."

Blackford understood. He'd have said the same thing at that age, no matter who had offered him cohabitational shelter.

They talked about several family members in Mexico whom Blackford especially cared about. Tony's stay in Washington would not begin until the spring term, "at the earliest. Conceivably not until summer. Or even fall. I'll know all that stuff later today."

Blackford drew a deep breath. "Later today. Does that mean you are free to have supper with me?"

"Provided you don't question me too rigorously on my contacts today. We have security to keep in mind, you know."

They made a date. They would eat here at home. Mexican food cooked by Josefina. Just the two of them.

CHAPTER 32

Blackford Oakes had been thirty-six years in the agency. He had operated in several theaters, winning the respect of his colleagues. His superiors also valued his work. They knew, however, of his tendency to act independently. More than once he had interposed his own judgment at critical moments. One of these had resulted in his discharge from the agency for insubordination. Not much later, he had been brought back in to take on a very delicate mission for which he was thought specially qualified.

This morning he flashed his credentials at security and submitted to having his briefcase examined, though with that little trace of impatience that reveals that you have got out of the habit of the daily security routine.

He went to the director's office on the seventh floor and told Miss Wheelock he'd be in his own office and available whenever the director got back from the White House. It was

Wednesday morning. The Director regularly attended a White House meeting on Wednesday mornings.

In his own office at the end of the hall, Blackford sat down to a large pile of agency summaries dating back seven weeks. One or two of these summaries prompted him to write on his notepad. He used a kind of shorthand he had been introduced to when taking training in the summer of 1951. "Speedwriting," as it was called, would certainly "not fool a cryptographer," the trainer told him. "But it's a convenient way of throwing off casual bystanders." Blackford had got accustomed to speedwriting, and used it even when security was entirely irrelevant.

The telephone rang. The director was in his office. "He will see Mr. Oakes now."

It had taken a few months for Blackford to get used to the director's little formalities. Blackford remembered when, as a student in college, he had got an appointment to interview J. Edgar Hoover. He had sat a good half hour in the waiting room, rereading the issue of *The Nation* that had excoriated the director as archetypally fascist, errand boy for Senator McCarthy and entrepreneur of other villainies.

Blackford was doing this interview for publication in the Yale *Daily News* and was pleased that his petition to see Mr. Hoover had been granted. But he was beginning to be irked by the delay, now over thirty minutes. The words of the receptionist stayed in memory: "Mr. Hoover will see Mr. Oakes now." No doubt Bill Webster had come to use that kind of language after serving for so long as Director of the FBI, beginning only a few years after the legendary Hoover had left. And of course most people still called him "Judge Webster," after his years on the court of appeals.

"Webster knows everything." Anthony Trust had chatted

with Blackford soon after President Reagan made the appointment in 1987. "But nothing about intelligence."

"That's okay," Blackford said. "We can fill in for him."

But Webster was affable and penetratingly intelligent. Blackford's dealings with him in the last six months had been pleasant and productive. Judge Webster rather enjoyed a little banter in his meetings. That may have been one reason Reagan appointed him.

"How you doing, boss?"

"Well, I'm okay. How about you? You got our daily reports while in Moscow?"

"Yes. I like the way"—Blackford carried on the conceit—"you plant your news in *Pravda*. Not easy to read, but if you stick to it, there it is. '*Minister Pleshkov flatly lying about Soviet production rate of MIRV missiles.*' That was very useful to me. Also the one in the next day's *Pravda*, '*Project Wiretap-the-Kremlin successfully completed.*'"

"Glad you caught those. Anything to worry about, Black?" Webster was now all business.

"I don't think so, Judge. My guess, and it's pretty well informed, is that the nascent plot was stillborn. The two principal players have been pulled out of the scene. The civilian contender for general secretary when Chernenko died— Dmitriev—is now a prisoner. We don't even know—and that was more than two weeks ago—what he's been charged with."

"That wouldn't have worked in Missouri when I was judge."

"It's not quite like the old days in Moscow, but a far cry from the way you did things in Missouri. In any case, Dmitriev's in no position to pull off a coup d'état. The other guy, the general, has been demoted. We did learn that Boris—

I don't think you know who he was, Judge; no reason to. But Boris Bolgin was an ace KGB operator, Gulag survivor, who locked horns with me a few times over three decades. He became the chief KGB operator in Europe. He retired and—defected. Only he and the Pope knew this. And me. He tipped me off to the plot a year ago, a very live plot, to assassinate Gorbachev. I went over there to tell him he had to get it called off. He shot himself the next day. I've put it together that before pulling the trigger of the pistol in his mouth he blew my cover. Maybe they'll go back and dig it up from a year ago. The general who was demoted—General Baranov— was in charge of the secret commission that investigated the assassination plot."

"So. Nothing that ties us to it in any way we don't want?"

"No, sir. Gus Windels undertook some pretty adroit sleuthing. So—I'll write the report and get it to you in the next couple of days. Is that okay?"

The director said yes, that was fine. "And, welcome home, Black."

CHAPTER 33

Philby went to bed soon after Graham Greene left. Greene, a night owl, said he intended to walk to Pushkin Square and go on from there to his "terrible hotel. Tell your spy network to avoid *both* the Cosmos and the Sovietsky."

Philby was up early in the morning. There was a burr lodged in his mind. After his first cup of tea, he was able to yank it from the subconscious. He stared hard at it.

What is this guy Harry Doubleday up to?

Further: Who *is* Harry Doubleday?

A simple emissary of the USIA and U.S. publishers? Not "simply" anything. Simple people weren't likely to capture the roaring passion of Rufina's old friend, the ultra-sophisticated Professor Ursina Chadinov.

Philby rarely did this, but after he had chewed down his breakfast roll, he went down to the ground floor, a mission in mind. He opened the door and signaled with his hand. His full-time security detail across the street would catch the signal, and act on it. He was never given a telephone number he could simply ring up in such circumstances. No matter. In less than a half hour, his case officer came up the stairs and knocked on the door.

Philby didn't want to share his conversation with Rufina, and so he asked the case officer, Yegor, to walk back downstairs with him. There in the lobby he told Yegor he had urgent reason to check up on an American who had been doing work on the cultural exhibit in Gorky. Philby gave the name and all the details he could summon immediately to mind.

Yegor took notes.

An hour later, Yegor came back to him and said that his superior in the Lubyanka wished Comrade Martins to come by the office.

A car was waiting outside. Philby called out to Rufina to say he would be gone a little while. She called back from the living room that she was on the telephone with her brother, who complained of a terrible headache.

"Give him my best," Philby said, grabbing his coat.

It was always so in the security world that you spoke as sparingly, even to your own colleagues, as possible. Philby was talking now to Captain Kuzmin, with the great head of black hair. Philby had no way of knowing whether Kuzmin knew anything at all about the Professor Chadinov scandal of Monday, and no reason to suspect that he might know anything.

What Kuzmin wanted to know was what had given rise to Andrei Martins's request. A request that he had classified as urgent, to look into the KGB file on the American, Doubleday.

"Captain, you will simply need to act on my suspicions. Mine are refined suspicions. If you feel I should call on Colonel Bykov, I am of course prepared to do so."

That had the desired effect. Colonel Bykov was not to be trifled with. Evidently he and Andrei Martins had a working relationship of some sort.

"Tell me what you want from us."

"What I want is to know from our people in Washington: Is there a Harry Doubleday"—he paused to write out the words for the captain—"associated with the United States Information Agency in Washington? If the answer is yes, I wish to know whether Mr. Doubleday has recently traveled to Moscow, and if so, when."

Kuzmin looked up from his notes. "That is a fairly simple assignment. We can do that. But I will need the authority of Colonel Bykov to proceed."

"Go ahead, Captain. Tell him that Andrei Fyodorovich thinks it important."

He was driven back to the apartment on Uspensky Street.

He found Rufina in distress. Her brother, Kostya, living in Kiev, where he worked as a curator in the museum, was suffering from a severe headache, the cause of which no one had successfully diagnosed. Kostya had been only six years old, ten years younger than Rufina, when their father died, and Rufina had helped to rear him. The siblings were very close, and twice Kostya had visited at Uspensky Street. Philby liked the studious and informal Kostya and admired his manual skills as electrician, plumber, and carpenter. He referred to him as "Comrade First Aid."

"I may have to go to him. I can get a lower-priced ticket using my Economics Institute I.D."

"Of course, go if you have to, Rufina."

It passed through his mind to put in a phone call, through channels, to Artur Ivanov, whom Rufina had spoken of as the Soviet counterpart with whom Harry Doubleday had conferred on the Gorky exhibit.

But what would he say to him? "Did you notice, Artur Filippovich, anything queer about the American, Doubleday?"

"Just who is calling? What do you mean, 'queer'?"

He ruled that out.

And what were the special powers of this Mr. Doubleday? Only Ursina could answer that question. But Rufina was right, Ursina should not be troubled. Presumably she was teetering from her experience, struggling to stand upright. She'd be under pressure from the Ministry of Culture and the security apparatus.

That was when the doorman rang up. Rufina walked down the two flights. She came back carrying a large brown envelope, her name neatly penned on it, over the Uspensky Street address. It had been delivered by messenger.

Philby was seated in his favorite armchair with a book when she opened it. She read the contents carefully. "Andrei. It's from Harry Doubleday."

He looked up sharply. "What does it say?"

"I'll read it to you. 'Dear Rufina, I am sorry I did not have an opportunity to call and say goodbye to you and to Andrei. I have to get back to America on business, but will return as soon as feasible.

Looks like someone spilled a coffee on this page

"'Rufina, you know Ursina's condition, because she told me she had confided it to you.'"

"Ursina's condition?" Philby interrupted. "What's that all about?"

"Ursina," Rufina said quietly, "is pregnant."

"You never told me that."

"I only knew yesterday. She told me confidentially. Shall I go on?"

"Of course. Yes. Yes."

She found her place in the letter: "'. . . she told me she had confided it to you. I will certainly discharge my duties as father of her—our—'" Rufina tilted the paper to receive the daylight. "He crossed out *her* and wrote *our*. '. . . our child. Ursina told you I was flying off. I wanted to make an emergency provision and so wrote out a brief testamentary letter, which I would very much appreciate your keeping until my return. I do not wish to leave it with Ursina, because of her recent troubles with the regime. Thank you ever so much, and my best to Andrei.'"

"I assume it is some instrument conveying something or other to her and the child. Odd he couldn't just keep it until his return."

"Keep it with whom?"

"Well, that's a point. Presumably not with the U.S. ambassador. 'Dear Mr. Ambassador: I have knocked up a Russian professor. If she calls on you for help, please tender her the care owed to the pregnant party.'"

"Oh Andrei, you can be so skeptical, so cynical. I'll put the letter in my file of family papers." She paused. "Andrei, I take it you do not wish to discuss what it was that took you away this morning?"

"Some things we never discuss, dear Rufina. You know that."

"Yes, that's true. I know that, and that's as it should be."

At noon the next day, Philby found a cab for her. They embraced and he helped load her bag into the trunk. She was off to her sick brother in Kiev.

CHAPTER 34

The tall, lithe official in the Soviet Embassy in Washington received early in the morning the special packet of documents from Moscow, for distribution as prescribed. He read the dispatch concerning one Harry Doubleday. It was marked "For Immediate Action."

When Mikhail Lebedev was seventeen years old, studying ballet in Kiev, he was told one morning after the class on Marxist doctrine that he was to take immediate action to correct his ongoing delinquency, which was his indifference to the finer points in Lenin's thought. Mikhail affected to be concerned, but actually spent his time pursuing his dancing, and one day he was sent to a reform camp in Siberia, where he stayed for six years and forgot everything he ever knew about dancing. But he forgot nothing about the need to take immediate action when directed to do so.

This directive, involving one Harry Doubleday, he decided to tackle himself. It could prove quite easy to probe. It was before nine in the morning when he scanned the Washington telephone directory, then the one for nearby Virginia. He found an M. H. Doubleday in Alexandria and rang the number using the special telephone. This phone was replaced every few days, which protected against the crystallization of fingerprints in surveillance antennae.

A woman answered the ring. "Who is calling?"

"Pan American Airways, ma'am."

"What about?"

"We have something in Lost and Found with the name Harry Doubleday on it."

"What is it?"

"We don't know, ma'am. We don't open packages left by passengers."

"Well, Mr. Doubleday is out of town. Will you leave me your number?"

Mikhail was ready. He gave her the number for Pan American. "Just ask for Lost and Found."

"All right."

She hung up.

Mikhail didn't want to call the number again, not for a while, anyway. On the other hand, immediate action was what had been requested.

He cabled back to Moscow. "INFORM ME IF POSSIBLE WHEN SUBJECT FLEW FROM MOSCOW."

In twenty minutes he had a reply. "PAN AM MOSCOW–NEW YORK, JANUARY 26, FLIGHT 27."

It was time to contact the New York consulate. "CHECK ARRIVAL MANIFESTS, PAN AMERICAN, JANUARY 26, FLIGHT 27. WAS A HARRY DOUBLEDAY LOGGED AS ARRIVING?"

That took a little longer, but not much. "AFFIRMATIVE. SUBJECT ARRIVED."

Mikhail shot back, "ATTEMPT ASCERTAIN IF SUBJECT LISTED ALEXANDRIA, VIRGINIA, AS HOME ADDRESS."

In another half hour he heard back. "AFFIRMATIVE. 34 QUAKER LANE."

Not good enough, Mikhail reflected. He would bring in Josey.

In forty-five minutes, a middle-aged woman, her shoulder-length gray-brown hair neatly brushed, arrived at Quaker Lane. She carried over her shoulder a navy blue tote bag, marked "Washington Post." Josey knocked on the door of 34 Quaker Lane. An elderly woman wearing an apron came to the door, opening the top half of it.

"Good day, ma'am. We are conducting a survey—"

"It's a cold day to be conducting surveys."

The visitor said, "That's real nice of you to worry about me, ma'am. That doesn't happen every day. Some people are real nice."

"I didn't exactly ask you to come in. I just said it was cold."

"Well, ma'am, if you prefer, I can just ask you these few questions standing out here. The cold isn't bad at all."

"What kind of questions?"

"Are you satisfied with your delivery of the *Washington Post*?"

"It comes in every day, don't it? You got trouble at your end of the business?"

"No no, just making sure you've got no complaints." Josey checked a line on her clipboard. "How many members of the household see the paper?"

"Just us."

"Yes, ma'am. Just you and . . ."

"Me and my husband. He's away a lot."

The inquirer entered another check. "Do you save the paper for when your husband gets back?"

"Save it? Sometimes he's away for two, three weeks."

Another check mark. "Would your husband be willing to fill out a questionnaire sent to his office?"

"He don't have an office. He works here."

The questioner registered surprise. "I thought you said he traveled a great deal."

"He does. He takes his office with him when he travels."

Josey laughed indulgently. "Yes, some people do that, traveling salesmen."

"He's not a traveling salesman. He's a book jobber. He sees that the bookstores have books in stock."

Josey took a deep breath. "That must have taken him to Frankfurt last week."

"Frankfurt? What do you mean?"

Josey seemed puzzled. "I thought everyone in the business went to the Frankfurt Book Fair."

"Last week, until Monday of this week, my husband was here. Now he's in Chicago."

"Well," Josey smiled. "I like to think that he'll pick up the *Post* at the airport."

"Hope that's all he picks up in Chicago. Look, I've got housecleaning to do. You got everything you need?"

"Yes," the visitor said. "Thank you very much. I have everything I need."

It was just past eleven. Nineteen hundred hours, Moscow time.

It was almost nine when Philby's telephone rang. It was Captain Kuzmin.

"We have the word from Washington. I'll read it. It says, 'HARRY DOUBLEDAY OF 34 QUAKER LANE ALEXANDRIA NOT SAME MAN AS SUBJECT.'"

"Thanks, Captain."

Philby was ecstatic. His suspicions were correct. Harry Doubleday was a phony.

It was good that Rufina was away. He walked quickly to the corner of the bedroom where she kept her writing desk. He dived into the file drawer and flipped to the folder marked FAMILY. He opened it and pulled out the sealed envelope marked for Ursina.

He must be cautious, but he knew well this, the technical end of the business, and ten minutes later he was passing the envelope over the flow of steam, easing open the flap. He put the envelope on the kitchen table and pulled out the enclosure.

It was a single page, written by hand in dark blue ink, and witnessed by someone whose name Philby did not recognize.

He read the text. It was an averment of the writer's love for Ursina Chadinov. A second averment acknowledged that he was the agent of her pregnancy. The last paragraph registered his intention, on his return to Washington, to confirm this instrument naming Ursina Chadinov heir to one-half of his estate.

It was signed, *Blackford Oakes.*

CHAPTER 35

Kim Philby had been up late. Over the years his friends, and in particular Rufina, had remarked the rages he would sometimes get into. Almost always these furors were, if not initiated by drink, intensified by it. Philby had already had several drinks when the telephone call came in from Captain Kuzmin, but before he scurried to Rufina's desk to find and pull out the letter, he had another slug. When he slid open the letter, his hands were shaking with excitement. And then his eyes saw the name at the bottom.

He poured out a full glass of whiskey and cursed. He closed his eyes to recreate the scene of his wedding reception. —That man, surveying the books in *his* library, was the most renowned agent in the enemy intelligence system. The same man who had confronted, and twice outwitted, Boris Bolgin. *He had been in this very room!* Receiving Philby's hospitality. And, perhaps that *very same night,* only blocks away, impregnating a Russian woman. A Russian woman who was his own wife's best friend. An illustrious professor of medicine. Just a couple of kilometers away, sitting there— *lying* there, legs apart, screwing a woman who used to be a prime Soviet citizen. Oakes, ejaculating into her not only his seed, but also the poison of Western capitalist thought. And now he proposes to give her one-half of the capitalist wealth he has accumulated by his services to capitalism and to the arms race and to opposing the march of history.

Philby interrupted his drinking to light another cigarette.

He was very glad, the next morning, when he recovered his ability to think, glad that Rufina was not there. Her table-cloth was stained with tobacco . . . turd.

He wiped up the mess and prepared for himself Rufina's potion: three cups of tea and three aspirin. He added one shot of brandy.

Life was becoming faintly tolerable when the telephone rang. Maybe it would be Rufina. And she would have news of Kostya. But it wasn't Rufina. "Comrade Martins. I am call-ing from the office of Colonel Bykov. He wishes to see you. A car will be outside your door in ten minutes."

Philby dressed and walked down the two flights of stairs. In a warm black woolen coat, his fedora plopped down on his head, he stepped into the waiting car.

He was led straightway to the third-floor office. The re-ceptionist looked up and nodded. He followed her, and she opened the door.

Bykov was seated at his desk, a lamp with a green shade illuminating one end of it. A floor lamp lighted the other end. The colonel rose, shook hands, and indicated the chair next to him, where Philby sat down.

"Now, Andrei Fyodorovich, what the hell is going on?"

A half hour later Bykov leaned back in his chair. "Andrei Fyodorovich, you have been a long time here without a cigarette."

Philby was not wholly surprised. The men who peered over at him every day and followed him wherever he went, every week, every year, would certainly have reported on his personal habits. Still, it was a little exhibitionistic for Bykov to rub it in, Philby's addiction to tobacco. He would have hugely enjoyed replying, "Oh no, Mikhail Pavlovich. I gave up smoking five years ago." *None of that, Harold Adrian Russell Philby.* Besides, he longed for a cigarette. He accepted the one proffered to him.

Bykov did not take one himself, but put the pack down on his desk. He leaned back again. "Comrade Chadinov has presented us with a very serious problem. It is one for which we are technically responsible. But in the last two days I have read our full file on the professor. There is nothing whatever to indicate any suspicion of political untrustworthiness. There are reports that she is outspoken, a bit imperious"— he was looking down at some notes under the lamp—"ambitious, inventive, a good student, good teacher . . .

"So we made no obvious mistake in designating her as one of the twelve welcomers. It has to be as you suspected, that her lover transformed her. And how ironic"—Bykov began amused, yielding to indignation—"that she should have been seduced physically *and* intellectually by one of the foremost spies." He gave a half smile. "Foremost *American* spies. You of course, Comrade Andrei Fyodorovich, are *the* foremost spy."

Philby acknowledged the compliment with a nod.

"But her prominence on the program, and the fact that dozens and dozens—that's the way these things always

happen—notice it and start talking about it—that puts attention on her case, attention that is very unwelcome. Our conventional arrangements would only draw more attention at
this moment to her defection. The culture minister would not
welcome that, and certainly not the general secretary, when
his stress is on 'changing ways.'" There was a faint derision
in Bykov's pronouncing of those words.

"Has she done anything . . . indiscreet since Monday?"
Philby thought himself at liberty to ask.

"No, and she has been carefully watched. The American
spy left at noon on Tuesday. She has been instructed to make
no overtures in any direction until she has met with the culture minister. That appointment with Comrade Roman Belov
is set for next Monday. Much thought needs to be given to
what he should say to her, to what we . . . will do with her."

Philby detected the dismissive motion of Bykov's hand. It
said, "Our meeting is over."

Philby got up. "I have a personal interest in this case,
Colonel. As you probably know, the suspect has been a very
close friend of my wife's. And the American—he has been,
for many years, a major antagonist."

CHAPTER 36

The ideological orientation of the peace forum's schedule was carefully planned to be unexacting. This meant—Culture Minister Belov nodded, on being advised by diplomatic expert Anatoly Dobrynin, the influential former Soviet ambassador to Washington—"leaving plenty of time for cultural pursuits, in which the subject of nuclear disarmament is just a benevolent backdrop." The delegates were invited to visit museums, to attend the ballet, and to explore Moscow's historic churches. The churches they visited were of course "nonfunctioning." And there was the program Gus Windels had described in his memo, featuring Kris Kristofferson's call to eschew women and whiskey and to think in terms of world peace.

On Thursday, the day before the final assembly that would vote out a resolution, Pierre Trudeau, former prime minister of Canada, issued a few invitations to a private social gathering to be held that evening in a suite at the Cosmos Hotel. Trudeau had strong political instincts and made it a point to invite one or two guests who were not the kind of people to whom he'd naturally gravitate. Yoko Ono was invited, as also three Latin American writers. Not one Soviet representative was asked. "Just tell your boss," he said to Aleksei, the Soviet official who had been put in charge of looking after him and making him comfortable, "that I'm not inviting any of your people because I think of them as hosts. This little get-together will be for guests, not hosts." Aleksei didn't argue the question, and the invitations went out.

Only a about a dozen delegates showed up, there being so many competing events. Trudeau, standing near the door, dressed in a light gray suit, perfectly tailored, was listening to Mexico's Carlos Fuentes when from the corner of his eye he spotted Graham Greene. Fuentes had been talking about the liberation movement in Nicaragua and others being fomented in Colombia and elsewhere in Latin America. Trudeau nodded and shot out his hand to greet Graham Greene. He motioned him to join in the conversation. "And I'll get you some real champagne," Trudeau said. "I wish I could say I had brought it from Canada, but Quebec separatism hasn't got *that* far. Accordingly, we have had to rely on French champagne."

Greene took the glass and sipped from it.

"That was a stirring speech you gave," Trudeau said. "It is a novel idea, that the time has come for Catholics and Communists to work together."

"Not all that novel, Pierre. I have hinted at that theme in several of my books."

"Of course. And you have derided the notion that the differences between the two faiths are irreconcilable. On the other hand, Graham, you have derided the notion that sin and non-sin are irreconcilable."

"I didn't say quite that, Pierre."

Trudeau smiled impishly. "I was in London when *The End of the Affair* came out. The wisecrack I remember—in *The Tablet,* I think it appeared—was, 'Mr. Greene seems to be saying that Christ preached, "If you love me, break my commandments."'"

Greene laughed, though not heartily. "Carlos here will explain to you what I am talking about."

"Señor Fuentes—"

"Please, Prime Minister, call me Carlos."

"Pierre, please. Well, Carlos, you, like Mr. Greene, have spent time in Cuba since the advent of President Castro. How can Catholics in Cuba be expected to work together with Fidel Castro, when Castro persecutes the Catholics?"

Greene broke in. "There is a great deal of exaggeration on that subject, Pierre. I have been in Cuba several times and spent some time with Mr. Castro—"

"Spent some time with him! You are recorded as having been with him until five o'clock in the morning."

Greene smiled and refused the tray of hors d'oeuvre being passed, but then changed his mind and picked out a cracker thick with caviar. "Yes, Castro keeps late hours. Some people tend to do so. Are you up late at night, Pierre?"

"That depends on the alternative. I suppose it is appropriate to pledge that we should all stay up late at night if required to avoid nuclear war."

Greene did not think that especially amusing. "I have

stayed up late at night, without feeling any inclination to do so, ever since Ronald Reagan was re-elected president of the United States."

"Yes," Trudeau said, picking up the remaining cracker with caviar. "In fact, I remember your saying four years ago that you would desert the West to live in a Communist country if Reagan was re-elected."

"That alternative was exaggerated."

"By the press, or by you?"

Carlos Fuentes spoke up. "But, Prime Minister—Pierre— what Mr. Greene spoke of Tuesday afternoon is a real phenomenon, not just a figment of his imagination."

"Graham Greene has a very famous imagination. In *Our Man in Havana,* he wrote as if in Cuba—it was merely laughable, back when the novel was published—a Communist dictator was actually in the wings!"

There was silence. The irony was difficult to cope with. Then Fuentes said, "I know, of course, that Castro has . . . insisted on . . . having his own way in Cuba. But we surely would not deny, Pierre, the good that he has done?"

"I would not deny it. No. But neither would I deny the indefensible that he has done. Graham, for many years you refused permission for your books to be published in the Soviet Union, protesting the denial of human rights."

"Yes, but the situation is much improved under Mr. Gorbachev."

"I think that's true, and let's drink to that."

Gregory Peck interjected himself. "Prime Minister, may I join this exclusive little enclave?"

"You are most welcome, Mr. Peck. You are one of my favorite actors."

"I wish I had been tapped for a role in *Our Man in Havana*."

"Oh?" Greene said. "Which part do you think you'd have been especially suited to play?"

"Oh gee, I forget, Graham. But of course, actors should be able to play any role."

"We are doing that here, aren't we? The role of international leaders."

Fuentes shook his head. "You are certainly qualified to play that role, Pierre. You have four times been elected leader of your country."

"Indeed, yes, Carlos. I wonder how I'd have done running for president in Cuba."

"Some time in the future," Gregory Peck said, "that kind of thing can be expected, but only if we proceed to a non-nuclear age."

"Hear hear!" said Carlos Fuentes, raising his glass.

"Hear hear!" said Pierre Trudeau, raising his own.

CHAPTER 37

En route home to Uspensky Street, Philby thought to ask the driver to detour to the post office building on Tverskaya Street. He would walk home from there after checking his mailbox, which he did once a week. He picked up the occasional letter and the non-Russian journals he subscribed to. He stuffed the letters into his pocket and carried the London *Sunday Times* in his hand. Back at Uspensky 78, Philby climbed up the stairs and went to his study, sinking gratefully into his beloved armchair. It had been left to him by classmate and fellow Soviet agent Guy Burgess. Rufina was always citing the relatively continent Burgess when trying to persuade Philby to drink a little less.

It crossed his mind that at some point he would need to eat something. Rufina always kept cheese and bread and beans, which could quickly become bean soup. All of them combined well with Madeira. He liked especially the Madzhari from Georgia—"even though," he had teased Rufina, "its alcoholic content is wimpishly low. It is no doubt produced by capitalists." The telephone rang while he was heating the soup. He lowered the flame.

It wasn't Rufina calling from Kiev. It was Ursina.

"Ursina, Rufina is not here," he said, hoping his tone of voice did not betray his revised attitude toward her after the events of the last few days. "She is in Kiev. Kostya is ill."

"I'm sorry. So, as it happens, am I—ill, I mean. You know, because I authorized Rufina to tell you, that I am pregnant. It develops that I have an ectopic pregnancy. Do you know what that is?"

"Well, I think so. A tubal pregnancy? Where the egg is stuck in the Fallopian tube instead of going down to the uterus?"

"That's correct. I have bleeding and dizziness and that means"—she struggled to keep her voice even—"it means that in surgery the doctor has to . . . well, what it amounts to is . . . remove the fetus."

"Oh my goodness, Ursina."

"If Rufina had been in Moscow, it would have been nice to have her at the hospital with me. But the operation can't be postponed, because I am bleeding. They have to act quickly when that happens."

"When is it scheduled?"

"For 6 P.M. tonight."

"You will have someone call to tell me everything went all right? I will call Rufina then, not before. It is hard to get through to Kiev, and I would only need to call her again after the operation."

"I will get through to you, Andrei Fyodorovich."

———

Philby finished heating the bean soup and sat down at the kitchen table with his opened bottle of Madzhari. He began to spoon the soup into his mouth. Abruptly he stopped. He got up and went into his library.

One of his three thousand books was a medical encyclopedia. He turned to "pregnancy, ectopic," and read down the page.

"The major health risk of this condition is internal bleeding. Before the nineteenth century, mortality from ectopic pregnancies exceeded 50 percent. By the end of the nineteenth century, the mortality rate dropped to 5 percent because of surgical intervention."

He paused at the kitchen table to put a slice of cheese onto a piece of bread. He ate distractedly, and finished hastily. He grabbed his coat and went down to the entrance. Opening the door, he once again waved his hand to hail his guardians across the way.

He waited outside for the guard to get to him.

"I need to go right away to Colonel Bykov at the Lubyanka. It concerns the matter we spoke of this morning, and I have important information for him."

"Can you wait for the car, or do you wish me to hail you a cab? I would accompany you."

"Get a cab," Philby said.

In fifteen minutes he was again at the office in the Lubyanka. But this time he had to sit down and wait. "The colonel is at lunch. He should back very soon."

In his career, Philby had often had to wait, sometimes for a very very long time as, in Spain, he had twice needed to do

in order to ambush his targets. But he could not, this afternoon, summon the old, patient frame of mind. He fidgeted.

Might he smoke?

"Not here. If you like I will lead you to another room in
the building."

Forget it.

He picked up an illustrated history of the Bolshoi Ballet.

Colonel Bykov had evidently entered his office through a
private door. He had not passed by Philby when the receptionist, responding to a light, announced that Colonel Bykov
was ready to see him. She led Philby, for the second time that
day, back to the inner sanctum.

"Good afternoon, Andrei Fyodorovich. You have news,
clearly."

Philby had thought through what he would say and how.
He would, invoking his rank and his experience of more than
thirty years, speak directly.

"The state unquestionably acknowledges that our movement would be better off if Ursina Chadinov were dead, re-
lieving us of several problems."

Bykov sat motionless.

"She called me just now to give me critical medical news.
She will be operated on at 6 P.M. for an ectopic pregnancy. It
may be that you know the relevant data, but in the event you
do not, I have looked them up. She is bleeding, she tells me,
and is dizzy. This requires immediate medical attention—any
delay threatens life." He paused, not without drama. "It
seems to me that an unusual opportunity presents itself."

Bykov picked up the phone. "Get me Dr. Drishkin."

The call went through quickly.

"Drishkin, Bykov here. Are you familiar with ectopic

pregnancies? . . . Yes, I have been told as much. Have any of our prison doctors officiated, in surgery, on ectopic pregnancies? Shumberg? . . . Well where is this Dr. Shumberg? . . . Lefortovo? That was Beria's favorite prison. Good acoustics for torture. Wait." He cupped his hand over the receiver. "Martins, the surgery is scheduled where, in the university hospital?"

"I assume so, or she'd have told me."

Back on the phone. "Drishkin, you are to inform Shumberg that he is to preside over a surgery this afternoon at the university hospital. Then you will pass word to the doctor scheduled to perform the operation that we have arranged for our own specialist to do so instead. Shumberg's job is to go to the hospital and dress for surgery. He will then stand by until the patient is under anesthetic. . . . Yes. That could be quite useful, what you say—that Professor Chadinov informed us through special channels that she wished to go to great lengths in order to save the child, even though, if I understand you, such measures can imperil the mother. . . .

"Advise Shumberg how to be in touch with me."

He put down the telephone. This time he did light one of his cigarettes, after offering the pack to Philby.

After a few drags, he said, "Listen now, Andrei Fyodorovich, to the sequence.

"—Professor Chadinov calls you and tells you the operation is scheduled. She asks whether you could use your special contacts to secure the services of a doctor who, having faced such problems in the past, has succeeded in saving the life of the child.

"—You come to me. I call a medical doctor who knows well the specialists in Moscow. He nominates Dr. Shumberg as the very best. But Dr. Shumberg is at his dacha and is out hunting.

"—My office makes every effort to reach him and does so. He is driven to the university hospital but arrives only just at six. The patient is already under anesthesia. Dr. Shumberg dresses and enters the operating room, telling the attending doctor of his recruitment for this operation. Shumberg examines the patient and proceeds with surgery.

"You could not hear that part of the conversation I had with Drishkin, just now, in which he informed me that Shumberg is very skillful at all aspects of assignments like the one he is being given."

Philby stood up. "Dr. Chadinov told me she would have me called to report on the operation, so that I could inform my wife, Rufina, in Kiev."

"We will see to it that someone calls you. Thank you, Andrei Fyodorovich."

"Always glad to be of service, Mikhail Pavlovich."

CHAPTER 38

It was just before eight o'clock that the telephone rang. Philby had paced the floor and smoked and drunk for two hours, awaiting the call. He had tried after his return from the Lubyanka to put in a call to Rufina, even though it would be too early yet to give her news on the . . . operation. He wondered why she hadn't herself got through to him. But long distance was difficult, and when the connection failed, he went back to his reading and lit another cigarette.

The call at eight was not from Kiev. The operator on the line said he was to hold for Colonel Bykov.

Bykov, in a minute or two, came on the line. Philby was not surprised by the formality in his tone of voice or by the salutation.

"Comrade Martins? Is this the correct telephone number for Comrade Rufina Ivanovna Martins?"

"Yes. This is her husband, Andrei Fyodorovich."

"Ah, yes, we have had dealings. Your wife is not in?"

"No, she is in Kiev."

"Well, be so good as to communicate the following to her. It has to do with her close friend Dr. Ursina Chadinov. It is a very short note from Dr. Kirill Shumberg, and I will read it to you.

"'The patient, Ursina Chadinov, submitted to abdominal surgery after she was diagnosed by the university hospital obstetrician with an ectopic pregnancy. The patient, Chadinov, a medical doctor and a university professor, made use of contacts in order to locate a surgeon experienced in this problem. My name was given to her because it is known that I have in the past twice preserved the life of the fetus, successfully moving it from the Fallopian tube to the uterus. This patient was most anxious to effect the survival of her unborn child. Unfortunately, she went into shock on the operating table and we were not able to save her life.'

"You will get that message through to Comrade Rufina Ivanovna?"

"Yes, Colonel."

"Now on the medical form Dr. Chadinov filled out at the hospital, where it asks the name of the father, she wrote down, 'Harry Doubleday.' For address, she wrote only, 'USIA, American Embassy.' The hospital will attempt to locate Mr. Doubleday by ringing the embassy tomorrow. And you will pass the news to Comrade Rufina Ivanovna?"

"Yes. But listen, Colonel, I have not been able to get through to Kiev. Would you do me the kindness of having someone in your office call me here with the code number for the long-distance operator who expedites telephone calls?"

"Yes, comrade. We can attend to that. Good night."

Philby rose from the chair by the telephone and moved to his armchair. He did not reach for his glass, nor light a cigarette. But after a while he stood and walked to one of his bookcases and took up a copy of his own book, *My Silent War*. In that book he had recorded, without emotional distress, elliptically, some idea of the deeds he had done for the Soviet Union and its movement over a period of twenty-five years, when posing as a British agent.

He had been careful, in the memoirs, not to dwell on details of his craft, of what he had done, which would have made for difficult reading for those Westerners who did not understand the totality of his commitment to his cause. There were no details of the men caught and hanged in Albania. There were over sixty of them, and the coordinates of their parachute landings had been handed to the Albanian security police by . . . himself. The Communist security force had lain in waiting and taken them, one after another, to the gallows.

Oh, there were other details of what he had done and of what followed from his betrayals, which he did not disclose in his memoirs. It was enough, in that book, to remind the reader, as he had done at the outset, that he was not an Englishman loyal to king and country who, along the way, had decided to betray king and country.

Why hadn't the telephone rung, bringing him the code?

He flicked open the book, easily found the right page, and read out loud the words in Russian: "All through my career, I have been a straight penetration agent working in the Soviet interest. My connection with MI6 must be seen against my prior, total commitment to the Soviet Union, which I regarded then, as I do now," he raised his eyes and head, as if to reaffirm what he had written twenty years ago, "as the inner fortress of the world movement." If he were producing a new edition of his book today, would he tell of his role in taking care of such a problem as Ursina had presented?

Of course not. If he were to recount today's proceedings—in which he took professional satisfaction—such a narrative would be kept in ultra-secret archives of the KGB, and the principals would not be identified by name.

Would he, in such an account—or in any account, ever—confess to the important subjective motive in what he had done? Certainly not. But he didn't have to conceal it from himself. The objective purpose was to relieve the state of the Chadinov problem—the professor of medicine who was prepared to denounce the whole Communist enterprise at a public gathering, an international public gathering! A gathering of distinguished guests of the general secretary! Yes, the state was now relieved of the diplomatic problem of administering justice to such a betrayer.

But, of course, he had another purpose in mind. He would hand it back to Blackford Oakes! Come to Moscow and seduce one of our prominent young professionals! Accept the hospitality of my own house at my own wedding—

The telephone rang.

"What is the number you are attempting to call, comrade?"

He gave it.

He heard the telephone ringing. It was answered by Natasha, Kostya's wife.

"This is Andrei calling. How is Kostya?"

"He is better. They think they know the problem. But he is still in the hospital, and Rufina is— Wait! Andrei, she is just at the door."

He held on, digging his nails into his palm.

"Andrei! I've tried three times to call you, but could not get through. Natasha says people always have this problem."

"I understand that Kostya is better."

"Yes, with thanks to Dr. Gulin. They have found the right medicine and already the pain is decreased."

"Rufina, I have very bad news. And I shall tell it to you directly. Ursina"—he hesitated for a moment—"Ursina was having abdominal pains and bleeding, and the doctor told her she had to have immediate surgery—"

"Oh my God. She *is* all right, I hope!"

"Rufina, dear Rufina. Ursina died on the operating table at seven o'clock tonight."

He could do nothing about her pain. He held the telephone in his hand and let her sob and weep.

After a minute or two he said, "Dear Rufina, I must hang up. There is nothing we can do. All love to you."

BOOK THREE

CHAPTER 39

At 373 Merriwell Lane, the Federal Express driver rang the bell a second time. If nobody was home, was he to leave the envelope at the door? He scanned the airbill, his eyes focusing on item number eight. The sender of the letter was supposed to "Sign to authorize delivery without obtaining signature." Had the sender done so?

The deliveryman could make out carboned traces of what had been the sender's pen, or pencil, but nothing like a legible signature. For the one hundredth time, the elderly carrier cursed silently the designer of the Federal Express airbill. What he was now attempting to read was the "FedEx Copy," *a carbon copy*, the original waybill having been retained by the sender. No telephone numbers had been given, neither the sender's in Vienna nor the recipient's in Virginia.

Okay. These things happen. He knew the practice: The home office would try one more delivery—tomorrow, same time—and then, if there was still no one home, send it back to—his eyes idled on the sender's address. Well, it had "strasse" in it. They all did, from that part of the world. Poised to return to his truck, he had lowered his cap against the setting sun when the door swung open. The Latino lady wearing an apron nodded her head.

"Package here for Mr. Oakes. Will you sign here please, ma'am?"

The woman with the Aztec face adjusted her eyeglasses and took the pencil in hand. "I don' write en English."

The driver pointed to the bottom of the page. "That's okay, ma'am. Is Mr. Oakes at home? To receive this?"

She drew forward, standing on the doorsill, to emphasize that the courier was not to come into the house. "Mr. Oakes is here. He is . . . Mr. Oakes is . . . Mr. Oakes is . . ."—she tilted her head, raising an open hand to her cheek—"slipping."

"Okay, well just—just make a check mark on this line"—he pointed.

She drew an X, returned the pencil, and accepted the FedEx envelope.

"Take care, ma'am."

"Yes," she said, with a quick smile. Envelope in hand, she turned, pushing the door shut with her rump. Inside the hall, she placed the stiff envelope on the broad mahogany ledge above the heater. She needed to push back the stack of un-read magazines to make room for it. She walked to the tele-phone in the coatroom, picked up the receiver, and dialed the intercom number 15.

"Llegó otra carta, está de Federal Express, señor." She spoke to Oakes in Spanish. Josefina González spoke only in Spanish. "I put it with the other mail.

"Will you let me prepare something different for supper? You have had the beans and cheese and the tortillas yesterday. And the day before yesterday. And the day before the day before yesterday." She had raised her voice.

But then she put down the phone, tightening her lips. Señor Oakes had hung up. Again.

Anthony Trust, tanned and relaxed, slim and well dressed in a camel's hair jacket, waited at the bar of the Chevy Chase Country Club. He was drinking a beer and knew to order an old-fashioned for Jake, who would appear in five minutes or so. Jake would never go directly to the bar after his golf game. He would go to the shower room, and come up after that. Anthony had once teased him on his inflexibility, but never again. "You're talking to someone who went thirteen months without a shower," Jake Shulz had answered, expressionless.

Drawing attention to his time as a prisoner of war in Korea had been unlike Jake. Seated at a table in the bar, working on his second old-fashioned, he had apologized for the melodramatic answer he had given. "I'm sorry about that— I'm sorry I made that reference there." He wouldn't even now use the word "shower," so embarrassed was he over having used it in the first place.

But Anthony was good in tight corners. He brushed back his long hair. "You want to hear a joke, Jake? Hmm. Joke-Jake. Jake-Joke. Quiet! I'll tell the joke and you don't have to listen to it. There was this guy I knew, just out of college, had never laid eyes on the director, not once. And he walks into the head over at the Dulles briefing section, pulls on the handle, and the door doesn't want to come open, so he gives it a big hard yank. It opens now and he meets the director, who's sitting on the can."

"When do we get to the joke?"

"Well . . . The director says, 'I haven't been to the can for thirteen months.'"

Jake's laugh was hearty.

Trust could do that to people. He and Blackford Oakes had labored and disported together for more than thirty years. It was Oakes he wanted, this March afternoon, to talk to Jake about. Blackford, their colleague in the agency for so many years; their boss on several missions. It had been more than a month since Blackford Oakes's abrupt resignation. He had given no explanation, leaving his resignation letter on the director's desk, with a note giving the name of Bob Lounsbury, his lawyer, if paperwork were immediately required. In the letter, he consented to meet, at the Merriwell Diner, only with the deputy director, if there was a need to discuss agency operations Oakes had special knowledge of. Summons to such meetings were to be given to Josefina. "Meeting today five o'clock" was all that was needed, and about all that Josefina could handle.

Jake was sipping his drink.

Anthony Trust talked to him now almost as if he were giving him a briefing.

"I've done a little sleuthing, Jake. We people know a little about sleuthing, don't we? Among the three of us we have, what? a hundred years in the agency? Black, me, you. Sleuthing is what we do to Soviet types, you're thinking, I know I know."

Jake nodded his head. Indeed, that was what he was thinking.

"Never mind that. It's been a long time since the day Black just up and quit." He looked down at a notepad. "February 1, 1988. Here are some bits and pieces I've put together. On February 2, he canceled his newspaper service. No more *Washington Post,* no more *New York Times, Wall Street Journal, USA Today.*"

"You got to envy him, somehow."

"I got through to . . . the right people in the phone company. His phone use is rare, but the service hasn't been canceled. Calls come in every now and then. Josefina turns the callers off unless the code word is spoken in Spanish—then she calls him to the phone. That has happened only two or three times. Outgoing, there's a long-distance call to Mexico City every Saturday, always at the same time—8:45 A.M. The number in Mexico picks up right away, before the second ring."

"He's calling Tony?"

"No. The call is to the old number, Sally's number. It was never disconnected. The call from Merriwell is actually to Sally's old maid, who still works there, does cleaning and laundry for Tony and the old lady, Tony's great-aunt. Beatriz González is Josefina's sister, Tony's old nurse. She knows—obviously—that the call that comes in regularly on Saturdays at 8:45 A.M. is from her sister calling from Merriwell."

Jake's expression was alarmed. The patch over his right eye made him look especially solemn when talking in this mood.

"Did you bug the phone?" He paused. "I mean, Anthony, you have a reputation for thoroughness."

"Jake. We're talking about trying to help a pal. No, we didn't put a bug on the phone. So we know only that Josefina has her weekly talk with Beatriz, and maybe reports to Beatriz, who maybe reports to Tony, that Blackford is—alive."

"But hardly well."

"But hardly well. What more can we look into? I checked at the Merriwell Mart. Black took me there once." Anthony's face brightened at the memory. "Sally was needing salt and pepper or artichokes or whatever it was she had forgotten, and she was hysterical because one of her guests had already arrived. Anyway, I told the guy at the Mart that I was with Pure Food and Drug and needed to check what had gone out to the house in the last few weeks."

"Was there anything worth looking at?"

"Well, no. Josefina does all the shopping. Merriwell Mart delivers about once a week, heavy on Mexican foods. The guy who runs it is Hispanic, and Josefina tells him what to bring on the next trip. Black's not going to starve. And he's not going to run out of whiskey."

Jake, his drink almost finished, signaled to the bartender for another.

"That's the kind of thing some people do, Jake. Right? Wife living in Mexico dies. After a while he's off on an assignment in Moscow. Comes back looking good as ever. Then—whatever happened . . . happened. He seems just to have quit life. You cut off your friends, tune out, and—"

"Try to drink yourself to death," Jake said, draining his glass.

CHAPTER 40

There was no formal connection between the invitation to Philby to visit Cuba, and his wedding to Rufina. Sentimental acts weren't entitled to recognition, in the orthodoxy of the society Philby lived in and had spied for. The Soviet Union was big on rewards, not valentines. But the invitation to visit Fidel Castro's Cuba did in fact arrive a few days after the wedding and was delightedly accepted. Of course there would be burdens, duties to perform in Cuba, but there were burdens in all of life, and the ratio here of exertion to reward was favorable.

They had originally planned to leave February 2, but in the shock of Ursina's death, Rufina begged to postpone the trip. Shock, but also duty: Ursina had no surviving family. Rufina, her closest friend, saw to all that needed doing. But she would be glad to get away later in the month, she told Andrei.

They would travel on a freighter, non-stop, Odessa to Havana. They would have a personal guide, Gennady, to look after them, and they would be looked after, upon arrival, by an official Soviet presence.

At sea for two weeks! Philby and Rufina treated this as if it were a honeymoon. Occupying one of the three staterooms on the freighter that carried goods for the straitened Castro regime, they would rise every morning and walk around the deck, discerning, whenever land was observable, just where they were on the globe. A very exciting moment came for Philby when the boat found itself within viewing distance of Eastbourne, on Britain's south coast. Through the morning fog, he thought he could make out his old school.

The crew was hospitable, and the couple's privacy was respected. It was surprising, given the sea traffic in the Atlantic, that they saw not a single other vessel after leaving the British Channel. There had been the one disturbing episode, an airplane overhead. A small plane, but it descended low enough to make the pilot visible. Gennady hustled his wards below. Did he really think there was any possibility of an alien force flying in that little airplane? Intending to do what? Call in a flotilla to wrest Philby back into the hands of Western justice? Silly. But Gennady was their escort officer and responsible for the success of the passage, so they followed his instructions.

They arrived in Havana after a fifteen-day passage and were greeted most heartily by the Cuban authorities. Examining the schedule they were given on landing in Havana, they were both pleased and appalled at the thoroughness of their itinerary, which would take them to all corners of Cuba. There were comfortable breaks, one of them in a luxurious setting in Baradero, with a beach stretching further than the eye could see in either direction. Philby declined to use that beach. He told Rufina he thought it a survival of capitalist degeneracy. But he did not deny her access to it, which she happily took.

Philby noticed that there was no place on the schedule that called for a personal meeting with Fidel Castro. His radio brought in daily BBC broadcasts, and he did not need to be reminded that Castro was fully occupied—for one thing, in simply feeding his people. That was a perpetual problem. There were specific distractions. Two men were arrested on suspicion of spying, both native Cubans, one of them an exile. And then there was the noisy defection of an influential general, who had flown himself in a Cessna, landed in Key West, and pleaded for asylum.

Never mind spending any time with Fidel Castro. But Philby did spend long hours, day after day, with Cuban officials who talked endlessly with him about the resources of the Communist world and about the inevitability, under Marxist direction, of victory.

Philby obliged his hosts most of the time, but now and again pressed his orthodoxy and gave rein to his crotchets. He and Rufina were to occupy a splendid section of the Dupont Villa, near Baradero, open to tourists. Philby accepted his quarters at one end of the villa but refused even to visit the grand palace, one more affront, a legacy of the period of capitalist exploitation. And when asked if he wished to see the house that Ernest Hemingway had lived in, his answer was that he had no interest in doing so. This did not involve a general boycott of Hemingway's haunts, however, and certainly not of the famous bar, the Floridita, renowned for its special daiquiris. The Philbys and their escorts were each served a daiquiri. One drink was never enough for Kim Philby, but when he motioned for a second, he got from his bearded Cuban escort lurid tales of the demonic strategic impact of this particular mix of lime and rum. The Cuban positively forbade the Philbys a second drink, even as he ordered another for himself and his two aides.

The only consumer item not rationed, Rufina noticed, was ice cream. All else was scarce. But she and her husband were not in Cuba to promulgate a commercial five-year plan, and their contentment was abiding that this critical island was in the hands of a Communist ally.

They weren't entirely sorry when, on the day they were supposed to depart, they were told that their sailing was postponed by two weeks because of a mix-up. The old familiar freighter had pulled away a day earlier than scheduled, which meant, for the Philbys, a fortnight more in Cuba, after which they were put aboard the *Yanis Lentsmanis,* and set out for another fifteen days at sea.

There were the exciting moments and the sharp changes, from the tropical sun to the cold of early spring. When they entered the Bosporus there was snow, but it was dark, and they could only just make out the road and lights in the house windows, including the house where Philby had once lived and worked. He had never traveled there to verify it, but it had been reported to him that his old house now bore a plaque: "Kim Philby, outstanding intelligence officer, lived here 1941–48."

CHAPTER 41

Dr. Vladimir Kirov was surprised by the nature of the call from Professor Lindbergh Titov. It wasn't surprising to be hearing from his old friend and fellow member of the Union of Scientists and Scholars. What surprised him was that the call hadn't been for the usual reason, which was, and had been for some years, to set a date for dinner and, often, on to the ballet. This time, Titov said he wanted a professional medical consultation. Kirov was in his early sixties, but had not slowed down as doctor and teacher.

"Of course, Linbek. I could give you an exact time to come in during the day. Or—you can come in any time after six. I stay in the office until just before eight. . . . Yes yes yes, we'll go for dinner after. I suggest the Hercole. The head-waiter there recognizes my eminence, and will take good care of us."

Comrade Lindbergh Vissarionovich Titov was just sixty. He was hairless, as he had been, at age twenty-one, when Kirov first met him at the medical school. After a brief exposure to Titov, Kirov speculated jocularly that the absence of hair suggested a furnace of intellectual activity, activity of such intensity that *something* had to give out—in this case, Titov's body hair. But everybody quickly got used to it, and the thirty-five students in the medical-research department of the university medical school soon stopped paying any notice to the hair, or lack of it.

Yet Titov was self-conscious, and took every opportunity to put on his cap, or, in colder weather, his knitted woolen hat, striped in red and gold, which he took with him everywhere. "Everywhere" included the laboratory in which he worked under the tutelage of Nikolai Sokolov, the only living Russian Nobel laureate in science when Titov entered medical school. Nikolai Sokolov was seventy-eight. His widely hailed accomplishment in radiology—he was father of the Sokolovgram—had been done in his twenties.

Sokolov had slowed down, but no one would suggest he withdraw from the research division of the medical school, and he had no desire to do so. He merely intensified his long-standing resistance to regular student seminars. Rather than simply teach or conduct seminars, he liked to walk about the classrooms and laboratories, watching the students at work, listening to what they were saying, hearing about the problems they were addressing, the threads of exploration that engaged them. Then, year after year, he would single out one student for a close personal association. In the spring of 1950, he had shown interest in the hairless young man who asked penetrating questions and who spoke and laughed a lot when in company with his fellow students in the refectory, or at ease in the courtyard, with a smoke, wearing, usually, his red and gold hat.

In May, Professor Sokolov addressed a note to the young Titov. He asked him to come to his office at five the next afternoon.

Titov allowed himself to speculate that, just possibly, the great Sokolov would select him as his special student. It was known that a fresh selection would be made after the incumbent protégé, the dreamy, longhaired Stepan, graduated and left Moscow to join the radiology department at the university in Leningrad. Such an association with Sokolov meant academic preferment, but, more important, meant intensive exposure to someone whose mind had dazzled scientists even in other fields. Titov was breathless at the thought that he might be picked, and so he was, after one hour's conversation in the great man's office.

Sokolov had opened by asking a question Titov had frequently heard. "Let me begin, Comrade Lindbergh Vissarionovich, by asking for an explanation for your extraordinary first name."

Titov very nearly blushed, as he sat, like a boy, answering that question. "Comrade Nikolai Semyonovich, my father was an aviator. He was in the Soviet Air Force. An accident in a fighter plane, the Ant-4—the first all-metal plane with two engines—resulted in the amputation of one leg. We were very poor, but we did have a radio, and my father's excitement in May of 1927 was—"

"You are going to tell me about Charles Augustus Lindbergh?"

Titov broke out in one of those ear-to-ear smiles that lighted entire rooms. "Yes, that is what happened. Now, although the English name isn't that hard to pronounce in Russian, people find it outlandish, so I've simplified the pronunciation to Linbek."

"Very well, comrade Linbek Vissarionovich. I note that your patronymic is the same as that of our . . . august leader."

"Yes, comrade. My mother felt it might give a little protection against any suggestion that we were pro-American because of my first name if she gave me the same patronymic as Comrade Stalin's. So she changed my father's name to Vissarion."

Sokolov paused. "That is a burden in life."

Titov did not reply directly. He simply smiled again, and admitted that in his dreams—"in my happy dreams"—he was an aviator.

After nine months superintending Titov, Sokolov went to the office of the dean. He recommended that the student Titov, now given the title Medical Scientist, be made a Fellow and excused from any formal obligations in the graduate-studies program. "He is a very rare bird, comrade. A free, unfettered, curious, imaginative mind. He is as familiar with the isotopes and the positron as with members of his own family. *Leave him free and unmolested*, Comrade Anton Dmitrievich."

It was so, and Titov's freedom from constraints pleased him greatly, a manumission he hastened to tell Kirov about, his close friend, the classmate who had locked into urological studies. "Where is your research taking you, Linbek?"

"I am not certain. But I *am* certain that I must arrange to visit Hiroshima."

Dr. Kirov now positioned his friend and patient over the special urological examining bench. Kirov's gloved fingers reached deep into him.

"Oy. *Oyyyyy!*"

"It's almost over."

"You mean my life?"

Kirov chuckled. "I will need a culture, and some urine."

Titov, dressing himself, asked, "What do you think it is, Volodya?"

"I think you have an enlarged prostate."

"Does that mean I can't have more children?" he laughed.

"You have a fine son."

"Yes. But after he was born, Nina had two ectopic pregnancies in a row. I think you knew that. I don't suppose anything you can do with my prostate could correct that!"

"Linbek, if the test is positive, then you will get treatment. There are basically two kinds. There is radiology, a specialty of yours, and surgery, a specialty of mine."

"Let's not talk about it at supper."

"As you like. But don't be tense about it. These things happen. Life goes on."

"My prostate's life would not go on, would it?"

"That can depend. On the precision of the radiological treatment. Or on what the surgeon discovered there."

The two scientists had finished their meal—Caucasian spiced chicken and rice, cake and coffee—and had almost finished the second bottle of wine. "You know something, Volodya?" Titov addressed his companion. "I have in my laboratory, I am convinced, the concept and the constituent parts of a procedure that would immunize against radioactivity."

Kirov was startled. "You mean, someone who was immunized would never have to fear X-ray treatment?"

"Correct. And if exposed to nuclear radiation—even at the level of Chernobyl—would have the means of neutralizing it."

"Is the work you are doing widely known?"

"Not widely. Two of my assistants are of course aware of what I am doing. So is Dr. Shumberg, our old classmate."

Kirov's face tightened. He thought to bring up the matter of Ursina, but quickly changed his mind. He could not trust himself to contain his tears at the mention of Ursina. "That is exciting, what you tell me."

"Yes, it is very exciting, but I must go home now. I am at the laboratory at six."

"I'll give you your medical news on Tuesday."

They exchanged a bear hug.

CHAPTER 42

At six-thirty, Titov arrived at the office of his doctor and friend, the red and gold hat tight over his head. On the phone, earlier in the day, Kirov had asked him to allow an hour or so. "I need to talk with you about another matter."

"There is no other matter than my prostate."

"I'll see you at six-thirty, Linbek."

The analysis had been done. The prostate was cancerous. "There is always the possibility of metastasis, and that is something to be watched. My recommendation is that you submit to twenty radiation sessions. I would be wasting the time of the principal student of radiology in Moscow—perhaps in the world—to instruct you in the matter of radiation treatments. What I have here for your radiologist is a very precise location to bear down on."

"Volodya, can I have . . . normal relations with my wife?"

"You certainly can, some weeks' time after the treatments. During the period of treatment you may not achieve satisfactory erections."

"In that case I will have to keep Nina entertained with bulletins from my radiological institute. But Volodya, you had some other matter on your mind. What is it?"

Kirov had not been informed by Ursina on that Friday, two weeks earlier, about her scheduled ectopic operation later in the day. She hadn't even told her old friend that she was pregnant—or that she had a lover, let alone an American lover. But in a telephone call from a public site (he assumed) the previous Monday, she had told him, excitedly and defiantly, about her encounter with the culture minister.

"What exactly did you have in that speech?"

"Not much you'd approve of, my dear friend."

"Maybe you should let me read it."

"I'll do that, Volodya. In the next couple of days. I'm going to be . . . busy for a day or so."

He loved Ursina Chadinov as he'd have loved his own daughter. He had taken Ursina under his wing when she was nineteen, at the behest of Dr. Roman Eskimov, his own, aging mentor, who was married to Ursina's aunt. Kirov had provided academic counsel, social direction, and warm company. There had been the brief estrangement. Ursina had invited Kirov, even though twenty years her senior, as her date at the medical students' end-of-second-year party. This party was, traditionally, unrestrained. The seventy students were tense from the ordeal of their examinations, anxious for a night's uninhibited relaxation.

Ursina, lively with wine, her eyes radiant with excitement, motioned to Vladimir—who was wearing a white shirt and his very best gray suit, his decoration from Moscow University prominent on his lapel—to follow her. Ursina led him to one of the rooms provided by the hostelry. "Then, Volodya"—she had never before used the diminutive with him, her mentor and professor—"I can express myself on how much I love you and owe to you."

Kirov followed her into the little room and accepted her hot embrace. But he grabbed her hand at a critical moment. "No further, dear Ursina. I am, in these matters—different."

She gasped, and in mere seconds was entirely sober. Her eyes were tearful. "I'm sorry, Volodya. But I love you just as much as if—"

"As if I were normal."

She bit that one off deftly. "If you were normal, Volodya, I wouldn't feel the love for you that I do."

The evening had ended on that conciliatory tone, but for some weeks, meeting each other in the corridors of the medical school, there hadn't been the old, easy intimacy.

Gradually, this returned, and when Ursina became a full doctor of urology, she was everywhere thought of as the special protégée of the learned Dr. Kirov, whom she had now informed of her disgrace with the culture minister.

Seated behind his desk, as if still talking doctor to patient, Kirov said to Titov, "I am personally and professionally interested in Dr. Ursina Chadinov."

"Isn't she the professor who was to follow me as welcomer at the peace forum?"

"Yes. That's she, and the talk she had prepared was the

cause of her political trouble. A lovely woman, gifted practitioner, and assiduous researcher."

"What's her trouble?"

"She is dead. I learned only after her death that she was deeply in love with an American and had conceived a child, apparently very soon after they met. He flew back to Washington soon after she found out—"

"Oh, one of those. 'I'll send you a Christmas card, dear—'"

"No no no. He loved her totally and intended to come back to Moscow—to do what exactly, one doesn't know. But Rufina Martins, who was Ursina's roommate for years, right until she married, became involved. She returned from Kiev, where she had gone to tend to her sick brother. She loved Ursina deeply and is ablaze with fury and indignation over her death."

"Death from *what,* goddammit it, Volodya?"

"Her pregnancy was ectopic."

"So? My wife had two of those. I've said that."

"We are told that she telephoned to Dr. Shumberg—our classmate, Kirill Olegyevich Shumberg. I don't know how she got his name."

"He's a big cheese, very involved with the government. I may have told you that he keeps a careful eye on my own research. But he is also a skilled practicing surgeon. He did the ectopic operations on my Nina."

"Here is what I've pieced together, talking with her regular doctor and with the surgeon who was all set to proceed with the operation. Ursina apparently was told that Shumberg was very skilled and sometimes had succeeded in saving the life of the baby as well as the mother."

"I have heard that that can sometimes be done. When he operated on my wife there was simply no question of doing any such thing. It is very unusual. But you told me Ursina was dead?"

"Yes. She died on the operating table."

"But that is inconceivable!"

"No, Linbek, it is not inconceivable. I have done research on the matter. It can and does happen, every blue moon. What is inconceivable is that the mother should be permitted to die if the surgeon sees that there is no chance of saving the fetus."

"Is that the same thing as telling me, Volodya, that Shumberg committed a very gross error?"

"That is one explanation for Ursina's death, Linbek."

CHAPTER 43

Nina Titov, petite and lively, with short dark curly hair, was a full-time wife and mother. She had known from the beginning that her husband, Lindbergh Vissarionovich, was wedded to his laboratory work. She promised on their wedding night that she would not seek to understand what it was he was doing. He greeted this news gratefully. In odd mentions of his work, Linbek stressed less its confidentiality than its inscrutability. "To understand, Nina, you would have to be a fifth-year student."

Nina did not probe the mysteries of radiology, but she paid close attention to Linbek's personal requirements, looked after his comforts, and worried over his occasional blue moods. Almost always these had to do with problems, direct or indirect, in getting on with his work, and in communicating his concerns to foreign scientists, getting from them their intelligence and insights, even as he sought to give them his own.

Their first-born son, Aleksei, was a surmounting joy for Nina. When he was three, she once again became pregnant, but this time, after a few weeks, she knew that something was wrong.

She called Linbek's old classmate, Kirill Olegyevich Shumberg, the prominent obstetrician. He diagnosed an ectopic pregnancy and performed surgery. She was very distressed over the lost child, and when, two years later, she had yet another ectopic pregnancy, she hesitated a few days before proceeding to surgery. In college she had studied Russian literature. She knew practically nothing about medicine or human biology, but she knew all she needed to know in order to do research in any field. She went the next morning to the university medical library to read about ectopic pregnancies.

She got little encouragement from her research on the question that most interested her, which was: Might her baby be saved? If the second Fallopian tube had to be severed like the first, and the fetus killed, that would be the end of the Titov household's hopes for a larger family. She did find a reference to one or two historical successes of surgeons in saving the child. These were so rare as hardly to offer a realistic hope. But they had happened, in medical history, and after taking notes she made the appointment with Dr. Shumberg.

"Ah, dear Nina Aleksandrovna," said the polished surgeon, trained meticulously in his handling of patients, "you have again the cursed ectopic?" He did a physical examination and took blood and urine samples.

"It is not an immediate problem, not an emergency, you are not bleeding. But we will have to proceed to surgery." He looked at his calendar and called the operating-room nurse. "Friday 8 A.M.? Very good."

"But, Kirill Olegyevich, I wish to talk to you about this."

She pulled out her notes from her purse. "There have been cases where the surgeon has saved mother *and* child."

"Yes," Shumberg said. "But for that to be even the remotest possibility requires that the fetus be specially situated and specially protected by the surrounding tissue."

"Can you attempt to do this for me, Comrade Kirill Olegyevich?"

"Of course. In a way, that is always 'attempted.' But incidences of success are so rare, we don't offer any hope to the mothers."

"You are a great doctor, and I will hope and pray that you can save the Titov child."

He did not succeed. Nina hadn't told Linbek about her research, or about her conversation with Shumberg. She didn't want him to have hope when none such realistically existed.

Seated at the dinner table back home after his meeting with Kirov, Linbek related what Kirov had just reported to him. He told Nina of the death of Ursina Chadinov.

Nina was perplexed. "Shumberg told me, when I raised the question of saving the baby, that there was virtually no chance of success. I wonder why this Ursina called him so specially? And when last did a mother die in an ectopic operation? According to my research, that would have been more than fifty years ago."

Titov chewed on his chop and took a glass of wine. After giving the matter some thought, he said: "I'm going to find out what day Shumberg will be coming to the laboratory. He comes usually once or twice a week. I will ask him about Ursina Chadinov."

Reaching the lab the next morning, he waited until nine, by which hour it was reasonable to expect Shumberg to be in his office and taking calls.

Linbek got through. "Kirill Olegyevich, are you coming today to the laboratory? There is something I want to talk to you about."

That afternoon, Shumberg followed Titov to an empty classroom. "Kirill Olegyevich, I want to know about Ursina Chadinov, who was a friend of a dear friend."

"Yes, that was very sad."

"I know it's sad, Kirill, when a forty-one-year-old woman dies. But I think it is more than sad when she dies under the knife of a very competent doctor."

"Linbek, staring hard at the tube when I had cut open her abdomen, I realized there was a critical difficulty with her breathing. I called out to the attendants. They did everything. But she was dead. There was no alternative than to assign shock as the cause of death."

"Kirill, what could have brought on the shock?"

"Are you asking me a question fit for a medical-school quiz?"

"No, a question fit for a famous surgeon operating on a woman in apparently good health."

"One can't always know what induces shock. It can have been a vessel suddenly blocked—"

"Is there anything you did that might have blocked an artery?"

"No. The incision in the abdominal wall went very smoothly."

"Recount to me, Kirill, how it is that you got called into this case."

"I had a telephone call from Chadinov herself."

"Where?"

He hesitated for a moment. "At my dacha."

"How is it she knew how to reach you at your dacha?"

"I cannot answer that question, Linbek. She would hardly be expected to take time telling me how she got through."

"What did she say to you?"

"She said she was scheduled for surgery that evening at the university hospital and she hoped I could perform that surgery."

"Why?"

"Because, she said, she had heard of my special skills."

"Did you give her to understand that you might save the life of the child?"

"I certainly did not 'give her to understand' any such thing. I did say of course that I would be willing to inspect the tube to see what could be done."

"Did you speak to the surgeon you relieved about your conversation with her?"

"No."

"Did you speak with her in the operating room?"

"She was already under anesthesia. I had told her I would come to her as quickly as I could, but could not guarantee my arrival in time for her 6 P.M. deadline."

"Why did you not recommend postponing the surgery?"

"There was some fear that damage was being done. She was already bleeding."

"From whom did you know about that fear? Did you talk with the doctor you relieved?"

"No. It was clear that the operation would proceed. He had been told he would be replaced."

"Told by whom?"

"An assistant from my office, whom I advised that I would proceed to act on Chadinov's wish for my services."

"So your office heard from you, not from her, that you would be in charge? If she called you at your dacha, she must have had the number from your office. Is there a record of her conversation there?"

"My dear Linbek, you are being . . . well . . . intrusive."

"I may be intrusive. You are responsible for a dead woman. Did you order an autopsy?"

"No. There were no next of kin, so she was cremated."

Titov lost control. "I think you killed her, Shumberg."

"You can go to hell, Titov. Or perhaps you would prefer a different temperature. A Siberian temperature?"

Shumberg stormed out of the classroom.

CHAPTER 44

The car traffic on the spring evening was reduced, at that late hour, but it was not eliminated. Tony Morales had engaged a cab to take him to Merriwell. There was method at work here. If he was driving a rental car, and if Blackford Oakes was resolved to enforce his no-visitors rule, Tony could more easily be sent away. But if there was no car, Papabile was not likely to just order him out of the house. Outside 373 Merriwell, the cab having been sent away, was darkness—darkness. There were driveways and fields, neighboring houses only dimly in view. Expelling him would require calling a cab, and such a delay might cause Blackford to cool off.

Tony looked up at the second story. The light was on in the master bedroom his mother had shared with Blackford for so many years. At the other end of the house there was no light. And looking up at the third floor, he saw no light from Josefina's room. She would be asleep at this hour.

He left his heavier bag in the garage, and walked with the little overnight pouch to the rear of the house. He pulled the flashlight from his pocket and inserted his key into the kitchen-door lock. There was a moment's anxiety as he turned the key and feared the possible sound of an alarm. He couldn't imagine that Blackford had wired the entire house against intruders. He hadn't done so when Tony's mother was alive; surely he had little reason to do so now. But all was not rational in his stepfather's life these days.

Inside, he turned on the light.

Josefina kept a clean kitchen. The dinner dishes had been washed and stacked to one side. On the refrigerator door the familiar photographs were still scotch-taped. There were three pictures of his mother, a half dozen of himself. There was even one, beige from age, of Tony's father, whom Tony had never known. There were snaps of a few old friends. He recognized Anthony Trust and Singer Callaway. There was a picture of Blackford with CIA Director Richard Helms. Blackford Oakes was smiling and, in his left hand, concealing something. It was a medal, Tony knew, awarded to him by the agency. An off-the-record ceremony, celebrating one of Papabile's adventures, about which Tony knew nothing.

He and his mother would know only that Blackford's absence had served "a useful purpose," as he would put it on getting back. Or else that it had been "disappointing." Once or twice there were flesh wounds bound for repair; one time, a cast on his left foot. Tony remembered finding the *Washington Post* with a line drawn next to a foreign dispatch, highlights set off with his stepfather's characteristic little check marks. He remembered the checks around the sentence, "Premier Khrushchev declined to answer any questions on the withdrawal of the nuclear missiles from Cuba." Tony had persuasively speculated, at age seven, that Papabile had had something to do with the detection and removal of the missiles. The picture in the *Post* of President Kennedy speaking to the large crowd in Berlin had also been ticked. Tony had allowed himself to wonder, with mock concern, whether such ticks were, perhaps, indiscreet. What had Blackford intended to do with these papers?

Tony wanted to take a beer upstairs with him. There was the problem that there would be no bottle opener upstairs. He snapped off the cap using the opener tied to the refrigerator, and carefully tucked the bottle into his little canvas bag. It would not spill, wedged in as he had it.

He turned off the light and, the flashlight rekindled, made his way into the hall. He was startled by the accumulation on the shelf above the radiator cabinet, and on the table next to it. Weeks, he judged, of unopened mail and unread magazines, and even some packages unexamined. His padre was in a bad way. But he knew that, and even knew why. After completing his registration forms for Georgetown six weeks ago, he had left to catch his flight back to Mexico. And he had called his father from the airport.

When father and son had odd bits of information or comments to transmit to each other, beginning in Mexico City in Tony's early years, they had taken to speaking them in Spanish. Tony heard from Blackford now, in a hollow voice, "Está muerta."

Just those two words. Tony in a flash knew what that must mean: that Blackford's Russian fiancée, about whom he had spoken so ardently that night at dinner, was somehow, for some reason, dead. Tony thought to turn around and go back to Merriwell. But his father added only the words, "Regresa a Mexico. Yo te llamaré."

So he did. He returned to Mexico and waited day after day to hear from his father.

He reported to the senior partner at Morales y Morales. Oscar Guzmán was studious and exacting. He was respectful in his references to the American who married Sally Morales after her husband was killed, but he never quite managed to excuse Oakes for embroiling Antonio's father in that Cold War mess, which went on and on. And what was all the fuss about Castro dragging his Communist net over Mexico? Oscar Guzmán had made two trips to Havana on legal business. He did not pretend that Communism had done anything for the Cuban people except scare them to death, lighten their daily diets, and impose some pretty humiliating rules on what they could do, not do, read, not read. *Cojones.* He looked up at Tony. He was a dashing young man, as his father had been at that age, though there was the American mother there also, the blue eyes, the flirtatious smile.

Tony told him what the procedures were at the Georgetown Law School and showed him the curriculum of the division that specialized in Hispanic law and, in particular, in U.S.–Mexican experiences. "They have like maybe one hundred books in the library on litigation over U.S.–Mexican-owned properties. I could see one whole shelf devoted to the expropriation of oil by Carranza."

"Yes. Your father had a little interest in one of those fields. Now his firm has a big interest in litigation over it. Ándale. It looks very good, Antonio. You will not regret the

time spent in Washington. Only try, if convenient, not to fall
in love with an American girl. We can't continue forever di-
luting your Spanish genes."

Tony smiled. "I'll report to Great-Aunt Felicia later today.
I know she'll be anxious to hear about my Papabile."

The days went by, and then weeks. There were only the weekend transmissions, Josefina González in Merriwell, to sister
Beatriz in Coyoacán—to Tony. They told the same thing, that
el señor was alive but not seeing anybody or taking any calls.

Tony allowed this to go on for six weeks, hoping one day
to pick up the phone and hear Papabile say—something. Yesterday, after much brooding, he had decided it was time to
involve himself. So here he was, back in Merriwell, walking
quietly toward his old room, opening the door and shutting
it quietly behind him, though he remembered, from many
raucous childhood experiences with boys from school who
had come for a sleepover, how safely sequestered from his
parents' room, at the other end of the house, his own bedroom was.

Tomorrow would certainly be another day. He had left a
note for Josefina in the kitchen. "Wake me before he comes
down to breakfast." He had the impression, when Josefina
shook him awake, that it had been only two minutes ago that
he had fallen asleep. He jerked his torso up and returned
Josefina's embrace, as he had done when a little boy. "Ya
viene pronto tu papá." His father would be down soon.

Tony, dressed and seated, was waiting for Blackford in the
breakfast room.

CHAPTER 45

Tony caught a full view of his stunned stepfather, frozen at the doorsill, staring at his son, who was sitting there staring up at him.

Tony would not forget that sight. His Papabile was unshaven, the face gaunt, hair uncut. He wore boxer shorts and a sweater. He paused just long enough to let his eyes dissipate the sleep and focus on Tony. He turned about and walked slowly back up the stairway.

Tony closed his own eyes. Absentmindedly, he turned the pages of the morning's newspaper, as if concerned for any other news than what he now had. He knew what would come next: Josefina.

She spoke to him in Spanish, tearfully. "Your father says you are to take one of his cars—I have the keys to both in the kitchen—and go to the Merriwell Inn. He will call you there when he is ready."

"Nada más?"

"No, that's all. Está bastante enfermo."

"I can see that"—that his father was very sick.

They tarried only a minute or two in the kitchen. Josefina simply insisted—treating him as she once had as his nanny— that he pause to take a glass of orange juice and a piece of toast. "We have to hope he will call you soon. Do you want to take some books?"

"Thanks. I brought my own."

And he read them, page-turners like *The Iberian Tradition in U.S. Law.* At noon, he drove to Georgetown, met his cousin Adelaide Gutiérrez, and lunched with her at the Georgetown Medical School refectory. She had signed up as a volunteer for Michael Dukakis, who appeared likely to be the Democrats' candidate, opposing George Bush. "On the other hand, it will obviously be Bush who's elected. Unless Reagan gets us into a war."

"Gorbachev doesn't want war, Adelaide."

"I know. But Reagan does want war."

"Maybe with Mexico. Not with Russia."

"I'm sorry you don't vote in America, Tony. With your homegrown skills, if you voted here you could vote ten times for Dukakis." He took down her phone number at the hospital where she spent so much time doing her field work.

"Maybe I'll call later. My . . . dad is sick."

"I'm sorry." She gave him a kiss on the forehead.

The rest of that day went by. Late the next morning his phone rang. He put down his book. It was Josefina. She spoke very quietly. She'd have been calling from the kitchen; his father was presumably upstairs. "El señor se afeitó." His father had shaved himself. "Tal vez mañana." Maybe tomorrow he would call. She put down the phone sharply. Perhaps he was coming down the stairs.

Josefina called Tony the following day. Her words, exactly, were that his father would be grateful if he came by that afternoon at five, but that he might not have the strength to stay up for supper.

Tony renewed his room reservation at the Merriwell Inn for two more nights. Driving his father's Buick station wagon, he pulled in to the garage just before five. His heart was pounding as he walked around the side of the brick Georgian house to the kitchen, his usual access point. Josefina kissed him. "Te espera en la sala."

In the living room, Blackford rose to his feet. He did not spring to his feet, as he'd have done as recently as six weeks ago, Tony noted, returning the embrace.

"You were good to come, Tony. I had just about thrown it all away."

"Bueno. Tell me the whole story."

"It is incomprehensible. I do not know what to *tell*. That day I heard—when you spoke to me from the airport—I had a cable, it was read to me from my office. It was sent by somebody in the USIA office, not anybody I knew. And it said simply—I memorized the message, you won't be surprised—it said simply, 'Moscow University Hospital, pursuant to instructions from the deceased, herewith reports the death in surgery of Ursina Chadinov. This information is to be delivered to Harry Doubleday, address, USIA American Embassy.'

"That was it. The only thing I did was get Jerry Schwarzbach at the Russian desk to put in a telephone call to Ursina

Chadinov at the hospital. An operator said that Professor Chadinov was deceased. What she was doing in surgery I can't guess. I suppose it was a heart attack. It hardly makes any difference. How I wish you had known her. This seems strange to say, Tony, but how I wish your mother had known her. She was . . . a singular human being. Of course, so was your mother."

Tony was alarmed by his father's aged face, which he could inspect now that the whiskers were gone. "Don't be afraid of making me jealous, Papabile. I think I understand. Mother has been dead a while now. Your capacity for love and friendship and company did not die with her.

"*But,* Papá, you have been doing your best to end your capacity to do *anything*. If you want to kill yourself, there are six pistols, four rifles, and six shotguns in your locker over there. Take a pistol and do it, if you are through with life."

"My religion—and your religion—forbids suicide."

"You are committing suicide in another way. Surely the church—your Episcopal Church, my Catholic Church—forbids that too."

Blackford looked up at his poised, blue-eyed stepson. His style of speaking was Sally's, exactly. He could manage to say only, "I am not arguing with you."

"Papá, can you control the . . . whiskey?"

"You know about that? Josefina—"

"Josefina said nothing. I have made some inquiries in the past two days."

"It will not seem credible. But in fact I have not drunk since I laid eyes on you two days ago. I doubt I will ever drink again."

"If you say that, then you are not cured. If you are cured, you will feel at liberty to drink some time again."

"Perhaps. Now I must regain my strength and"—he stood up on his feet, putting his arms around Tony and struggling to get the words out through his tears—"thank God for the son he gave me."

He removed his arms. "Go back to Mexico, Tony. This time I *will* call you there. And I'll be happy when you come to Washington for a semester."

Tony knew it was best to leave. "I'll drive back here in the station wagon tomorrow morning and have a cab pick me up to take me to the airport."

In the kitchen he spoke for a few moments with Josefina, kissed her, and thanked her for everything she had done for his father.

"Pronto se va mejorar." He'd get well soon, she promised.

CHAPTER 46

After Tony left, Blackford walked about the house almost as if it were his first visit. He had not noticed anything, he had to admit, for ever so long. The living room where he had met with Tony was handsome, woodlined. There were bookcases at one end, opposite original paintings collected over the years. There was the tiled fireplace, framed by two semicircular sofas, an armchair at each end, a large coffee table between.

He passed into the hallway leading to the front door. Josefina had made some attempt at order, piling the magazines on top of each other, placing them on the shelf above the radiator. Correspondence was on the low table, sitting in a large silver bowl, oblong in shape, which Sally had brought up from Mexico. It was not entirely full, but it had now forty or fifty pieces of mail, many of them obviously bills.

He made a rough effort to separate the letters from the bills. He would take the letters upstairs, read them in the bedroom, perhaps during the stretches when he was unable to sleep.

"Señor?" He heard Josefina call out.

"Sí, sí." He had forgotten her first call to supper. In the dining room she brought him tortillas and cheese and a small tomato salad.

"No, gracias," he said to the proffered beer. He ate listlessly, then got up, walked into the living room and brought over the *Washington Post*. Michael Dukakis and George Bush, he learned, had both won primary elections.

He took the sheaf of letters upstairs. He thought to turn on the television, but changed his mind. But he did reach for a CD, and stuck on some Bach partitas, done by Rosalyn Tureck.

He sat down in the armchair by the bed and put the mail on the bedside table. He hoped to avoid letters from well-wishers inquiring after his health. There was one letter there, hand-addressed, from the director. It was kind of Bill Webster to write as he did: If and when Blackford changed his mind about the years ahead, "we are here waiting for you."

He came then to the FedEx letter. It had been posted in Vienna, early in February—he could not make out the exact date. He opened it.

It too was handwritten.

He was so startled by the opening lines, his eyes shot down to the signature, which read, "Harold Adrian Russell Philby."

Dear Oakes:

    That was quite a stay you had here. I have drunk to—am drinking to—your accomplishments. It was a fine touch that you were, among other things, my guest at our little wedding party. So you managed: One prominent Soviet woman seduced. Her thinking corrupted. She's egged on to deliver a sophomoric speech in the Great Kremlin Palace. We cherish our copy of it. No wonder she died, or was it that her system could not stand the thought of procreating another Oakes in this world? History, Harry Doubleday, is of course the great engine of the Communist world enterprise. Perhaps history had a hand in ending a perfidious life. Feel free to write to me in Moscow (I am in Vienna for only a few days) if I can be of any service. You may be considering defection. I am schooled in advising people how to conceal their allegiances.

Blackford thought to reach for the whiskey bottle in the cabinet.

But the thought was fleeting.

Questions crowded his mind, and sharp thoughts began to pump up his blood pressure. How did Philby know who he was? How did he find out? How had he got the Merriwell address?

Of course! Rufina! Rufina must have torn open his letter, the letter bequeathing half his estate to Ursina.

He closed his eyes, recreating the scene in Philby's apartment on Uspensky Street. He had not dreamed of the possibility that Rufina would open that envelope. But then he had never dreamed the nightmare of Ursina dead.

But how had Philby got hold of Ursina's speech, which Blackford himself had never seen? What could he have meant by saying that perhaps "history" had had a hand in Ursina's death?

He roiled at the ugliness of the letter. But then it was written by someone who had had no hesitation in betraying fellow citizens to ugly deaths. What could such a man ever do that was surprising?

He walked to the medicine cabinet and surveyed the bottles on Sally's shelf still sitting there. He swallowed a sleeping pill and made his way back, climbing now into bed, shutting off the lamp, and closing his eyes, waiting for the drug to do its work for him.

The next morning he called the special number in Frankfurt and gave the conduit the embassy number in Moscow. He was relieved that, in moments, he was talking to Gus.

"Hey Black. I hear you've been . . . vacationing a bit."

"Yeah, well . . . Gus, you know Vladimir Kirov? I never met him, but Ursina told me she brought him along one night to dinner with you."

"Sure. I remember sending him the schedule on the Gorky exhibit. He asked me for it."

"Well, he was very close to Ursina, and he's a medical doctor. Tell him I've been real sick, just coming out of it, and I want to know what happened to Ursina. Can you find out if an autopsy was done? And ask him something else, Gus. Ask him if the father of the child of an unmarried Russian woman has any rights, legal or conventional, when the mother dies the way Ursina did."

"Yeah, I can get through to him. —Black, some people are saying that Ursina saved the state a lot of trouble. Sorry to put it that way. But that's what they're saying. Anyhow, there are a couple of things popping here, but nothing to talk about over the phone, not even on this snug line."

CHAPTER 47

Blackford submitted to the medical examination Tony had urged over the telephone. "And, Papá, you should go to a physical therapist. Work out a couple of times a week. I have a cousin in medical school at Georgetown. She was telling me about a physical ed instructor she thinks is terrific who does individual training on the side. I'll call Adelaide Gutiérrez and have her leave a message with you or Josefina—the name and number of the phys ed guy. And you can talk to Adelaide about it if you want. Her number—"

"Yes, I have a pencil. In my line of work we always have pencils handy."

"I thought you were expected to memorize?"

"If there is any risk that the bad people want that information. Is Adelaide hot?"

"Papabile, such a question!"

"Well, don't let the bad people take physical therapy. They're dangerous enough as it is."

Eight days later, his letter to the director was answered by a telephone call. "Monday is fine as Reincorporation Day. Black, I thought of having a half-dozen people for lunch in my dining room. I thought Anthony Trust and Singer Callaway and Jake—Jake what's-his-last-name? I forget . . ."

"Jake Shulz."

"Yes. Our Congressional Medal of Honor winner. And anybody else you want."

"That would be nice, Bill. I'll give a speech on my blackout. You got something interesting for me?"

"As a matter of fact I do, Black."

"Well then, give me a good lunch."

Back at work, Blackford read a long cable from Gus.

"I accosted Kirov. I used just the approach you recommended: You were the father, and you felt you had responsibilities in the matter of Ursina. He dodged and dodged, didn't throw me out, but went on and on about how accidents happen. So I said, 'Vladimir'—that's what he told me to call him at the dinner we had with Ursina—'Vladimir, I need to see the report by the doctor who did the operation. Can you get that for me?' Kirov said he'd have to check with the legal people to find out whether I could have access to it. He said, 'You know, Gus, there is no way your friend Doubleday can medically establish that he *was* the father.'"

Blackford bristled. But his orderly mind got in the way of

his incipient indignation. One could hypothesize that someone else was the father.

The cable read on: "Kirov wasn't suggesting he thought
any such thing, but warning that a legal, court-of-appeal approach might bump into this, denying you rights you'd have
if you were the established father. I guess in the good old
USA in such a situation the presumed dad would demand a
DNA on the fetus. But Ursina—Kirov called her 'my dear,
beloved Ursina'—was cremated.

"So I said to him maybe the thing to do was for me to go
quiz the surgeon. He paused over that one. Maybe, he said,
you need a Soviet lawyer.

"What do you think? I'm inclined to go see the surgeon.
Kirov did give me the name—Dr. Shumberg. My cover would
be that I am drafting a report on Ursina Chadinov on behalf
of a U.S. citizen who was here helping Deputy Minister Artur
Ivanov on a project in which the U.S. and the USSR are
jointly engaged. Think about it and call me."

Jonathan Tuck, in the legal department at Langley, was a
friend Blackford had several times worked with when bump-
ing into questions that needed counsel from people who
knew, well, the law of the land.

Blackford explained the problem.

"I know, Jon, that Soviet officials can take the position
that any contact I had with Professor Chadinov was personal.
In one way it was certainly that. I intended to marry Ursina.
I have a good friend in the Moscow office, Gus Windels.
We've done things together in the past, and he's willing—and
I think eager—to go to the doctor who operated. The ques-

tion: Can he plausibly claim that I have the right to see the doctor's report?"

"Blackford, that is a novel question. I don't think anybody ever wrote a treatise on the subject. I'm going to have to ask you something off the record."

"Okay."

"Is Gus proposing to tell our ambassador what he's up to?"

"No. I'm not sure *what* Jack Matlock would say. As you know, Jack's a scholar and has intellectual interests."

"Yeah. And one of them is to keep the U.S. clear of unnecessary confrontations with the Soviet Union. And unnecessary—forgive me, Black—engagements with Soviet citizens."

Blackford managed a smile. "Granted. But I don't see this as a confrontation. Just a personal-service inquiry."

"I know somebody I can call who might have an angle on this. You'll be in your office this afternoon?"

Blackford nodded.

Two hours after hearing back from Tuck, he cabled to Gus. "Call me on the good line tomorrow 3 P.M. Moscow time."

CHAPTER 48

The nurse asked Gus what it was he wished to consult with Dr. Shumberg about. Gus said that he was on an ambassadorial mission, having to do with someone engaged in the cultural exhibit being jointly sponsored by Washington and Moscow. He was given an appointment for 6 P.M. that day.

Dr. Shumberg was well known in the little community of Soviet scientists who were sometimes called upon to discharge diplomatic assignments. He was known for his general affability and for the closeness of his ties with the KGB. When Gus arrived, pulling out his card, Shumberg's tone of voice was that of a man who, however important, was prepared to interrupt whatever he was doing in order to oblige this postulant.

Gus Windels said that he was asking questions on behalf of an American citizen who had recently been in Moscow on U.S.–USSR business and had sired a child who—

"You are talking, obviously, of Professor Chadinov's lover."

"Yes. The question has been raised: What exactly was the cause of her death? And, of course, you would be the authority on that subject."

Shumberg picked up his phone, looked down at a list of numbers in his drawer, and dialed.

"I am calling to speak with Professor Titov. It is Shumberg calling. . . . Titov. There is an American here who is beginning to ask me exactly the questions you asked, in the matter of Chadinov. I am fed up answering journalistic-type inquiries on the matter. If"—he looked down at Gus's card—"Mr. Windels wishes to speak with you on the subject, you can give him the medical information I passed along two weeks ago." He slammed the telephone down and turned to Gus.

"Is there anything else I can do for you?"

Gus read up on Professor Lindbergh Titov in the extensive file the embassy had on him. He was a world-renowned radiologist, Gus learned, said to be at work on a means of advancing positron emission tomography. The objective was a cancer cure and also a means of immunizing human beings against damaging ionization.

Gus thought it wise, instead of calling on the telephone, to go to the radiology laboratory and present himself at Titov's office. He introduced himself as a friend of Vladimir Kirov. "And of Ursina Chadinov. She was a special friend. In fact, it was I who introduced her to Harry Doubleday, on whose behalf I am undertaking this inquiry."

Titov's interest in the matter was obvious. Gus continued, "I went to see Dr. Shumberg, and he telephoned you while I was with him. I heard him say that he had answered every question on the matter of Ursina Chadinov, and that I should go to you, not him."

"That bastard! That shit! So *I* am now the source of knowledge on the matter of Professor Chadinov! All Shumberg did was operate on her! Mr. Windels. There is a great deal on my mind right now. But I am *intensely* interested in the matter of Ursina Chadinov. I will discuss the matter with you in—different circumstances. Are you willing to come to my apartment?"

"I would be honored, Dr. Titov."

They made the engagement.

"May I ask, Dr. Titov, have you seen the surgeon's report following the death?"

"Yes. I succeeded in getting a copy. Hmm! It is perhaps the *only* piece of information I have not been denied! Perhaps because it was not written by a foreigner, and isn't therefore suspicious. Anything written by a foreigner needs to be certified for ideological 'reliability.' I am surprised they permit me to use ultrasound waves in my laboratory. Some of them have not been cleared by security."

"I look forward to this evening," Gus said.

CHAPTER 49

Gus Windels arrived at Lindbergh Titov's large apartment at 6 P.M. It was a select address, with a husky doorman at the entrance, and an operator who took him up in the creaky old elevator to the eighth floor. Gus emerged into a hall with three doors, but only Titov's name was posted. He rang the doorbell.

It was opened by a lanky young man, his hair in fashionable teenage disarray. He wore blue jeans, a striped sports shirt, and, on his head, an old-model aviator's cap. Hanging down from his neck, suspended on a braided cord, were an aviator's dark glasses.

His expression was bright, and his diffident smile seemed genuine. "Hello. I am Aleksei."

"How do you do, Aleksei?" Gus extended his hand. "I have an appointment with your father."

He was taken through a living room with a half-dozen framed posters from scientific conferences and as many oil paintings, into a study with a very large table, on which what looked like a whole library of manuscripts were piled high.

"Ah, Mr. Windels, sit down. I was incensed by what you told me. I even called Shumberg this afternoon. I said to him, 'Shumberg, that is very interesting, suggesting to an American inquirer that I am the authority on the death—the killing—of Ursina Chadinov. *This call is simply to say that you will not get away with this ongoing deception.*'"

Gus said nothing.

"But I want to call in my wife—Nina Aleksandrovna— to hear what you have to say."

She came to the door, Aleksei at her side.

"Alyosha," Titov said. "Who called for you?"

"I wish to practice my English. Or"—he looked over at Gus, seated by his father's desk—"is he going to speak in Russian?"

Gus was pleased by the opportunity to say, "I was born in Kiev. I am happy to be talking in Russian, my native tongue."

Titov knit his brows. Even his bald head seemed concentrated on the question on his mind. "Why not? Alyosha is seventeen years old. Any additional data on the intransigence of the . . . of the governing class will be enlightening."

Nina upbraided her husband. "Linbek! Linbek."

"Do not worry, Nina, the authorities know how I feel in these matters. It is only my scientific eminence that keeps them from silencing me—that, and the fact that, unlike Sakharov, I have not spoken out publicly. But sit down. Nina and Alyosha, Mr. Windels was a good friend of the late Ursina Chadinov."

"We were saddened and perplexed by her death," Nina said.

"We didn't know her," Titov said. "But her mentor, Vladimir Kirov, is one of my oldest friends, and I have learned a great deal about her in recent days."

"You knew about her intended speech to the peace forum?" Gus asked.

"There was general comment on her absence. You know, I was one of the speakers, and she was scheduled to come next after me. Did you, Mr. Windels—"

"Please, Gus."

"—Did you, Gus, see the speech she intended to give?"

"No. But Mr. Doubleday, her . . . her affianced, told me before leaving for the airport that the text was, he had been given to believe, 'incendiary.'"

"How, 'incendiary'?"

"She apparently complained about restrictions in Soviet life."

"One of us!" Titov said.

"Mr. Doubleday, who had to return to America for a brief period, is a friend of mine. He asked me to deliver a document to Ursina's closest friend, Rufina Ivanovna, now married to Andrei Fyodorovich Martins."

"Did Mr. Doubleday tell you that he was concerned for her welfare?"

"No. But he did say that the culture minister had instructed her not to leave Moscow before meeting with him, after the peace forum was over. She was to explain her behavior. Did you, Dr. Titov, learn from anybody what was written in that speech?"

"We had only the rumors. And of course everyone in my institute wondered how she would be punished."

Nina left the room and came back with vodka. "You can get some soda pop, if you wish, Alyosha."

The boy looked up at Gus. "Were you alive, Gus—"

"*Mr. Windels,*" his mother corrected him.

"—when Charles Augustus Lindbergh flew over the Atlantic?"

"Alyosha! Were *you* alive when they stormed the Winter Palace?"

Titov laughed. "You say you were born in Kiev. When?"

"In 1958."

"But you have seen the *Spirit of St. Louis?*" Aleksei persisted.

"Yes. It is in a museum in Washington."

"Papa, will you take me there?"

"I promise," Titov said. "One day." His voice was solemn.

Gus was invited to stay for dinner. They talked more about Ursina. Titov's antipathy was plain. "I would not put it past Shumberg."

"And yet, when Nina Aleksandrovna had her pregnancies, you entrusted her to his care, as you recounted."

"His skills are celebrated. But my focus now is on the man, not on the obstetrician."

After dinner, Titov spoke of a forthcoming conference of medical research scientists in Vienna. "While I am away, Nina and Alyosha will go to his grandmother in Leningrad—Nina's mother. But none of that interests you, Gus."

"Your future interests me very much, Linbek Vissarionovich."

"I will remember what you said. And I will keep your card. Here is mine."

They shook hands.

In the hallway, Aleksei said, "Don't forget your promise, Mr. Gus. Though actually, it was my father's promise."

"I won't forget," Gus said, as the elevator door opened.

CHAPTER 50

Roman Belov, the minister of culture, was a longtime friend of Mikhail Gorbachev, going back to his election as a member of the Central Committee. It was merely weeks after Gorbachev's election as general secretary that he elevated his friend to culture minister.

Belov was by nature a sycophant, and at one point was even reprimanded. Gorbachev used plain language: "Roman Ivanovich, if you agree with *everything* I say, what is the point in my asking your opinion? Maybe I should make it impossible for you simply to agree with me. That would mean reformulating my questions to you. For instance, I could say, 'Belov, it *would be interesting to know* what I thought of Reagan's State of the Union Address last night.'"

Belov attempted to make light of this, but he caught the rebuke, and resolved at least not to sound, in future conferences, as if he agreed automatically with Gorbachev on everything. Belov now made it a point to try to sound, at least at first, ambiguous. He reminded himself of this resolution when summoned, the Monday after the peace forum closed, into Gorbachev's sacred private office to "share impressions on the events of the past days."

Thirty-seven years earlier, when Belov was assistant to Lavrenty Beria, he had accompanied Beria, head of the Ministry of Internal Affairs, to a meeting with Josef Stalin in this same room in which he now sat with Gorbachev. Belov had brought together data on the demographic distribution of students applying for admission to the Soviet Union's medical schools. "I am not absolutely certain what the general secretary is looking for," Beria had instructed him, "so bring the composite files, and also bring files on particular categories he might inquire into. Be sure to look at Jewish students. And look also at which specialties are attracting the most students."

Roman Belov remembered the sheer fright he felt on being shown through the door, in the footsteps of Beria. Stalin's greeting to Beria had been nothing more than the faintest nod of the head. Beria remained standing for an awkward few minutes, until Stalin pointed to a chair. Belov was panicked. Did this mean that he too was to sit on one of the chairs? Or was he to remain standing, unless specifically told to sit down? He would certainly need a surface on which to spread out his portfolio, when questioned.

He was standing for another five minutes before Stalin said to Beria, "Tell that icicle you brought in to sit down." He had had to guard the stability of his voice when Stalin then called on him for a few figures, which happily he had in memory, and so did not need to spread out his package of papers. Stalin then said nothing. He looked through the space between Beria and Belov, and fiddled with his pipe on his desk. Another full five minutes went by. "That will be all, Comrade Lavrenty Pavlovich."

The composition of the general secretary's office hadn't substantially changed, through the administrations of Bulganin and Khrushchev, Brezhnev and Andropov, Chernenko and, now, Belov's patron, Mikhail Gorbachev. Belov had been in this office briefly during the reign of Brezhnev, but, again, as a subordinate. Now he was a full minister, and Gorbachev's confidant in important matters.

He was comfortably seated in an armchair before Gorbachev said, cautiously, "What did *you*, Roman Ivanovich, think of our peace forum?"

Belov said he thought that it had been successful, and that this was largely owing to the acuity of Gorbachev in encouraging an ecumenical tone. He complimented Gorbachev on his own address to the assembly, in which he had stressed national developments, including the broadening of—Belov hesitated to say "human rights," a term used with antagonistic forethought by the enemy. "To use your words, Mikhail Sergeyevich, our new approach to 'the humanitarian problem' is there for all to see."

Gorbachev closed his eyes briefly. Opening them once more, he said, "What is this I have heard about your canceling one of the welcoming speakers?"

"That was most extraordinary. A bumptious young woman, a professor—"

"Why was she invited to speak?"

"She was invited by the committee on speakers. They

chose her because she was an academic, a practicing physician, and a woman."

"What was it she was going to say?"

"I have the copy of the text I confiscated when she came to my office for clearance. It is brief, a mere two pages, but highly incendiary. I put it aside in case we proceeded to prosecution."

"You have decided not to prosecute a citizen who sought to subvert a national purpose before seven hundred delegates?"

"Actually, Mikhail Sergeyevich, the point quickly became moot. The subversive woman died in surgery."

Gorbachev looked up. He paused. "How did you bring that about?" But quickly he laughed, as appropriate for an amusing, incidental gibe. "Well, so much for that. Now this is the point I wish to discuss with you: a program for following up the forum's good work by alerting culturally influential people around the world—people who are capable of listening to the Soviet view of things—to the extreme dangers of the U.S. decision to proceed with an anti-missile system. We need the professoriate, the clergymen, the entertainment world, to listen to our warnings, and to use their connections in their several fields to get out the word: Resist Reagan on Star Wars!"

Belov was taking notes on a pad whisked out from his pocket. "I think it would be prudent to introduce a resolution in the United Nations exactly to that effect."

"Yes. But we will wait a few months until our line has been assimilated by the intelligentsia. When we go to the United Nations, we must have more than the votes of Algeria and Vietnam supporting us."

Belov laughed. "Of course, of course. And we might plan a public demonstration outside the UN, with important speakers. Kris Kristofferson was very effective here at the peace forum, as was Yoko Ono, and—"

"Well, there is plenty of time to think about all that. Meanwhile I will press on with the call for a comprehensive ban on nuclear testing. Good work, Roman Ivanovich. I will be in touch with you."

"General Secretary, my thanks. I will continue to be guided by your star."

"Make certain my star is not shot down by their Star Wars."

Belov nodded slightly, and the aide standing by the door opened it for him to leave.

CHAPTER 51

It was after the close of the Vienna medical-research conference, which went forward under the banner of "Science for
Welfare," that the bomb went off. For several hours it had
simmered silently. The Soviet aide who had tended for five
days to Dr. Lindbergh Titov—organizing his living arrangements, escorting him to and from the assembly meetings and
seminar rooms, running diverse errands—now advised him
that his reservations were in order for the flight back to
Moscow the next morning at 0900.

Titov nodded, routinely.

"Do you need any arrangements made for tonight, Comrade Titov?"

"No," Titov answered. "I will stay in my hotel, perhaps
dine with one or two of my colleagues. Thank you, Preshkev."

"Very well, Comrade Titov. The car will be here for you
at 0700. We will arrive early."

The next morning, the black Mercedes, its uniformed driver, and the chunky Captain Yaroslav Preshkev were there at the Imperial Hotel's front door well ahead of time. Preshkev went into the lobby to wait. At 0700 he called up to Dr. Titov's room, but there was no answer. He must be in the elevator, Preshkev thought.

But Titov didn't emerge from the first elevator, or the next elevator. Preshkev froze. "Has Dr. Titov checked out?" he asked the desk clerk.

No, he hadn't checked out.

Should he be reported as missing? Preshkev brought out from his pocket the book listing all 190 participants of the Science for Welfare conference. He picked out the telephone number listed for the arrangements secretary. But there was no answer. What else to expect, he hissed to himself, calling an office at that hour of the morning?

He looked for another listing, hoping that someone would answer the telephone even at that hour. But no one picked up the phone.

Dr. Alberto Angelo! The conference chairman! He too was staying at the Imperial. Preshkev all but ran to the concierge. "Please ring Dr. Angelo."

"He is on Do Not Disturb."

"Ring him anyway!"

"Sir, shall I put you through to the general manager?"

Preshkev clenched his fists. Using a public telephone, he dialed the Soviet Embassy. The duty officer answered. Preshkev identified himself sufficiently to be put through to the ambassador at his residence.

The ambassador listened to the alarmed voice. "That is grave news. I will call Moscow. Do not report his absence to the police. Proceed to the airport, to the departure gate. Perhaps he misunderstood and made his own way there. If he is not there for the flight, have the car bring you here. I will have preliminary reactions from Moscow."

Colonel Bykov shouted at Captain Akimov. "Why did you let him go to Vienna with only a single security officer? Don't just tell me that Titov has traveled before to other conferences. The point is not that he may have traveled once or twice before with only one single security officer. The point is: *He is missing!* One of the two or three most important scientists in the Soviet Union is *missing*. Why did you let that happen? Were there any signs of disaffection? Bring me his files."

Bykov read them. He called Dr. Shumberg. He listened to Shumberg describing anti-state remarks made by Titov at their last meeting, a criticism which had been reported by Shumberg at the time, and duly entered into the Titov security file.

Bykov addressed Captain Akimov again. "*What is the use of files* if they are not acted upon? Here is *clear* evidence that Titov was a risk. But he is permitted to go to Vienna with only a single supervisor."

He put down the file. He told Akimov: "Order an immediate inspection of Titov's apartment. Let no one else enter the apartment or leave it. Get me a record of all telephone calls into and out of that apartment in the past week."

Bykov would learn in less than one hour that no one was home in the Titov apartment, though it hardly looked abandoned. "Everything seems intact—I mean, the furniture, all the usual things. Dr. Titov's desk has papers and manuscripts.

There are no signs of preparation for departure. The refrigerator is running, though it is without fresh food. The boy's room is full of model airplanes, scattered about. I don't know what to say, Comrade Mikhail Pavlovich."

Bykov called for his car and drove to the radiological institute.

He sat down at Titov's desk and called in the four scientists designated as senior.

He addressed them in solemn tones. "We are concerned for the welfare of Dr. Lindbergh Vissarionovich Titov. He is missing in Vienna. It is not inconceivable that he has been kidnapped. Dr. Astrey: Was Dr. Titov near to completion on any particular research project?"

"Well, Colonel. Yes. He had done all the projections on UL 242."

"What is *that*?"

"That is what Dr. Titov—what we have been working on for almost two years. A very exciting project. If I may say so, cosmically exciting."

"Is it something your staff can complete without him?"

"Oh no, Colonel. His role is indispensable. We would need him here."

Back in his office, Bykov called the mysterious and critical Esterhazy, at the office of the general secretary. He briefed him. "I propose to call out a general alarm in Vienna for Titov. And to report to the police that he may have been kidnapped."

"I think you had better talk with the general secretary. Stand by."

He was put on.

Gorbachev told him to proceed to issue that alarm.

CHAPTER 52

The U.S. Embassy in Vienna relayed the bulletin about the missing Titov to the State Department. A copy was sent simultaneously to the CIA. Director Webster called the American ambassador in Vienna. "Mr. Grunwald, I have the bulletin on the missing scientist, Lindbergh Titov. Do you know anything about it?"

"No," said Henry Grunwald. "But of course I know who he is. *Time* magazine did a profile on him only a year or two back. Quoted a lot of big-name scientists who said how important his radiological work was. There's a Soviet lobby working to get him a Nobel prize."

"Do you know anybody—any Austrian, I mean—who might have got some idea from Titov as to whether he had any . . . interesting plans? Some friend, or working contact?"

"Yes I do. My contact would know Titov professionally,

and was almost certainly there at the Science for Welfare conference. He's also anti-Soviet."

"What kind of leg room are the Soviets giving the KGB in Vienna?"

"Well, Vienna is, maybe only after Berlin, the center of the spy world, as you know. There are things they're not permitted to do, same things we can't do, but the prohibitions are only against military or paramilitary activity, and the Russians can always dress their generals in plain clothes. Do you know what language he has, Titov, that's useable in this part of the world?"

"I don't. But we're looking to find someone who's been in the Soviet Union who might be able to answer that. When you call back about your contact, I'll have that for you. I have to assume he knows some English, and maybe German."

The director called in Blackford Oakes and told him about Titov. "Black, do you know Vienna from first hand?"

"I lived there two months, 1976."

"Any live contacts?"

"No. But I remember the city layout pretty well. And my German isn't all used up."

"Did you make any contacts in Moscow who might have some idea what Titov is up to?"

"Yes I did. Vladimir Kirov was my Ursina's—my late lady's—mentor, and for sure he knows Titov, they're both high academicians. But who we ought to have in on this, Bill, is Gus Windels. He knows Kirov, and more important, he talked with Titov just a week or so back. Maybe he can come up with a lead."

The television station in Vienna, ORF—the Osterreichischer Rundfunk Fernsehen—broke into the evening's news with an announcement.

"*This is live news.* The missing Dr. Lindbergh Titov has just telephoned this station. He spoke with our representative and said that he has not, repeat has not, been kidnapped. Dr. Titov said that he was 'in retreat'—his words, 'in retreat'—in Vienna weighing alternative possibilities for his future. He then hung up. ORF will contact the Soviet ambassador and relay this message from Dr. Titov and request a comment. We will broadcast that comment as soon as we have it.

"On screen is a picture of Dr. Titov addressing the Science for Welfare conference at the University of Vienna. This picture was taken on Tuesday. The renowned Dr. Titov spoke about the promising role that radiology will play in human health.

"ORF has interviewed several participants. Nobody has an explanation for the disappearance of Dr. Titov. It is widely speculated that he is defecting. A question was put to the U.S. ambassador, Henry Grunwald, who was seen with his wife arriving at the Vienna State Opera, where *Don Giovanni* is being performed. He said there would not be any comment on Dr. Titov other than that Titov had not been in communication with the U.S. Embassy."

Blackford was on the secure line with Gus. "I'm sure glad you're back on the team, Dad. Now I think the world is safe."

"Gus, good to hear your voice, and thanks again for those cables. You had a full evening with Titov and the family."

"Yes. And I'm hardly surprised they're thinking maybe he's defected."

"Gus, you okay for an assignment?"

"Shoot."

"First, how is the Soviet press handling the Titov news?"

"By ignoring it. But that probably won't be what they're going to be doing tomorrow, especially if Titov says he's defecting."

"If he was going to do that, why didn't he do it today?"

"Maybe he's not ready to face the alternatives. He would have to plead for asylum in order to be allowed to stay in Vienna. Stay there, or go somewhere else. Somewhere he'd be accepted."

"In his case that would be like, everywhere, right?"

"I'd guess so. But these things take time."

"We want to be ready to do the right thing if he turns in our direction."

CHAPTER 53

After his "reincorporation" into the CIA, Blackford had taken to returning home in midafternoon. He hadn't recovered his old stamina and felt keenly the need for a "lie-down." He disdained the word "nap," which he thought appropriate for children and pregnant women.

He would reach Merriwell, climb the stairs, shake off his trousers, and be asleep in minutes, waking an hour later. He would then go down to his study and, seated in his armchair, read books and magazines. The mention by Director Bill Webster of Vienna prompted him this afternoon to dig out the handy German reader he had leaned on and mastered a decade before. He was reading, also, a life of Stalin that attempted to track Stalin's purges in the thirties, seeking also to get to the bottom of the so-called "Doctors' Plot," which had activated Stalin's complicated anti-Semitic dispositions.

The historian Robert Conquest shed some light on the point when he wrote that "Lenin himself (who was partly Jewish by ancestry) said that if the commissar was Jewish, the deputy should be Russian. Stalin followed this rule." Until the bloody end.

Blackford's attention turned to Tom Wolfe's *The Bonfire of the Vanities.* He picked it up where he had left off the day before, reading on with admiration and delight. He had at hand also *Spycatcher: The Candid Autobiography of a Senior Intelligence Officer,* by Peter Wright, and would give it his critical attention. For many years he had passed around précis of books he thought professionally interesting, and welcomed recommendations by fellow agents. With the afternoon mail, Josefina brought him a pot of tea, when normally he'd have taken a cocktail. One letter, postmarked Moscow, caught his eye. Before he had completed opening it, he sensed who it was from.

Again, it was handwritten, on the same quality stock as had been used in the letter from Vienna.

Dear Oakes:

I hope you are recovering from the death of "wife" and child. But you have had your life's ration, when you think of it. "Birth and copulation and death / That's all the facts when you come to brass tacks." That's how my old acquaintance Tom Eliot put it. You had the one, plenty of the second, and now, just a little ahead (I have reports about your ill health), the third. I hope you go as peacefully as your dear Ursina. I saw to it that she would experience no pain. She would pass away without having to parse her vagabond speech for the People's Minister of

Internal Affairs. My gracious, such language as you taught your Ursina to use! But she is at peace. Pending, to conform to Christian diplomacy, your reunion, which will surely not be too far distant.

    Ever your nemesis,

      Philby

At the bottom of the page Philby had scrawled, in the British fashion, "PTO"—Please Turn Over. Blackford did so, and read. To add to his fury, there was the need to acknowledge this terrible man's flair for evil piquancy. "You will perhaps have forgotten, Oakes, that you left, in care of Rufina, a testamentary will, duly witnessed, deeding one-half of your estate to Ursina. I have tracked down an aunt of Ursina's in Leningrad and I have dispatched to a lawyer there a copy of your will, with the suggestion that he consult the aged lady, who, as next of kin to Ursina, is indisputably her beneficiary, to advise her that she can press in American courts for one-half of your property. Does this include one-half of your files on anti-Soviet activity? Perhaps a settlement might be made. If you are so inclined, do not hesitate to be in touch with me. —P"

Blackford pondered the words. He needed company, needed the strength of another person. A friend . . . He called Singer Callaway. "Could you come by?"

"For a drink?"

"Yes. I think I will have a drink with you. I need to share something with you."

He tried to turn his mind away from the letter. He picked up the *Spycatcher* volume. He opened the cover of the bestseller.

The book was an account of the penetration, over three decades, of Western intelligence, focusing—he saw from the chapter headings—on the work of Guy Burgess, Donald Maclean, and Kim Philby.

He closed the book, and waited anxiously for Callaway.

CHAPTER 54

In their whispered planning, Linbek and Nina were moderately reassured. Nina's mother did indeed live in Leningrad. It didn't matter that her senility intermittently excluded rational discourse—that was not a Titov problem. What mattered was that Nina and Aleksei would have reasonable grounds for making the trip to Leningrad. There must be nothing suspicious about their departure from Moscow.

Titov had planned his own movements with great care. Leaving Moscow on Sunday, April 24, he would be in Vienna that night, comfortably ahead of the opening of the conference on Monday morning. Nina and Aleksei must remain in Moscow, to avert any suspicion of collective Titov flight plans. They must wait until Tuesday, April 26, and leave *then* for Leningrad. Titov's disappearance would not be effected until Thursday night. In Vienna, he would take a cab to the home of his old student, Dr. Valeria Mikhailov, simultaneously advising the Austrian Ministry of Security that he was at least contingently petitioning for asylum. Valeria, a woman of talent and determination, was delighted at the prospect of having a role in the escape of her old tutor from the country from which she had herself fled after completing her studies fifteen years earlier.

"So. On Tuesday evening, you and Alyosha will take the overnight train for Leningrad. On our Family Calendar"—he pointed to the closet door, left of the refrigerator, where a large calendar hung, on which social and professional engagements were noted—"you will write, for April 24, 'Linbek departs Vienna.' For April 26 you will write, 'Visit Grandmama, Leningrad.' For April 29, write, 'Linbek returns.' For May 1, 'Back from Leningrad visit.'"

All of that was carefully done. Even so, Nina was apprehensive on the Monday and Tuesday before the train trip of Tuesday evening.

She would not tell Aleksei what was contemplated until after reaching Leningrad. A friend would meet the train, ostensibly an old friend of the family. The driver would take them not to Grandmama's, but to a lodging house.

Inevitably she heard from her son, "Why aren't we staying with Grandmama?"

"I will tell you later."

She did tell him, during a walk in the park. She could easily have given him her secrets right there, at the little inn at Durkha Place 40. But habit, years and years of the fear of being tapped, governed her practices in daily life.

"Alyosha," she said, sitting down on a bench and savoring the spring air, "we are going to join your father in Vienna, but we will not be able to travel there by conventional routes."

"We are escaping?"

She should not have been surprised. Aleksei quickly penetrated circumlocutions and dissimulation.

"Yes. We are escaping. Your father is a very important man, and the authorities will not permit this to happen if they can help it. That is why we are staying at a little inn. And we will not even be visiting Grandmama. We do not wish to leave any trail, in case the KGB explores our whereabouts."

Aleksei was dismayed at leaving his school and his friends and, especially, his ten-year collection of airplane lore. But he sensed the tension of the moment and resolved to say nothing that might distract, or disappoint, his mother. So he said, "Let us hope to be soon with Papa."

Seated on the park bench, still wearing a winter coat and hat, addressing her son, who wore his long jacket and his aviator's cap, ear muffs hanging loose around his neck, Nina informed him of her detailed plans.

"You are to go to the ticket office of the Helsinki Ferry. If you follow this street"—she pointed—"to the square, you will see the bus station. Take a harbor bus. At the Finland Line, purchase two tickets to Helsinki on the ferry leaving tomorrow at 3 P.M. Here," she handed the leather packet to him, "is my passport and money. You have your own passport. If they ask any questions, tell them you and your mother are going on a visit of only a few days. *Be certain* to ask for round-trip tickets. When you have the tickets, find your way back to where we are staying. Do you remember the address?"

Aleksei smiled at her, impatiently.

"Where?" his mother teased.

"We are at Durkha Place 40."

"Of course, darling. I knew you'd remember the address."

"Mama, do you think we could visit where Grandpapa the aviator, my papa's father, lived?"

"No, dear. I don't even remember the address. And your Titov grandparents are long dead."

"That's too bad. I would have loved to talk to my grandfather about his days as a pilot."

"One day you will fly in an airplane."

"Like traveling from Helsinki to Austria? *Of course!* There's hardly any other way to get there!" He thought to tease her in turn. "Maybe when I buy the tickets to Helsinki, I should also ask for air tickets from Helsinki to Vienna?"

She batted him over the head with her glove.

CHAPTER 55

Aleksei set out briskly for the bus station. His mother had told him not to dally. He took her instructions so seriously that when the bus to the harbor drove by the widely advertised History of Soviet Aviation exhibit at the Leningrad Museum, he did not jump off the bus or even change his seat. He passed the museum by wistfully, but feasting, as the bus made its way, on large photographs and artistic depictions of MiG, Yak, and Su fighters.

He had got from the concierge at the inn a small street map of the city and followed the route of the bus as it headed north, stopping to pick up and discharge passengers.

The city seemed to him livelier than similar apartment and office blocks in Moscow. Perhaps it was the spring, and what it does to animal spirits. The great palaces, he learned from the guide printed on the back of his map, were, some of them, already open for tourists, and others would be opened in the early weeks of May. Peter's Palace and Catherine's Palace were special favorites of visitors, he read.

But that would be for another day. He took his responsibility gravely and, alighting from the bus, he walked with steady pace toward the ships and ferries he had spotted, a hundred meters from where the bus stopped.

He could make out the painted Finland Line sign and walked to the door, wedged open in celebration of the warm weather. Twenty people, most of them elderly, were in line outside the single window in the high-ceilinged room. He wondered idly why there should be a full ten feet of space above his head. He speculated that, in years gone by, resourceful travelers voyaging to Helsinki might have taken their own horse carriages on board. That would have been fun!—leaving St. Petersburg with your two horses and getting off the next day in Helsinki with your two horses.

The line was moving, and he reached the window. "Two round-trip tickets to Helsinki, with reservations for the departure tomorrow at 3 P.M.," he said to the elderly woman at the window. She was wearing heavy glasses, and had a sweater wrapped around her shoulders.

"Passports."

He pulled them out of his mother's packet.

"Open return date?"

"Yes, ma'am," he said.

She returned the passports, took his money, and fed out two strips of tickets.

Aleksei pocketed them and walked back to the door, stepping outside. Two men took hold of him, one on his right shoulder, the second on the left. One of them—he could not identify which—said: "Show me your passport."

"Who authorized you to see my passport?"

This was acknowledged by a kick to his left leg of stunning force. Aleksei found himself clutching the jacket of the man on his left just to stay standing. The pain eased. One man held him upright, the other frisked him until he found the leather folder in his jacket pocket. The man opened it, looked into a passport, and said: "Well, well. Aleksei Lindberghovich Titov." He turned to his fellow officer: "Vanya, we've got here the son of the great scientist Lindbergh Vissarionovich Titov. And look, the boy has his mother's passport too."

Aleksei, limping along, was half dragged to a waiting car and, a few minutes later, into a large concrete building painted, though not recently, gray. There was an official at the desk on the ground floor, but Aleksei's guards walked right by him, without comment, into a hallway. They rang for the elevator and took him down to a lower floor into a windowless room. Its furniture was a long sturdy desk at one end and a single upright chair in front of it. One guard maneuvered Aleksei over to the chair, and then pushed him down onto it.

Minutes later, a short, stocky man appeared, his black hair swept back, a collar, which appeared to be black velvet, open at his throat. He sat down and motioned to the guards to leave the room.

"Ah then, Aleksei Lindberghovich Titov. You were intending, with your mother, to flee the country."

Aleksei and his mother had not prepared for this interlude. Aleksei improvised. "We were going for a brief visit to Helsinki, sir."

"So. Who was going to take you around, when you arrived in Helsinki?"

Aleksei hesitated. "My mother has friends." He was encouraged by his improvisation, and decided to expand on his answer. "A schoolmate of my mother's."

"How convenient to have schoolmates in foreign countries where you plan to travel."

"Yes, comrade."

"And where is your father?"

"He is in Vienna, comrade. He is a scientist."

"Yes, we know that. Was he by any chance going to meet you in Helsinki?"

Aleksei had given no thought to this possibility. But then he remembered the promised flight—his first flight—from Helsinki to Vienna. "I don't think so, sir."

"Why don't you think so?"

He could hardly say that he expected to fly to Vienna. "I think my mother would have told me."

"Where is your mother?"

He knew intuitively that the challenge lay ahead. "I don't know, comrade."

"What address are you staying at in Leningrad?"

"I don't remember, comrade."

The interrogator reached into a drawer and brought out a black instrument, the length of his forearm. He pushed the buzzer on his desk and the two guards reappeared. "Hold him over the table."

One guard pulled Aleksei by the left shoulder, the second by the right shoulder, bringing him over the right end of the desk. They stretched his arms tight over the opposite end. His buttocks protruded over the edge.

The officer in charge stood and walked to the left of Aleksei. He brought full force to the blow on the buttocks. This brought a cry from Aleksei and a jolt from his hips.

"*Tighter*," the lieutenant said.

Aleksei's face was jammed onto the desk top. The lieutenant struck him again. Again Aleksei cried out. But he said nothing.

The lieutenant paused. With his finger, he pointed at Aleksei's waist. The first guard knew what that meant. While the other held him down, he moved to Aleksei's side and yanked down on his belt. But Aleksei was well built, and his pants did not slide off. The guard reached around Aleksei's waist and felt his way to the buckle, unfastening it. Now he succeeded, pulling the boy's pants down, and then his underwear. Aleksei lay naked below the waist, two great welts on his backside.

"That's better." The lieutenant struck again. There was another cry, this one more shrill.

"Are you going to tell me where to find your mother?"

Aleksei forced himself to think of Charles Lindbergh. He was over mid-Alantic and had fallen asleep, and recovered himself only just in time to keep from crashing into the water. He had met the challenge, the pain of keeping himself awake. But had Lindbergh's pain been so intolerable? Did Lindbergh weep? Were there tears? Aleksei was weeping and began to cry out, as yet another blow struck him with violent impact. Would he simply pass out? The truncheon struck again, and Aleksei gasped out, "*She is in Leningrad.*"

The lieutenant struck him yet again.

Aleksei found it difficult to speak, but the guard on the left said he could make it out. "She is staying at Durkha Place 40."

"Take him away. Come then to me, and bring the car."

CHAPTER 56

The envelope, marked "To be opened only by Soviet Ambassador," was brought to Ambassador Arkady Luzhin just after nine in the morning. His aide, on handing it over, said, "I thought I should not interfere with this. It could be from him."

Luzhin looked the envelope over carefully, without opening it. "It was mailed Saturday afternoon—from the railroad station post office."

He opened it carefully with a pair of scissors, running his eyes down to make out the sender's name. It was plain to see. "Lindbergh Vissarionovich Titov."

"Close the door behind you."

Left alone, Luzhin read the letter.

It was surprisingly long-winded. It recounted a dozen problems Titov had run into in the past year or more having to do with his and his associates' need for manuscripts, books, journal articles, and, above all, addresses, postal and electronic, of—Titov had listed the names of six scientists in the United States, West Germany, Sweden, and Israel. He wrote of his frustration at not being able regularly to communicate with these and other scholars.

Luzhin read the third page with amazement.

"I have reflected that it is not possible for me to continue my work in the repressive conditions of the Soviet Union. Accordingly, I have resolved to leave Moscow.

"But in recognition of my Russian blood and of my love for my motherland, I am amenable to an accommodation. If the Ministry of Education and Research can arrange to transport my past work and my archives to Vienna, I will undertake to continue my studies without formal estrangement. You would need to arrange for two of my associates"—he gave their names—"to take up residence in Austria.

"I assume that the required technical resources are available here, perhaps at the University of Vienna Medical School. If that should not prove to be the case, the ministry would need to arrange to ship to me materials that I will itemize if we agree to proceed.

"I intend to be in daily contact with the Austrian Information Office, Ballhausplatz 2. Herr Peter Jutzeler has consented to relay messages addressed to me."

The letter was signed, in Titov's ornate script, "Lindbergh Vissarionovich Titov."

In Moscow, Nikolai Paval, the Deputy Minister of Foreign Affairs, called his meeting for six o'clock. Summoned were

Mikhail Bykov, for security; Roman Belov, minister of culture; and Rodion Rodzinsky, dean of Moscow University's medical school.

"I cannot imagine anything so . . . grotesque as what is here being said to us by Titov," the deputy foreign minister began. "He wishes us to patronize a continuation of his work *in a foreign country*. And to supply him with *Russian scientists* to do this. And with archives and laboratory equipment!"

"Why does he not ask," Colonel Bykov said with heavy sarcasm, "that we supply him with the answers to his research questions?"

"It is all so strange," Culture Minister Belov said. "For instance, there is nothing said about the needed consent of his associates to such an arrangement. Nothing is said about their families. About *his* family." Bykov scribbled on in his notepad.

The deputy foreign minister said, "It is important, and it is heartening, that he makes no profound ideological statements here, no repudiation of the Communist cause. His complaints are specific and personal. In this frame of mind, it is our challenge to induce him to return to us."

He turned to the dean. "His complaints. Are they serious? Is it only irksome, what he has objected to, in the matter of his freedom to do research?"

"More than just irksome, comrade. It can be paralyzing, to be hindered in spontaneous communication with foreign students and academic researchers. Even when the material sought after isn't flatly barred, sometimes weeks and months go by because the security bureaucracy—forgive me, Colonel Bykov, if I am rubbing my feet over the face of one of your children. What is truly difficult, and sometimes impossible, is to secure permission to send out research done by Dr. Titov and his team."

The deputy foreign minister's interest was keen, and he motioned the dean to expand on his point.

"The problem is that if a researcher doing work in a laboratory in Chicago wishes to coordinate his work with Titov's, he cannot do that unless Titov can send him what *he* has. But the security people usually forbid this."

"On what grounds?" Paval asked.

"On the grounds that Soviet research should not be shared with anybody. On the grounds that to do so is to give away a national property—"

"Suppose we were talking about research into missile interceptors," Bykov interrupted. "You would hardly expect that we would make such research common property, Comrade Rodzinsky?"

"Are you then saying that we should begin by simply denying Titov the freedom he is after?"

"Comrades, comrades," Deputy Foreign Minister Paval cut in. "To me it is clear that we have here an opportunity for negotiation. It is possible that after some discussion, and some reassurances, and an invitation to Dr. Titov to reflect on some of the . . . incongruities of what he proposes, that we can persuade him to return. Meanwhile, there is to be no mention of his absence in the media. Dr. Titov is, we shall record officially, on a leave of absence and traveling in . . . Europe."

"Are we to inform the Austrian police that we have no further interest in his whereabouts?"

The door opened. Bykov recognized the intruder, and rose to ascertain why he was there. The two talked for a few seconds in whispers. Bykov returned to his seat and apologized.

"An important development, Comrade Nikolai Vasilievich," he addressed the deputy foreign minister.

Paval went back to what he had been saying before the interruption. "Yes, in answer to that question. The Austrian police are to be told that all is well in the Titov matter. Meanwhile our detachment in Vienna is to do everything possible to locate him. An emissary is to contact the Austrian go-between, Jutzeler, to ask him to set up a meeting between our representative and Titov."

"Who will be our representative?" Belov asked.

"On that point I will wish to confer privately with Comrade Mikhail Pavlovich."

The others left the room.

Bykov stayed. "The interruption, Comrade Nikolai Vasilievich, was to advise me that our KGB in Leningrad have . . . picked up Nina Titov and her son. Attempting to leave the country."

CHAPTER 57

It was Tuesday late morning. Colonel Bykov had made up his mind how to proceed.

He sent for Comrade Andrei Martins. "Bring him here right away."

Philby was there an hour later. Bykov briefed him on the Titov defection.

"You have once or twice asked to be given another mission, Andrei Fyodorovich. Today we have one for you. You are to go to Vienna. Your mission is to get Titov back here. You will have substantial help. To begin with, Dr. Vladimir Kirov will be with you. Do you know Kirov?"

"I met him once, Mikhail Pavlovich. He was the mentor of Professor Ursina Chadinov—"

Bykov looked up. Philby thought he could see a wink. "The late Professor Ursina Chadinov."

"I stand corrected." Philby, too, suppressed a smile, or almost.

"Most critical, here, is that Kirov was a classmate of Titov and continues as close friend and confidant. I have already talked with Kirov, and he is willing to go to Vienna. But he has reservations. He says he is hardly in a position to contradict Titov on the matter of his complaints about access to data and to foreign scientists."

"You will have to fill me in."

"Ah! Of course. You are not aware of the demands made by Titov? The conditions he set down before agreeing to return?"

"No, Mikhail Pavlovich, I am not."

"He demands—of course—the safe arrival of his wife and son. That is a story on which I will need to expand. Then he demands future unimpeded access to foreign data and foreign scientists. Deputy Foreign Minister Paval is anxious to make that concession, whereas I am insisting that there be surveillance of Titov's conversations with foreigners—especially after this! And that a committee evaluate any request for a transfer of data or material he wishes to have sent out.

"Call that a negotiable point. And—listen, Andrei Fyodorovich, to this: He wishes two of his colleagues at the institute to emigrate to Vienna to work alongside him to continue joint researches."

"That is truly wonderful! I find that truly imaginative! You have of course not spoken to the select two?"

"Of course not. They are not even aware that they are playing a role in all of this. Bear in mind that Titov's colleagues are not even aware that he is . . . estranged. We have arranged to pass on the word, through the dean, that he is taking a brief vacation. But of course even here," he offered Philby a cigarette and lighted his own, "word gets out. And there is the matter of his wife and son."

"You were going to tell me about them."

"Our branch in Leningrad acted very quickly, very commendably. In a routine check at the ferry terminal, they spotted the young man—his name is Aleksei—buying tickets to Helsinki. He was apprehended, refused to give the address of his mother, and was taken to the security building, the Balukla—"

"I know the place. I lectured there, if you remember, to three hundred of your colleagues."

"Yes, well, there he was interrogated by Vasily Trail. Lieutenant Vasily Trail."

"Who is he? Why is his name important?"

"Vasily Trail was a young assistant to Blokhin. V. M. Blokhin. Comrade Blokhin believed in direct action. He—" Bykov aimed an imaginary pistol to his head—"singlehandedly executed 7,000 Poles—individually—in twenty-eight days, in Katyn, in 1940. We have to be grateful that the young Titov did not resist Lieutenant Trail for too long. Trail had not been advised that we have an interest in the health of Titov's wife and son."

"Was the boy . . . maimed?"

"No. But he will not be fit for several days to be seen by his father. In short, we must keep mother and son sequestered, but available by telephone, if and when we think it useful that they speak to Titov. Proof that they are alive."

"If not well."

"He will recover."

"What is my role?"

"We can assume that the Americans will have an aggressive unit in Vienna to talk Titov into defecting. We do not know what inducements the Americans will come up with. We can assume that they would find no problem in funding a continuation of Titov's work in a select university."

"Are the research facilities he needs very—special?"

"They are certainly special. But presumably within reach of a scientist working in Vienna. *Your* job, Andrei Fyodorovich, is to make yourself aware of exactly what is going on, what the Americans are offering, what Titov is thinking. At the right moment, I would suppose that you would speak directly with Titov."

"My Russian is serviceable, but not . . . resourceful."

"A member of your team will serve you as an instant translator, Russian–English."

"What am I to say to Titov, beyond stressing the professional concessions you have spoken about?"

Bykov drew on his cigarette. "Andrei Fyodorovich, you are by reputation the wiliest intelligence agent in the world. We will be substantially guided by what *you* recommend. Your mission is simple: Get Lindbergh Titov back to the Soviet Union."

"Reunited with wife and son?"

"If Titov does not come back, wife and son will stay here."

"Dead or alive?"

"Dead or alive."

CHAPTER 58

The Titov project went quickly to the top of the pile on the desk of CIA Director William Webster. He called in Walter Jacobs from the Soviet desk. What Jacobs liked most about the director was that even when saying not a great deal, Webster could communicate a shelf-load of thought.

This time Webster opened by saying: "Why do we want Titov so badly? Have you thought about that?"

"No."

"Well, let's think about it together."

A half hour later, Webster got through to Ambassador Henry Grunwald in Vienna. Grunwald, before taking on diplomacy in his retirement, had reached the pinnacle of the profession of journalism—editor-in-chief of all the publications of Time,

Inc. Webster had talked with him a few times before his retirement as a journalist and had the measure of the speed with which Grunwald caught on to whatever the problem at hand was. Grunwald was about the same age as Henry Kissinger, and they had arrived in the United States as refugees from Hitler at about the same time, speaking English with about the same Germanic coloration.

"I'm sitting here with Walter Jacobs, Henry. Obviously we want Titov the scientist to come to us. Who wouldn't? But is he of any use to us as an anti-Communist? Hang on, I'm going to put you on the speakerphone so Walter can hear what we're saying."

He pressed the requisite button. "You hearing me, Henry?"

"I hear you fine. You are asking me if I know whether Titov is an anti-Communist."

"Well, sure. In the sense that he resents the repressions on research, we can assume that, yes, he is. But before we exert ourselves totally, it would be good to know whether, if he gets out, he will be willing to speak up."

"You mean, speak out on . . . the basic things? Human rights, Soviet totalitarian practices, that sort of thing?"

"Yes. That sort of thing."

There was a trace of laughter. " 'That sort of thing,' Bill, goes a long way . . . Well, in the past ninety-six hours I've read everything I could put my hands on about Lindbergh Titov—I even found out that he was named after Charles Lindbergh, born the same year Lindbergh made his flight."

"Have you had any experience with Gus Windels, one of our guys in Moscow, hangs out at the State Department—Public Affairs?"

"No. What's he got on Titov?"

"Maybe a fair amount, because he briefly dated Ursina Chadinov. The late Ursina Chadinov. Chadinov and Vladimir Kirov were very close, and Kirov was a classmate and long-time friend of Titov."

"So. What can I get from Windels, on the phone from Vienna, that you can't get, on the phone from Washington?"

"Not much. But we're bringing Windels in. He'll arrive in Vienna later today, or tomorrow morning."

"I'll expect him to call me. Meanwhile—"

"Yes, he'll know to do that."

"Meanwhile, I know where Titov is hiding out. Not with the man I first thought of. But I should have thought of this lady. She defected, after getting her graduate degree in biology at Moscow U., and that was fifteen years ago. She teaches now at Vienna U. The go-between, Peter Jutzeler of the Austrian Information Office, has been placed in charge of this little mess by the Austrian government, and he has told me to come by to see him."

"When did he tell you that?"

"About the time, Bill, you began this phone call."

"Okay. We'll hold. Get back to me as soon as you can."

"As soon as I can will still be early, Eastern Daylight Time."

"You know the number. They'll find me."

"They'll put me through on a secure line?"

"I'll arrange that—wait a minute, Walter has a question."

Webster leaned to one side and Walter Jacobs bent his head toward the speaker phone. "Mr. Ambassador, this is Walter Jacobs."

"How do you do, Mr. Jacobs."

"The scientist who defected fifteen years ago, with whom Titov may be staying, is her first name Valeria? V-a-l-e-r-i-a?"

"Yes. Valeria Mikhailov, graduated Moscow U. School of Medicine 1972, defected to Austria 1973."

"Thanks. We have a file on her."

"I haven't met her, but word is she's a tough lady and pretty vocal anti-Communist."

"Okay. I'll turn you back to the director."

"Henry, I'll wait to hear from you. Hear from you on two counts"—William Webster was methodical. "(1) What Jutzeler is asking, and (2) whether Valeria Milker—Milkkervich—"

"Mikhailov."

"—Mikhailov is willing to put you in touch with our quarry."

"Gut. Auf Wiedersehen."

The ambassador's car pulled in at the Austrian Information Office, an annex of the Foreign Ministry. It was once a palace for a neglected Austrian queen, who was left to console herself with her ninety-seven-room abode. Ambassador Grunwald stayed in the limousine, sending an aide to expedite contact with Jutzeler. Grunwald was, after all, ambassador of the United States of America. He had driven here from a relatively modest residence, though it was adequate to have served as the meeting place of Premier Nikita Khrushchev and President John F. Kennedy when they met in 1961 to confer on the Berlin crisis. Grunwald was ready to do what he could to bring Titov permanently to the West, and preferably to the United States.

It made a difference, leaving the Soviet Union and taking up work again in the United States. Solzhenitsyn had discovered this, though he too had allies, not in Vienna, but in West Germany.

Grunwald wouldn't be sticky about protocol, certainly not to the point of remaining immobile in the car until Herr Jutzeler came to get him. He would get out of the car and follow his aide, if informed where exactly to go, and that Jutzeler was standing by.

Meanwhile, sitting here for who knew exactly how long, he would steal a look at his paperback—he always had something by him to read, to avert idle moments. This was the long-awaited biography, in German, of Albert Einstein. But he put it down quickly when he saw Rick, his aide, approaching the car, leading to it a gentleman dressed formally in dark blue, wearing glasses, his blond hair in a crew cut, his tie also blue, though lighter in color than his jacket. His tiepin bore the white-cross Austrian crest.

Rick opened the door and Grunwald stepped out. Herr Peter Jutzeler bowed his head slightly and extended his hand. Jutzeler led his guest through the waiting room and into a hallway, from which they entered a modest meeting room. It was decorated along the sides with gilt sconces. A chandelier hung over the highly lacquered table, an onyx fireplace at one end. A tray with tea and cups and pastries sat on the table.

Jutzeler motioned Grunwald to a chair and took the one opposite. He smiled: "We hardly need an interpreter, Herr Ambassador. But if you prefer?"

Grunwald laughed. "Speak in whatever language you like, and I'll do the same." To Rick: "When we are through, I'll pick you up in the waiting room."

The two diplomats sat down.

———

Professor Valeria Mikhailov, tall, resolute in appearance, her straight blond hair framing her face, spoke, in her spare apartment, with her guest, Linbek Titov. "I suggest we both go to the airport in my car, if you don't mind riding in a ten-year-old Fiat. That will save us the cab fare to the airport, which is considerable. When your wife and boy arrive, we can then hire a cab, which I assume will be required even if they don't have much luggage. I will drive with your son, and you and your wife can take the cab. I have to confess to you, Linbek, I have very little money. I send a check every month to support my mother in Volgograd. I need to make every schilling count."

"I have sensed your problem. The allowance extended me for incidental expenses during the conference gave me no slack. My wife will arrive with almost six hundred dollars in U.S. currency, carefully accumulated over the years. That will certainly tide us over until I have made a fresh connection."

"Yes, of course. These are the least of our worries. And a friend on the fourth floor is leaving tomorrow for a week in France. She will let me use her apartment, but that begins only tomorrow. Tonight we will be squeezed into mine."

"Valeria, this is such a very happy day for me. And adventurous. I think not of our privations, but of those that are had by our countrymen left behind."

They were at the airport a half hour ahead of the flight from Helsinki. "I will wait for you in the baggage area. You can greet them at security and have your private family reunion. Then come to me, at baggage level."

Dr. Titov was standing, excitement mounting as he saw

the two-engine Russian-made jet draw up, and the airport passenger staircase wheeled out to the cabin door. In a few minutes, the passengers began to file out. His heart was pounding. Finally, young Aleksei would have realized his ambition to fly. His dream fulfilled—an airplane flight! Helsinki to Vienna. And, incidentally, to life in the free world.

The file of passengers thinned down. A very large man emerged. No doubt he had held up the passengers behind him.

Two minutes after the fat man had got past the gate, it hit Lindbergh Titov like a shaft of ice-cold air to the heart.

Nina and Aleksei were not on board.

"I've got a bagful of news, Bill." Ambassador Grunwald was speaking to the director of the CIA. "I put the top of the news into a cable to State a half hour ago. I'll give you more details, which you'll want. First thing: Mrs. Titov and the son were supposed to arrive on Saturday. They were not on the scheduled plane. If they had had trouble at the Finnish end, they'd have gotten word to Valeria Mikhailov. They had her number. It means only one thing: The Soviets got them."

"Where? Where, I wonder."

"I don't think the KGB would have taken any chances trying to kidnap them in Helsinki, so I figure they were stopped before boarding the ferry. And you know something? There is *not one thing* we can do about it. They've become just . . . a Soviet bargaining chip. Their absence makes our job much harder."

"Right. Well, we'll alert Moscow to listen hard for any clues. What about Jutzeler? Herr Jutzeler?"

"I had an hour with him. Very formal gentleman. But here is what the Austrian government says:

"In order to observe neutrality, they want conferences with Titov conducted under Austrian auspices, in a chamber under Austrian security. Soviet and U.S. representatives may confer privately with Titov, but only in quarters the Austrians designate. There is to be no effort made by Soviet or U.S. representatives to approach Titov elsewhere."

Walter Jacobs approached the speakerphone and asked, "Does Jutzeler know where Titov is? I assume he does."

"I thought he probably did. But you know, I'm not *sure*. It could be that Titov is calling in over the telephone. I didn't press him, obviously. And of course I never let on that we think we know where he—probably—is hiding out.

"Now. Herr Jutzeler informs me that the Austrian Foreign Ministry stipulates that there shall be not more than two emissaries designated to represent the conflicting interests. No separate security. The emissaries' names are to be given to Jutzeler. Just two Russians, two Americans."

"Well, we'll give one of our two spots to Gus Windels. His native Russian is a terrific advantage. We already spoke about him."

"And the other?"

"I'm thinking."

"You'll need to act quickly. The Russians have already given the names of their representatives. I don't know what Titov plans to do now that the family has been stopped. Captured. Conceivably he'll just give up and go home."

"That would be . . . terrible," Webster said. "Also, sad."

"Do we know anything about the Soviet representatives? Who they'll be?"

"Yes, and here is their biggie: Professor Vladimir Kirov. An important figure as a teacher and medical practitioner. But what really counts is: He and Titov are old friends, going back forty years. Classmates."

"And the other?"

"I don't know anything about him. His name is Andrei Fyodorovich Martins. Odd surname."

"Okay," the director said. "We'll get back to you, Mr. Ambassador."

Webster called in Anthony Trust. "Walter Jacobs will fill you in, Anthony. I'll be back in a few minutes. I have to put in a couple of calls, and I'd better speak to George Shultz. As Secretary of State, he'd certainly be interested."

Webster left the room, and was back in a half hour.

Seated, he spoke to his two senior consultants. "Anthony, Walter: A bulletin just came in. Gus Windels had one of our people in Moscow ring Titov's apartment on the telephone. No answer. She went around to the address. There were two goons very prominent in the lobby, checking people going in and out. Obviously the mother and son—her name is Nina, his, Aleksei; he's seventeen years old—are on their way to Austria, or trying to get there. Or in detention somewhere. Our gal in Moscow doesn't know, obviously, about the Helsinki flight they were supposed to be on."

"Yes," Jacobs said. "There is that possibility, that they tried an overland route. That would explain why they couldn't call—you know the phone service in that part of the world."

"Well, we'll have to focus on the Vienna scene. We need one more man there. Ideally, we should send Blackford Oakes. Nobody beats him in skill and experience. He knows Vienna from ten years ago, and he has worked with Windels.

Oh, and just this winter he spent—no comments, gentlemen—six weeks in Moscow. There's just one thing I worry about—"

"His health?" Walter Jacobs asked.

"Yes. I'm concerned about it.

"Anthony, you're his oldest friend. —Say. Is it *true* that you had the job of holding him down when his headmaster in England flogged him?"

"Well, yes. We don't talk about it, a bad memory for both of us. Ten years later I made it up to Blackford by covering him in a shootout and saving his life. Though come to think of it, the bullet did graze him. On his ass!" They laughed.

Trust went on, "I agree with the director, Black's health isn't so good. He pulls out late afternoons, most days, just to rest up. But there's nobody better than him, sizing up situations, acting quickly. I'd say: Give it to him, if he wants it."

"If he doesn't take it, I think Roger d'Aubisson is good," Jacobs said.

"I'll talk with Blackford," the director said.

A half hour later, Blackford Oakes was in the room. He had got a quick briefing from Walter Jacobs.

"We have Gus Windels arriving in Vienna tonight," Webster said. "We need somebody from here."

"I'll go, Bill."

Blackford sensed the director's reservations.

"You're not looking too good yet. We ought to think a little about your health."

"Fuck my health."

Webster looked at him, hesitated, then said, "Okay, Black. Go. Have Walter fill you in on the latest Vienna developments. And when you get there, Grunwald will be up on anything that's happened while you're flying. You've been given the two Russian names. Do those names mean anything to you?"

"I've never met Kirov, but he was like a godfather to my . . . lady. And"—Blackford gripped the arms of his chair— "*Andrei Fyodorovich Martins is Kim Philby.*"

"Kim Philby! I didn't know he was still doing missions."

"He gets into a lot of missions, Judge. Including hospital operating rooms."

"Well, okay, Black. Good luck. If you get a chance, kick Philby in the ass for me."

"I promise I'll do that, Judge."

CHAPTER 59

They met at the café in the venerable Bristol Hotel. Oakes had been there a decade ago and it hadn't changed, though in 1988 there were more young Austrians and tourists than back then. He recognized the distinctively recognizable headwaiter with the walrus moustache and the bronze chain hanging low from his neck. The headwaiter affected to recognize Blackford, but didn't, really. Blackford looked much more than ten years older than when he had last frequented the Bristol. Gus could understand the headwaiter's confusion: Gus wasn't sure he himself would have recognized Blackford, from just a few months ago, let alone what he must have looked like ten years back.

They met with an embrace, never mind the formalities—you're not supposed to embrace men who are traveling about under cover. But their joint experiences on two missions, and the natural attraction of the Ukrainian-born twenty-nine-

year-old for the sixty-two-year-old legend was keen, and reciprocal. Blackford had arrived at noon and gone instantly to
the Bristol Hotel for his much-needed nap. Gus had come in
from Moscow the night before, and in the morning headed
directly to the U.S. Embassy to confer with Ambassador
Grunwald.

When the two men got together that evening, neither of
them mentioned the death of Ursina, let alone the cause of
her death. But Gus did speak about the buzz on the matter
of her failure to speak at the welcoming ceremony. "I think
you could get a thousand rubles for a copy of the speech she
intended to give. You never actually saw it, did you, Black?"

"No. I know the culture minister, Belov, got a copy,
and so did Rufina. That means, of course," Blackford's voice
tightened, "that Philby saw it. I have to assume that Ursina
had her own copy, but she never showed it to me. I was surprised, but after the shock of that afternoon's meeting at the
Culture Ministry, I didn't want to press her for it."

"God knows what she said in it." Gus moved his hand
out of the way so that the beer pitcher could be set down.

"We're not ready to order," Blackford said in impressive
German.

"Some people are saying—I actually heard this from a
university student; I mean, the student told it to my driver,
who told it to me—that Ursina, in her speech, urged all those
attending the peace forum to rise up and storm the stage and
kill Gorbachev when he came on later in the program."

Blackford managed a smile. "I guess I wish I did have a
copy, so that stuff like that could be disproved."

"They'd probably think the copy you exhibited was a for-
gery. Only the minister of culture could suppress those rumors
and—you want my guess, Black? I think he wouldn't want to.

The more extreme Ursina's speech is taken to have been, the more reason for suppressing it."

"Yeah. I guess they wouldn't want to be accused of suppressing a speech on the labor theory of value."

"Well, let me tell you, because I've got a lot to tell you—" He quaffed his beer. "God, that's good stuff. I spent the morning with Henry Grunwald, and the procedures are crystallizing."

Gus pulled up his notebook:

"(1) We are to have as many meetings as Titov wants, before he makes up his mind which way to go.

"(2) They are to be held at a little bierhaus on Friedrichstrasse, Friedrichstrasse 49. Jutzeler goes there a lot at relaxation time and knows the owner. It is locked tight until 6 P.M. every day. Jutzeler's got the keys and knows where the light switches are. In fact, he knows how to make the beer flow, not that that's likely to happen. Though I don't know, after a speech by Philby, I may need a beer, either to drink or to ram up his ass."

"Gus, I'm not getting it all. What exactly is to go on at the bierhaus?"

"All of this, Grunwald reminded me, is subject to the final okay of Titov, but the arrangements reflect what he has demanded of Jutzeler, and the preliminary plans are approved by Kirov."

"Is Kirov the chief guy? Or Philby?"

"Kirov. He is your counterpart. Philby is mine. To get on:

"(3) If Titov confirms, our first meeting is tomorrow at 1300. There will be Austrian security guards at the front and at the rear door of Otto's—that's what the bierhaus is called, Otto's. Twenty minutes before rendezvous time, the Russians will be admitted through the front door by Jutzeler and will take their places at a table at the south end of the main room. They are Kirov, Philby, an interpreter, and—the Russians insisted on this—a bodyguard borrowed from the Soviet Embassy. They weren't allowed to bring any from Moscow.

"(4) Ten minutes before rendezvous, Jutzeler will go to the back entrance of Otto's and lead in the U.S. delegation. That's you, me, an interpreter, and we too have to have one bodyguard—Jutzeler is making a big production of absolute equality, both sides. Grunwald's looking around for a likely guy. There are no U.S. Marines in Vienna, not since the treaty, and that was thirty-two years ago! We'll be seated at a table at the north end. Got that?"

"How big is Otto's?"

"Small. The distance between us and the Russians will be about twenty feet.

"(5) At 1300, Jutzeler will escort in three people, to be seated in the center, opposite the bar. They are Titov, who insists on bringing along his 'escort, companion, consultant, friend,' Valeria Mikhailov. He's been staying with her. She's a former student of his who defected fifteen years ago and teaches biology. Nobody could object to her being there.

"Then . . . then the third person. He is a retired judge who, way back then, represented Austria in the long U.S.–USSR deliberations that led to the peace treaty. He established a reputation for rigorous neutrality. He has agreed to sit in and listen to, and rule upon, complaints."

"Jesus Christ. It sounds like a fucking courtroom. Is there an appellate body standing by?"

"Ease up, Black. The rules are that the Russian representative gets to speak for fifteen minutes to a half hour. Then you speak for the same period of time. Then Kirov—obviously there is instant translation all the way through—can ask you questions, if he wants to. You can ask him questions, he can ask you questions. Both sides can object to questions as irrelevant. Judge Waldstein rules. Titov has the authority to overrule the judge. If he wants to hear your answer to a question by Kirov, you can give that answer, whether Waldstein says it's relevant or not."

"My, you people were busy in the last twenty-four hours. While you did all that, all I did was pack up, go to the airport, fly to Frankfurt, connect to Vienna, check in at my hotel, and sleep for an hour."

Gus grinned. "Actually, it came together quickly. Titov wanted to hear both sides and wanted both sides to be free to comment on what had been said. He didn't want this to stretch over an age.

"At the end of the day, unless Titov says, '*Halt! No more!*,' we agree to come back the next day, same drill. At some point, Titov turns to you and says: 'Kindly help me to get re-established in' —read Vienna, the United States, wherever, in the West. Or he turns to Kirov and says, 'Vladimir Spiridonovich, I am ready to return to Moscow.'

"Both sides are pledged not to interfere with Titov's movements at any time, in whatever direction he travels."

"That's worth thinking about with another beer."

"I second that." Gus hailed the waiter.

Blackford fondled his glass. "We've got one great thing going for us: the prospect of a free life. Kirov has two things going for him: reintegration into an institute Titov founded and into a community he grew up with, and—the blockbuster—reunion with his wife and son."

CHAPTER 60

The outside of the bierhaus was Alpine-style, its wooden roof slanting down at both ends, the door and shutters a deep green, white wooden frames around the windows. Etched into the wood, and gilded, the words on the sign read, "Otto—1938."

Well, Blackford thought, sitting in the minivan across the street, maybe the house was built just in time to welcome Adolf Hitler to Vienna. Herr Jutzeler, standing outside the bar, was keeping careful track of the time, and at 1249 he signaled to the van across the street. Blackford opened the front passenger door, Gus and the interpreter, the rear doors. They filed out and followed Jutzeler on the stone walkway around the building to the rear.

Blackford took a deep breath as he felt his way through the narrow passage toward the tables in the main room. The next time he raised his head, he would be looking into the face of Harold Adrian Russell Philby, traitor and woman-killer. He had rehearsed his face to register no reaction to that ugly man.

The room was adequately lit, as it would be in the evening, Blackford surmised, when the company of serious beer drinkers would weave in and out. There were no lit candles, but the yellow lamps at either end of the bar were aglow. And also the lamps at the ends of the room, where the opposing sides' representatives would sit behind the tables, over which green felt had been placed.

The interpreter took the leftmost chair, Blackford the next, Gus on the right. They spread before them notepads and a bound folio. The lamps from behind gave ample light.

It was then that Blackford looked up. Opposite, on the left, was the interpreter. Next to him, Professor Kirov. His hair was gray and tidy, his brow furrowed. He wore glasses and kept his head tilted down toward his notes.

Next to him was Philby. His demeanor was anything but furtive. He looked not directly at Blackford, but immediately above him, as though he were interested in examining a beguiling piece of art. He was a tall, well-built man, his hair a white-gray, matching his suit, and he was wearing a tie that, Blackford thought, was—could it be? The tie of a Cambridge graduate? Was there a special Cambridge tie for a graduate who had betrayed his country? If so, there must be a shortage of them, Blackford reflected: Philby, Burgess, Maclean, Blunt, Cairncross. Were there others?

All eyes turned to the entrance as Jutzeler came in, followed by a visibly nervous Lindbergh Titov, his collar open, his eyeglasses clutched in his hand, his eyes examining everything in the room, left and right. Behind him was Dr. Valeria Mikhailov, a blonde and sturdy northern type, self-assured, wearing black pants, a white blouse, a red vest, and pearl earrings. She was carrying a large handbag, one end of a manila folder protruding. A very small old man was next, perhaps in his early eighties. There was a solemnity in Judge Waldstein's manner that suggested there would be no trifling with him. He was followed by an interpreter.

They took their seats and straightened their papers on the table. Herr Waldstein looked about, as if in search of a gavel. Finding none, he tapped his water glass with his pen, looked down at his notes, and began to speak. "We are here, in this informal, indeed quite novel, convocation, in order to permit Professor Lindbergh Vissarionovich Titov, of the Moscow Radiological Institute, to deliberate his future. He has requested this special forum so that he can fully examine the alternatives. On my left," he gestured, "are Soviet representatives who will make the case for his return to Moscow. Their identity is known to the U.S. representatives, who will make the case for Professor Titov to stay in the West— whether in Austria or the United States would be for him to decide.

"I note that it was Dr. Titov who asked that the deputation advocating asylum should be made up of Americans, not Austrians. That choice, and others, were his to make.

"We will begin the proceedings following a schedule suggested by Dr. Titov and submitted to both parties. There will be statements, followed by questions and cross-questions. Dr. Titov may interrupt the proceedings at any point. The advocates, however, will need to be recognized by the chair before interrupting to ask questions or make comments.

"We will hear first from Dr. Kirov, a distinguished professor of medicine, and a colleague of Dr. Titov's of long standing. Professor Kirov."

Kirov fumbled with his chair getting to his feet.

"There is no need to stand. You may speak seated."

He sat down again.

Kirov recited for a full five minutes the history of his association with Titov, beginning when they were both students at Moscow University, Titov under the special supervision of the renowned Nikolai Sokolov; continuing through their professional careers, Titov's as a researcher with brilliant insights into the world of radiology.

"We, loyal sons of the Soviet Union—my colleague Comrade Martins is not a native of our motherland, but a distinguished Englishman who elected many years ago to leave the West, to find haven and purpose in the Soviet Union. He traveled east, as I hope my old friend Linbek Vissarionovich will, on reflection, resolve to do.

"Dr. Titov has made demands—requests—having to do with professional matters. The Education Ministry has examined these and found many of them reasonable, and if Dr. Titov elects to enumerate these, we are prepared, Your Excellency, to respond to them one by one. I believe my time is up."

Waldstein: "Dr. Titov, do you have any questions at this point?"

"Well, yes I do. And I say this to my old friend Vladimir Spiridonovich: How would I know that if such reforms as you approved were to go into effect, they would not be rescinded later—a month later, or two years later?"

"Dr. Kirov, would you answer that question?"

Blackford's hand pressed down on Gus's forearm. "No comment," he directed in a whisper.

Kirov said that the good faith of the commitments of the Ministry of Education and Research would certainly bind everyone involved to such reforms as were agreed upon.

Titov nodded and returned the chair to the judge.

Waldstein looked over to his right. "Mr. Windels, you are taking the floor in place of your senior colleague?"

"Yes, Your Honor, and I shall be speaking in Russian to Dr. Titov."

Waldstein nodded.

Gus introduced himself as a foreign service officer especially familiar with the Soviet Union, inasmuch as he had been born in the Ukraine and had lived there through his fourteenth year. The United States, said Gus, had a single interest in these proceedings. It was to make it known to Dr. Titov that if he sought asylum, the U.S. government would pronounce him qualified to have it.

He spoke for some minutes on the subject of other Soviet citizens who had undergone experiences similar to Titov's. Not long ago, he said, one such was Svetlana Stalin herself. No one was more familiar than she with life and practices in the Soviet Union. These—life and practices in the Soviet Union—were affairs for the government of the USSR to decide upon, but Dr. Titov might wish to weigh, in his deliberations, the experience and resolutions of Svetlana Stalin, and also of the ballet dancers, the whole lot.

"We are not here, Your Excellency, to argue the merits of life in the West. It is for Dr. Titov exclusively to weigh these. We are of course willing to answer, or try to answer, any questions he puts to us. Our mission is to assure him, quite simply and directly, that if he *chooses* to immigrate, we will honor his decision and act upon his claim for asylum."

"Professor Kirov, do you have any questions?"

Kirov whispered to Philby.

"I yield to my associate, Comrade Andrei Fyodorovich Martins."

Philby spoke in measured tones. "Is it not true that in the past, Soviet citizens who have moved to the West have been harassed, isolated, removed from normal life? I give the example of Anatoly Golitsyn. I will quote a letter he wrote to his sister in Odessa, which came to our attention."

He quoted the letter in which Golitsyn complained that he had been forced to live in a remote corner of New York State and forbidden to travel except with the permission of the FBI.

"Your comments, Mr. Windels?"

Blackford spoke up instead. "Your Excellency, the letter just now quoted by Mr. Martins was written by a defector who feared for his life. It was only with the purpose of protecting him from retaliation by agents of the Soviet government that he was subjected to such restrictions as requiring permission to travel.

"It is so, Your Excellency, in both environments. The British diplomat Harold 'Kim' Philby published his memoirs in 1968—*My Silent War*, the book was called—and spoke of restrictions on his life in Moscow, including the requirement that he receive permission to travel.

"We should add this point, Dr. Titov"—Blackford was looking now not at Waldstein, but at the bald, attentive man at his side. "Golitsyn and Philby were spies, men engaged in espionage. They changed loyalties, and thus were, hypothetically, special targets of retaliation. You, Dr. Titov, if we have been accurately informed, do not aspire to life as a secret agent. Our understanding is that your intentions would be simply to pursue your profession. Such have been the resolutions, we have been told, of Dr. Valeria Mikhailov, seated at your side, who also sought asylum, and has not been restrained in any way in her life in Austria—again, if we are correctly informed."

The faces of the Communist delegation were frozen.

There was a pause. Waldstein asked Dr. Titov if he had any questions.

Yes, he said, he did. His wife and son were evidently detained in the Soviet Union. "They were to arrive five days ago. And I have heard nothing from them. I wish to ask Professor Kirov, or Comrade Martins: Why have they not been released?"

The two men spoke to each other in whispers. Kirov was pleading his own views, but clearly Philby prevailed, and Kirov would be the spokesman of the position arrived at.

When Kirov addressed the meeting, he looked away from Titov as he said his words. "The matter of *other* concerns and demands by Dr. Titov necessarily rests as simply one more demand, which cannot be addressed individually, needing to be considered alongside answers to the whole question." Kirov fixed his eyes on his notes.

Titov addressed the judge. "Your Honor, if my question is not answered satisfactorily, instead of in doublespeak, we cannot proceed with this exercise. I request a suspension of this forum until I have considered the implications of what Vladimir Spiridonovich has said. My old friend Vladimir Spiridonovich." Titov looked, his eyes moist, down at the floor.

"You have the right to suspend, indeed to terminate, these proceedings. Do you wish to schedule another session?"

"Yes, Your Honor."

"We will, then," the judge looked down at his notepad, "meet tomorrow, at the same time as today, following the same procedures. The order of withdrawal from this chamber will be as specified."

He got up, followed by Titov and Mikhailov and the interpreter. Oakes led Windels and their interpreter out through the back door. The Russians went out the front.

CHAPTER 61

The next day, Judge Waldstein began by saying that the deadlock reached in the closing period the day before would continue unless the parties could agree to a procedure. "I suggest that Dr. Titov agree to put off any reference to reunification with his family on the understanding that after other matters are dealt with, that question of reunification will then logically be faced.

"If this is agreed upon, we can proceed. If it is not agreed upon, I do not see how we can go forward. If we put the family reunification in abeyance, it can be done with the understanding that unless that question is resolved to the satisfaction of Dr. Titov, all other agreements are canceled."

There was a stir in the room. Titov whispered briefly to Valeria.

"This motion," Waldstein continued, "will require that the parties present here consult among themselves. There are rooms upstairs. The first room on the right is reserved for Dr. Titov. He can consult with Professor Mikhailov there. The first room on the left is reserved for the Soviet delegation. The adjoining room, for the U.S. delegation. I will remain here and make myself available to anyone who wishes to consult with me."

A half hour later, Valeria Mikhailov reported to Waldstein that Titov was prepared to proceed on the understanding the judge had specified.

A knock on each door established that the others were also ready to proceed.

There followed an hour's discussion, during which, using his notes, Titov enumerated his specific complaints when at work at his institute. Several demands were dealt with acquiescently by Kirov. Two of them he said he would need to consult with Moscow about before conceding.

For almost the whole of the subsequent half hour, the parties stalled on the question of the freedom, asked for by Titov, to send to scientists abroad, on his own motion, research developed at his institute. Kirov said that he had been "instructed" that a high-level committee of the Ministry of Education would need to weigh any proposal to share research.

Time was spent on just who would participate in such a committee, and a few names were mentioned. It was embarrassing to Titov when Martins gave the name of Kirov as manifestly qualified. Titov proceeded as though he had not heard the nomination.

By about three o'clock, the fatigue of all the parties was palpable. But Waldstein wanted them to get as far as they could. There had been nothing at all for Blackford and Gus to contribute, except to answer questions about the nature of censorship in the United States. Blackford admitted that scientists in America at work on secret projects could not simply share their research with anyone else. "But that would not apply to medical research."

"What about medical research with military implications?" Waldstein asked.

Kirov broke in. "I will not ask Dr. Titov directly, in this forum, to opine on whether his research has military implications. But it would seem obvious that, however tangentially, it does. This may be one reason why Dr. Titov traveled two years ago to Hiroshima."

Everyone looked up at Titov.

"Those of you who are not informed in medical science," he said, pointing his finger first at Waldstein, then at Blackford, "cannot know that research of almost any kind can have military uses. Stopping quickly the loss of blood is thought a purely medical expedient. On a battlefield it can be a critical military asset.

"But with your permission, Judge Waldstein"—Titov's impatience broke through—"notwithstanding the earlier agreement, I must insist that unless I am reunited with my family, I will no longer discuss any subsidiary matters."

Waldstein sipped from his water glass. He saw that Martins's hand was raised for recognition.

"Yes, Herr Martins."

Philby cleared his throat. "I am instructed to advise Dr. Titov that his wife and son will under no circumstances be released from the Soviet Union. There will be family reunification only if Dr. Titov returns to the land that raised him, educated him, and furnished him with the equipment that made possible his research."

Titov turned pale. He looked at Valeria. Blackford's low hiss of frustration could be heard by Gus. Kirov's face was again turned down to his notes. Philby was silent. Everyone was silent.

Waldstein sipped again at his glass of water. He addressed Peter Jutzeler, seated by the entrance door. "Herr Jutzeler, we shall have to adjourn. I shall not reconvene this meeting until you request me to do so after hearing from Dr. Titov and from the Soviet delegation that they are prepared to proceed. If United States participation is required in formulating an agreement, you are to so advise Mr. Oakes."

He rose.

CHAPTER 62

Late in the afternoon, Blackford called Jutzeler, using the telephone number he had been given. Blackford had spent an hour at the embassy, conferring with Ambassador Grunwald and then, on the secure line, having a long exchange with Director Webster, who in turn had spoken with the secretary of state and the national security adviser.

"I have a proposal I need to communicate to Dr. Titov," Blackford said to Jutzeler, "and it's going to require spending a while with him. Can you take us—Windels and me—to him?"

"Yes. At least, I think I can. Before I say yes finally, I must call Waldstein. I want to . . . make sure that it is not explicit—or even implicit—that neither of the parties may talk privately with Titov, even in my presence. Where will you be?"

"What I have in mind to communicate cannot be done in your presence. Inform Judge Waldstein that, reciprocally, we

will raise no objection to a private meeting between Dr. Titov
and the Soviet delegation."

"Very well, I understand. Again, where will you be?"

"I will be in my hotel room with Windels for a half hour.
Then we will go to the dining room. But we'll leave word that
we are expecting a call."

"I will try to get through to you before dinner."

He did, and Oakes and Gus met with Titov and Valeria
at their selected restaurant, near the Schwarzenberg Palace.

Soup and wine were served, and Blackford set forth his
proposal.

Titov's soup grew cold while, for twenty minutes, he listened attentively to Blackford and exchanged quick reactions
with Valeria. Finally, he asked Blackford to give him an opportunity to confer privately with Valeria.

"Of course. But I think Gus and I will order something
to eat while you deliberate. Maybe you should do the same
thing?"

"Is that medical advice?" Titov asked with a smile. Gus
interpreted. Feigning offense, Blackford observed huffily that
he was able to understand a phrase that basic without the
help of an interpreter.

"It is something of a gamble, but we can hold out hope,"
Titov concluded, when the four conspirators joined up for
coffee.

Valeria, when she and Titov were at a separate table, had
said she thought Blackford's idea was surely worth attempting. "There is an element of cowardice in these bullies. It dis-
appoints me that Kirov seems so humble, so subservient with

that Martins creature. But we can count on the KGB giving final authority to the man closest to a KGB turn of mind, and that would certainly be Andrei Fyodorovich Martins."

Titov used the restaurant telephone to call Jutzeler. Jutzeler called Waldstein, who got word to the other parties that they would convene again the following day. Same time, same procedures.

The heavy spring rain and strong winds confused the regimental drill devised by Jutzeler, as the principals coped with umbrellas and raincoats and hats. Blackford found himself distressingly close to body contact with Philby, bound for their separate entrances. But all was soon in order, and Judge Waldstein recognized Titov.

Titov said that he had thought through the negotiations they had had in this room and had resolved what would be his principal decision. He had conferred with Mr. Oakes on such compromises as might then be made in which the United States would concur. "My decision, Judge Waldstein, is to petition the United States Embassy for asylum and to emigrate to the United States to pursue there my calling as a radiological researcher."

Philby looked over at Kirov, but Kirov's head did not move.

Titov went on. "I will expect the Soviet Union to deliver my wife and my son to me here in Vienna. I would request, also, that they bring me two filing cabinets. I grant permission to copy everything to be found in those cabinets.

"I further agree, and would execute such an agreement with all attention given to legal enforcement, to communicate any future developments in my work to the Moscow Radio-logical Institute, including 75 percent of any commercial value that derives from any work I do in the next ten years.

"I further undertake to avoid any publicity that would otherwise attach to my departure for America. I would not meet with the press or grant interviews. I would pledge, again for ten years, not to pronounce a single word of criticism of the Soviet government, not to join with any other emigrant in any public protest of any policies undertaken by the Soviet government.

"I would, in short, be an all-but-invisible scientist, mak-ing his way in a new environment."

The statement stunned both Kirov and Philby into silence.

Waldstein waited a moment and then addressed them. "Is there any comment you wish to make at this point?"

Philby said that there was a Russian expression for what was being proposed—"Dr. Kirov can give it to you in the original, but that's hardly necessary. It says, You take the horse and leave us the hay. We informed you yesterday, Your Excellency, on what terms the Soviet government would agree to release Madame Titov and her son."

Kirov raised his hand and was recognized.

"I would like a copy of Dr. Titov's statement. Is there one available?"

"Yes," Titov said. "I have here two copies." He handed them over to Waldstein.

"Would you care to comment on the statement by Herr Martins?" Waldstein asked Titov.

"Yes. Comrade Martins, I understand your position, and I began by attempting to describe what benefit I thought the

Soviet government would derive from a covenant of the kind
I proposed.

"We can go in the other direction. Far from my simply
disappearing, a refusal to disgorge my wife and child would
result in at least the following:

"(1) I would call a press conference, amply advertised
ahead of time. I would describe the detention of my family.

"(2) I would describe the burdens of life in Russia for scientific researchers, imposed by Soviet censorship, repressions,
and suspicions.

"(3) I would quote the paragraph from General Secretary
Gorbachev's speech in January, at the International Peace
Forum. You will remember, Comrade Gorbachev said to the
assembly, 'Our new approach to the humanitarian problem
is there for all to see.' I would ask how to reconcile such a
statement with his refusal to permit one woman and one boy
to rejoin their husband and father.

"(4) I would say at that press conference that a letter was
being sent to the seven hundred participants in the peace
forum at which Comrade Gorbachev spoke. I would include
in that letter statements made by participants upholding
human rights and applauding the Soviet Union's moves in
that direction.

"(5) I would describe my willingness to forfeit all commercial proceeds not only from work already done, but from
any work I completed in the next ten years.

"(6) I would announce the formation in Washington of a
committee that would bind together all emigrants from the
Soviet Union in total and unrelenting commitment to the effort to release two human beings to their husband and father.
And we could call for general relief for all other claimants to
the humanitarian relief Comrade Gorbachev spoke of.

"And I have two copies of this declaration as well, Your Excellency." Titov handed over the papers.

No one spoke.

Philby raised his hand. "We move for an adjournment, Your Excellency, until further notice."

Waldstein turned to Blackford, who shook his head—no, he had nothing to say at this point. Waldstein turned, finally, to Titov, who also shook his head.

"This meeting is adjourned."

He rose. The principals, reaching for their umbrellas, followed suit.

CHAPTER 63

Moscow. The same participants sat again around the green baize table in the office of the deputy foreign minister. The officials he had summoned were seated when he came in: the minister of culture, Roman Belov; the dean of the medical school, Rodion Rodzinsky; and, of course, Colonel Mikhail Bykov, for the KGB.

Nikolai Paval, whose mode of speech was direct when dealing with his peers in close quarters, began to speak as he lowered himself into his chair. "Well, gentlemen, this is a shitty situation you people have put in my lap. You, Bykov. You advertised the disappearance of Titov by sending out an alarm in Vienna—"

"But it was called off in twenty-four hours!"

"So everybody who was dead during those twenty-four hours never knew about it. And you, Rodzinsky. Dean of the entire medical school, without any idea that you were nurturing a traitor and someone bent on discrediting our cause."

"Comrade Nikolai Vasilievich, there was nothing in the files—"

"Yes there was. There was the report from Dr. Shumberg that Titov was dissatisfied with the official reports on the activity of . . . yet another traitor you managed to nurture, Rodzinsky, the woman Chadinov. But"—Paval turned to the other side of the table—"it was *your* responsibility, Bykov, to act on Shumberg's report that Titov was going about saying that Chadinov had been killed intentionally in surgery—"

"Not quite, Comrade Nikolai Vasilievich, not quite. It is *only* Dr. Shumberg whom Titov questioned. There is no evidence that he was, as you put it, going about saying that kind of thing."

"Which does not answer the question, How is it that, with the Shumberg report in your files, you let Titov go to Vienna, where he sits now happily bent on bribing the Soviet government?"

He looked down at his file. "At least you picked up the woman and the boy in Leningrad, and I suppose I should congratulate you"—he looked down at his file, as if to read fine print—"for not actually killing the boy, though your agent evidently tried heroically to do so. Perhaps he is out of practice.

"Now. Which course of action should we take? My inclination is to confront ugly developments realistically. Accept the consequences of our own derelictions, send the woman and the boy to Vienna, and to hell with them."

"Comrade Nikolai Vasilievich," Bykov raised his hand. "This would be an act of capitulation of profound consequences. Word of it would spread through the entire cultural community: Defy the Soviet Union, and the government will take no effective steps of reprisal—"

Dean Rodzinsky interrupted. "The only act of reprisal, as you put it, Comrade Mikhail Pavlovich, that we could undertake is the detention and imprisonment or even, I suppose, the liquidation of the family. But what is the point in a reprisal if it does not further your objective? Keeping the family in detention is not going to bring Titov back, and is not likely to fortify the loyalty of other members of the research community."

"What *would* be guaranteed if we kept them here," the deputy foreign minister said, "is huge publicity, as word gets around not only in the Soviet Union, but all over the world, as Titov proceeded with his"—he picked up a sheet from the portfolio—"his catalogue of defamations. And unless we shot the woman and the boy, there would be no end to the hue and cry for their release—not tomorrow, not the next day. It would be another Sakharov case. And if we *do* shoot them, just consider! There'd be grounds for major anti-Soviet propaganda, infinite propaganda.

"Now"—Nikolai Paval, thirty years in the army, was experienced in calling people to order—"turn for a moment to other aspects of the suggested 'covenant,' as Titov described his proposals. What about his files, Comrade Rodion Arkadievich? If we permitted Titov to recover his files, after we had copied them, would this cause damage?"

"No, Comrade Nikolai Vasilievich. Moreover, we could arrange for a very quick copyright, which would hold him to his promise to give us the proceeds, if ever there are any, of a commercialization of that research."

"How quickly could all of this be done?"

Roman Belov was finally heard. "I could supervise it all very quickly, Comrade Nikolai Vasilievich. If I may suggest it, I think the entire business—getting the Titov woman and the son without publicity from their present quarters, bringing together the files, dispatching them all to Vienna—would be most efficiently done using one of our transports. Load the files into the plane here in Moscow, land in Leningrad, load the passengers, and on to Vienna." He looked around the table. "And the transport could pick up Kirov and Martins and the two agents you sent there, Comrade Mikhail Pavlovich, for contingent purposes."

"Yes." The deputy foreign minister paused. "Yes. Let us put it together in that way. You attend to the details, Comrade Roman Ivanovich."

Colonel Bykov turned full face to the deputy foreign minister, his pen in his right hand pointed consecutively at his three colleagues. "Comrade Nikolai Vasilievich, I formally request a ruling on this question from the general secretary."

"Very well, Comrade Mikhail Pavlovich. It is now five minutes to twelve. If you"—he turned his head to Roman Belov—"have not heard from me to the contrary by 1215, you will proceed on my—on our—understanding."

CHAPTER 64

Peter Jutzeler conferred closely with his superior about final arrangements. The foreign minister was anxious to expedite the—heartily welcome—closing of the Titov episode. It had been a great victory for the West, but the conciliatory terms would be met: There would be no publicity, none whatever. The press blackout had worked very well. It had been nine days since the twenty-four-hour alarm over the disappearance of the Russian scientist. But when the minister's office had sent out the word that all was well—that the "missing" scientist had simply been taking a tourist's sojourn in Vienna—the pressure had lifted, and there was no longer any journalistic curiosity on the matter. The press knew nothing about the drama in the bierhaus, not one word about it having leaked.

Jutzeler had done a good job, and would now preside over the ending of it.

It would be important for rudimentary reasons of tact

and diplomacy—the minister agreed with Jutzeler—to separate into two distinct events the arrival of Frau Titov and her
son, and the departure of the Soviet delegation.

Perusing the rosters brought together by Jutzeler, Minister Hauptmann was annoyed at seeing that the outgoing Soviet party would include two "Soviet agents"—whose presence
in Vienna he had had no knowledge of. Obviously they were
a part of the security detail sent in to conclude the Titov affair.

"Well, Jutzeler, it isn't as if we actually *controlled* the
coming and going of agents, Soviet, American, Argentinian,
Congolese. They have visas?—they get in. These two people
leaving tomorrow on the Soviet plane were here to exert a
strong arm if they thought it was needed. Either to protect the
two Soviet delegates, Martins and Kirov, or to aggress against
Titov. The fact is, they did not interfere. We certainly won't
impede their departure. For the hell of it, check when, exactly,
they got into Austria, in case I decide to make a scene."

Jutzeler had responded immediately to the telephone call
from Titov that morning, requesting that the U.S. delegates,
Blackford Oakes and Gus Windels, be present at the airport.
"They must have an opportunity to be there at the consummation of their important initiative," Titov had said excitedly.
"They will, with their own eyes, see my wife and son descend
from the airplane. You will kindly expedite this?"

Yes, Jutzeler said, that was easy to do.

So, there would be three cars departing from Kärntner Ring 16
at 1315 and arriving at Schwechat Airport at 1350, ten minutes
ahead of the scheduled landing of the Soviet transport plane.

Jutzeler would ride in the first car with an aide and an Austrian policeman. In the second car, Dr. Titov would ride alongside—he had insisted—his old friend Valeria Mikhailov, who had stood by him during his turbulent stay in Vienna. In the third car, Oakes would be at the wheel. He had rented a car and knew the road well, he told Jutzeler's office. He explained that although Windels was expected as a member of the retinue and had clearance, he, Oakes, would in fact be alone in the car. "Mr. Windels has other urgent business to attend to. If he gets done with that, he can come to the airport in a cab."

Jutzeler thought to give the disembarking detachment one half hour's lead. That would provide time for the family reunion, Titov with wife and son; for unloading the baggage, including the research files of Dr. Titov; and for refueling the plane.

At 1430, the Soviet detachment would arrive in two cars. Jutzeler had assumed that Martins and Kirov would drive in one car, the agents in the other. But Kirov said he would prefer to travel with one of the agents in one car, leaving the second for Martins and the other agent.

The cars would go directly to the Düsseldorf gate, reserved for charter and diplomatic flights. An official of the immigration service would be there to stamp the passports of the departing Soviet delegation. They would proceed up the stairs to the plane. Jutzeler and his aides would return to their car to drive back to the city, but departing only after the engines of the transport had been fired and the taxiing to the runway had begun.

As planned, Gus Windels arrived in the restaurant of the Imperial Hotel at eight. Blackford was seated in one of the booths, the candlelight illuminating the rich red velvet and the gilt sconces over each of the carved-wood booths.

Blackford was reading a paperback. In front of him, face down, was a menu displaying the imperial Habsburg seal, which a hundred years earlier had adorned the grand hotel as one more of the emperor's palaces.

"Let's have something to eat," Blackford said routinely, after a slight throat-clearing. They looked down at their menus but were interrupted by the headwaiter. He brought in an ice bucket and a bottle of Moët et Chandon champagne. "Herr Oakes, this bottle was ordered to be served to you with this card."

Blackford opened it and handed it over to Gus. "You handle this. It's in Russian."

"It says"—Gus ran his eyes up and down. "It says: 'In anticipation of my . . . reunion with . . . my wife, Nina, and son, I salute you and Mr. Windels and my new country.' " Gus looked over at Blackford. "That's it, Dad. That's what it says."

"That's real nice."

In German, the waiter asked, "Shall I open it, sir?"

"Danke, yes," Blackford nodded.

Gus ordered pheasant and a bottle of burgundy wine. Blackford selected pariser schnitzel. Gus was lively, inflamed even, and talked on with great spirit, recalling one or another detail of the tumultuous six days. He didn't like to praise Blackford, guarding against any taint of sycophancy. That would have interfered with a professional relationship that had developed profoundly in their partnership of a year ago, when they had traveled about as father and son, and now during the weeks of their new mission in Moscow, followed by these days in Vienna. But the wine overcame his reserve, and he said, "Dad, that was some thing you pulled off. Calling the Soviets on a blackmail move and making them retreat! That's going to take twenty-five years of seminars by the Soviet High Command to digest."

Blackford managed a smile, a grateful smile. He was only fiddling with his veal. Gus said, "Come on, Black, eat something. Do some justice to our two wines. Every now and then, in our trade, we have to live it up!" He raised his glass, Blackford his, though his eyes didn't match the movement of the glass. They remained level as the glass came to rest on the table. His eyes focused on Gus Windels's face.

"Gus, I've got things on my mind. I thought of not telling you about them, but I figure I've got to do it. Here's the first thing I want you to have." He pulled out an unsealed envelope from his pocket. "Take your time. Read carefully."

Gus read Blackford Oakes's resignation from the Central Intelligence Agency, dated May 8, 1988. Yesterday.

"What's this all about?" Gus was shaking his head and the great body of hair it commanded.

"Let me tell you, Gus. I know you'll disagree"—here Blackford did draw the glass to his lips, and drank—"but I knew what I would end up doing the minute the director told me to go to Vienna. And if he hadn't sent me, I'd have resigned and made my way to Moscow, to do it there."

"*I know what you're going to say, Blackford.* I know I know I know."

"Yes. I'm going to kill Philby. It isn't just that Philby must die, it's that I must kill him. And he must know that it's me. He killed Ursina and our child, but he didn't kill me. It's my turn."

———

As Gus listened, Blackford started reminiscing. He didn't do very much of that, habitually, but an event from the past was sharply etched in his memory and he was engrossed tonight in the telling of the one story.

"You remember the month I spent in the Philippines? I mean, you remember I told you I was there a few years ago, on a tricky assignment?

"President Marcos—President Ferdinand Marcos—was told about the operation that we had accomplished. He was very grateful. And he invited me to have dinner with him and Imelda, that's his wife—'The Empress Imelda,' they called her. At dinner—it lasted three hours—he told me about his father. His father was an important Philippine official. When the Japanese came and conquered and took the father away to prison, the younger Marcos organized an underground group to swoop down on the prison and stage a rescue. The Japs got wind of it at the last minute, and a Japanese sergeant went to the senior Marcos's cell and shot him through the eyes. Ferdinand Marcos was ten yards away when it happened. He escaped.

"He told me that his mission became to find that Japanese soldier and shoot him. He said he tracked him for two years during the occupation. He found him one afternoon at his station in a compound. 'I had my pistol in my hand and could have just pulled the trigger,' he said. 'But that wasn't what I needed to do. So I called out—I knew his name— "Yishita!" He whirled about, a few feet from me. I said, "This is Marcos Jr." That gave him the time I wanted him to have, to know that it was me. That I was there to pay him my father's debt.'"

Gus said nothing.

"That story became very important to me after I learned the cause of Ursina's death. That's how it has to be, and I'll do it tomorrow, at the airport. He'll know it wasn't just . . . an Austrian sniper."

Gus thought to draw Blackford's mind away. Perhaps spend a minute or two on technical matters. He must not just say to him, "You are not to do it." It must not even cross Gus's mind how to prevent Blackford from doing it. *Though it did in fact cross his mind.* He could contrive to have Blackford detained tomorrow!—he could figure out *some* way to make that happen, giving Philby time to get to the airport and back to Moscow. But as he fingered the edges of his idea, he knew he must not do it.

So he turned to other matters. "Black, you got a gun?"

"Yes. Pistols aren't hard to find in Vienna."

"Where will you hide out waiting for Philby?"

"There's a hangar alongside. It's used for VIP receptions and for when it's raining. There's a men's room there. I scouted it this morning."

"You will of course escape. Now, I'll be riding with you to the airport—"

"No. I know it was set up that way, but I don't want you there. I already told Jutzeler you wouldn't be there. I don't want you in the way. I'll drive myself."

"Well, okay, so you drive yourself. Our car—your car—is one of the three official cars, so it will be sitting there, right outside the Düsseldorf gate. You will run for it after the shooting, run for it and get the hell away. I don't think there'll be motorcycle cops around on this operation. Then . . . then head for Andau, the Hungarian border, south. It's an hour away, the international bridge. I don't have to tell *you* what to do, when you're in Budapest, making your way out through resistance channels—"

Blackford raised his hand. "Thanks, Gus. Let's just say—whatever happens, happens. We'll leave it there. Okay?"

"Okay," Gus said, but he ducked his head toward the menu, so that Blackford would not see the tears in his eyes.

"No, I won't have any dessert."

Conversation trailed off. Gus didn't finish his last glass of wine.

Late the next morning, Blackford came in as scheduled to Gus's hotel room. Gus greeted him. "We have a half hour. I'll walk with you to the car. We'll have to stow your bag. Have a look at what I've got here for you. Amazing what you can come up with in the midnight hours. Takes knowing the right people."

Blackford examined the passport. The man whose face was on the photo I.D. wore a moustache. Phony moustaches are easy to stick on the face. The likeness was passable, if the immigration people weren't especially curious. The eyes, on the fake Oakes, were usefully squinted—Blackford could squint as well as the next man. The entries in the U.S. passport looked authentic, and were entirely plausible for an American tourist day-tripping to Hungary. The canvas bag contained toilet articles, shirts and underwear, a book in German, and a bottle of vodka.

Blackford handed over the bag he had prepared for Gus to take away. "I ran through the papers in my folder in there. No problem, mostly bureaucratic stuff. I looked for the two letters from Philby. But then I remembered, I gave them to you yesterday."

"Yes. And what I did was write out a Russian translation of them, and make copies. I had one set delivered to Kirov last night. You remember that Titov told Kirov he personally believed that Ursina had been killed? Well, now he'll *know* she was killed. And who killed her. Here are the originals back."

Blackford did not reproach Gus. He stuck the letters into the bag Gus would be taking away. "You might find these useful, I don't know. Dr. Shumberg's colleagues might be interested." He looked at his watch. "I've got to go."

It was a fine sunny day, and passing by the flower vendors they could smell the Austrian spring. They reached the Fiat sedan and put the bag in the trunk.

Blackford extended his hand. Gus did not take it. Instead, he walked to the passenger door, opened it, and got in.

"I'm going with you," he said.

Up the street, directly ahead, the doors of the two lead cars were open, the first for Jutzeler and his aides, the second for Titov and Valeria. Standing outside, Blackford opened his door, and got in.

"You shouldn't have done that."

"We're off, Dad."

At the airport, two Austrian officials stood at the curb in front of the Düsseldorf gate. They acknowledged Jutzeler, pointing to the lead parking space reserved for him. The Jutzeler car edged in, followed by Titov's car, and Blackford's. Titov and Valeria stayed in their car. So did Blackford and Gus. They sat. Blackford's eyes looked over at the gate through which the passengers would be passing. It had been freshly painted, but already flowers clung to the sides.

A minute before two o'clock they heard the airplane engines. Moments later, the AN-26 touched down. Jutzeler hailed Dr. Titov. Leaving Valeria in the car, Titov almost ran the thirty meters to the gate. A few paces behind him, Blackford and Gus followed. When the gangway was lowered, all eyes were on the plane as a woman's shape became visible. Blackford eased into the adjacent hangar and opened the door to the men's room. Inside were two stalls, a partition between them. He sat on one of the toilets, keeping his eyes on his watch. Eight minutes went by and someone entered the other stall. Blackford waited several minutes, then stood and affected the sounds of a man vomiting. He flushed the toilet repeatedly until the other person had left. He sat down again and trained his eyes on his watch.

It was nearing two-thirty. Putting a handkerchief to his mouth, as if gagging, he looked out from the hangar. He saw first Kirov, then Philby, stepping out from their cars, the agents alongside. They walked now toward the gate. When Philby was abreast of the hangar, Blackford stepped out, his pistol in hand.

"This is for you, Philby, from Ursina and me."

A shot rang out hitting Blackford on the shoulder as he discharged his own shot, piercing Philby's throat. From the ground, he attempted to raise the pistol again, but this time the guard's bullet hit Blackford between the eyes.

The Soviet guard who had shot Blackford shouted to the Austrian airport police. They raised Philby from the ground, carrying him toward the gate. The second guard shoved Kirov forward, but Kirov would not move except toward his wounded fellow delegate. Looking down at Philby he said in clear tones, speaking in the language Gus understood, "*I hope he has killed you, Andrei Fyodorovich.*"

He consented only then to be led through the gate, leaving it for others to resolve whether the wounded Martins should be carried onto the plane or be taken for emergency treatment.

Gus knelt beside the body and waited, immobile, until the ambulance came, then looked on forlornly as the sheet was drawn up over Dad's face.

ACKNOWLEDGMENTS

In 1987–88, the Soviet Union, we would learn in a very few years, was actually winding down, but there were no signs of fatigue in the implacable underworld of spies and espionage and mayhem. The story here told returns to life the experienced CIA agent Blackford Oakes, who quickly encounters a very real-life figure in the U.S.–Soviet rivalry. Other real-life figures appear in this novel, but the scenes in which they appear are imagined. This is a work of fiction, and accordingly I have taken chronological and other liberties.

In preparing this book I read widely in books and periodicals that touched on the life of one of the protagonists. I was especially interested in the biography by Rufina Philby, *The Private Life of Kim Philby;* as also *My Silent War,* by Kim Philby; *Stalin: The Court of the Red Tsar,* by Simon Sebag Montefiore; *The Cambridge Spies: The Untold Story of Maclean, Philby, and Burgess in America,* by Verne W. Newton; *Our Man in Havana,* by Graham Greene; and the indispensable *Facts on File.*

I brought with me to Switzerland, where the book was written, Jaime Sneider, a young graduate of Columbia. Jaime had done editorial intern work for *National Review,* and had gone then to California to write speeches in the campaign of William Simon Jr. for governor. Jaime is busy now preparing his own book and writing and doing research in Washington, D.C. In January/February 2004, he saved my life with his computer skills as I worked my way through these pages. He is a splendid researcher, skier, and companion, and if Blackford were to rise again, I'd think it inconceivable that he should do so save under the supervision of Jaime.

My associate Linda Bridges did intensive work on the manuscript, helping to edit it page by page and pointing out its strengths and weaknesses. I am deeply grateful to her. And, as always, I am indebted to my oldest editorial friend on earth, Samuel S. Vaughan, renowned editor, sometime president of Doubleday, editor and catalyst of the book *Buckley: The Right Word* (Random House, 1996). At first glance he was appropriately skeptical about the manuscript, so that his enthusiasm for the final draft, which incorporated his suggestions, was especially heartening. If memory serves (and if it doesn't, he will correct this), this is the 30th book of mine that he has superintended. Those he didn't are not worth reading.

Frances Bronson of *National Review* has been secretary, office manager, and animated friend and colleague, on whom I have continuingly relied. André Bernard, publisher of Harcourt's trade division, has provided critical enthusiasm, and I am also indebted to Harcourt's managing editor, David Hough.

I did not send the manuscript for comments to the bene-factors I have relied on in the past, primarily, as I pause to think about it, because two of my liveliest and keenest friends have died in the interval since my last novel. I remember Tom Wendel and Sophie Wilkins, with everlasting affection.

W.F.B.
Stamford, Connecticut
December 1, 2004